Love Beyond Orbit

Aloha in the Future

The sequel to
Brent and Edward Go to Mars

Richard Jeffery Wagner, PhD

Auctus Publishers

AuctusPublishers.com

Published by Auctus Publishers
606 Merion Avenue, First Floor
Havertown, PA 19083
Printed in the United States of America

ISBN (Print): 979-8-9928526-1-5
ISBN (Electronic): 979-8-9928526-2-2
Library of Congress Control Number: 2025939734

Contents

Introduction

It is now highly feasible to take care of everybody on Earth
at a higher standard of living than any have ever known.
It no longer has to be you or me. Selfishness is unnecessary.
War is obsolete. It is a matter of converting high technology
from weaponry to livingry.

—Buckminster Fuller

S et in the future and meeting various definitions of science fiction, this book has flying cars, robots, rockets, and other tropes of science fiction, but it is also a love story with some detective work, philosophy, and travel blended in. This is the third in the Brent and Edward series that begins with *The Zombie Philosopher* followed by *Brent and Edward Go to Mars*. In this book, after their return from space with their friend Cindy Fairfax, who had accompanied them to Mars and back, the protagonists have adventures in Hawai'i.

This novel is in the subcategory of *hard* science fiction because the projections of future technology and society are based on science. That is, there are no imaginary or fantastic contrivances: they are all realizable technology. It is also an exploration of social change propelled by economic change driven by technological improvements. These innovations include intelligent machines eliminating the need for human labor, described in the first book, and a water economy in space enabled by abundant fusion power,[1] described in the second book.

Society benefits from automation, and human labor will not be required in the future. A socialist system must develop to provide a fair distribution

---

[1] Practical fusion power is one technology that might not be realized. However, I am optimistic that it will be available in 150 years, so my science fiction books rely on it as a heat source for various engines in space and on planets.

of wealth. Naturally, such social changes will be strongly resisted, but also naturally, the advancing tide cannot be held back.

This book continues the story of the two friends, Brent, a philosophizing robot, and Edward, a young software engineer. Although drudge work is no longer required for people to live in this projected future, many choose a professional or artistic career as part of a fulfilling life. In the future, robots designed for work in a human environment will have a human-like form. Other robots will have different forms. Can friendships arise between humans and robots? My books in this series answer in the affirmative.

Brent and Edward take a ballistic rocket trip to Hawai'i, and while there, encounter many words and phrases in the Hawaiian language. Hawai'i, by its constitution, has two official languages, English and Hawaiian, and that will remain the case in the future in which this book is set. In general, foreign words are italicized in literature. In Hawai'i, Hawaiian words are not foreign so they are not italicized. I use the diacritical marks, the 'okina (') and the kahakō (macron), for some Hawaiian words except when a word has been Anglicized, such as *Hawaiian*. That word occurs in English but not in Hawaiian. The Hawaiian term for the Hawaiian language is *'ōlelo Hawai'i*.

All my books, fiction and nonfiction, have footnotes. They help readers better understand the story with supporting information. Given the choice between footnotes and parenthetical inserts, footnotes are the better option because they allow readers to skip them if they like. If footnotes bother you, as they have at least one critic, skip them. The book reads fine without them, but I hope that the science, history, and language aficionados among my readers will find them useful or interesting.

As my readers may have noticed I am also fond of quotations from notables at each chapter head. These are usually relevant to the chapter they kick off, and add force, I think, to the philosophical ideas expressed. The main thing is to enjoy the ongoing story of Brent and Edward and I hope that you do.

Sweet April

One of the first conditions of happiness is that the link between man and nature shall not be severed, that is, that he shall be able to see the sky above him, and that he shall be able to enjoy the sunshine, the pure air, the fields with their verdure, their multitudinous life.

—Leo Tolsto

Brent, Edward, and Cindy in freefall moved hand over hand to their seats in the shuttle, having left their compressed air jetpacks in the space hotel lobby. As they got into their semi-reclining seats and strapped in, the autopilot announced to all the passengers that they would feel one gee of acceleration in a few minutes. Then the brief countdown began.

"Time to wake up now." In the flying car garage tower, not far from Nā Hōkū[2] Spaceport, the timer daemon she had set awakened Maxine from her nine month slumber. She saw through her camera views that a bipedal robot was polishing her dark blue surface. She inspected her sensors and actuators: all operational. Her liquid hydrogen fuel tank was full. She did a test spin-up of her two turbine engines and sent a summary message to Edward Collier's personal device: she was ready for his arrival at the spaceport.

The winged shuttle descended from Hotel Leo in low earth orbit, came out of supersonic flight regime, and glided through the troposphere, nose and wings cooling, to a runway landing on the northern continent in the western hemisphere. Edward Collier and his robotic valet, Brent, were among the passengers. So was private investigator, Cindy Fairfax. The three friends were returning from their trip to Mars after 283 days off-

---

[2] Hawaiian for *the stars.*

planet. Brent and Edward had gone to Mars for pleasure, Cindy, with a Ph.D. in archaeology, for business.

After debarking the shuttle, the three friends obtained their luggage. Brent, in his valet uniform, pulled both wheeled space trunks, while Edward and Cindy carried their own lighter bags. Edward also carried Brent's valet satchel. They made their way outdoors onto the sidewalk leading to the air car landing area. In the bright sunlight a paparazzo drone zoomed down and accosted them. "Go away!" yelled Edward.

Brent was more accommodating and he politely answered the paparazzo's questions. Yes, he planned to remain in valet service, no, he would not quit writing on philosophy, and so on. After the drone flew off, they resumed their progress to the air car pickup and drop off location. Brent explained to Edward, "Being nice to the press will help me sell more books."

"You are right, of course," replied Edward who then pointed, "Over there, I see Maxine waiting for us."

As the trio approached, Maxine popped open her luggage boot and opened her doors. Brent put the space trunks in the boot, and they three got into Maxine. She closed her doors, revved her turbines, shot upward to cruising altitude, and headed to Edward's home in the country.

Illuminated by the sun low in the clear blue eastern sky, air car Maxine approached Brent and Edward's house from the west. The birds and squirrels in the tree-filled yard saw her rapidly appear to grow larger. As the whine of Maxine's turbines and the whoosh of her swiveling thrusters grew louder, birds scattered, and squirrels hid on the far sides of tree trunks. Maxine's flight was fast and rock steady. She descended quickly and touched down firmly but gently on Edward's landing pad at his rural home, a safe distance from the trees around his house. Maxine powered down her twin hydrogen turbines, opened her doors, and her three passengers climbed out.

Cindy looked at the trees surrounding Edward's home and the country road leading to the town, not far away. "This is lovely," she said. The two-story pale blue house looked well built and solid, with long eaves and plenty of windows.

Edward was a rather ordinary-looking software engineer, not tall, nor short, not fat, nor thin, with dark brown hair and brown eyes. He inhaled deeply the smells of springtime. "It's good to be home and on solid ground."

Argent-faced Brent, wearing his valet uniform of white shirt, black tie, slacks, shoes, and a black bowler hat, replied, "Indeed sir, the familiar sights are welcome to my mind."

Edward and Cindy had developed a romantic relationship on the space liner returning to earth and Edward hoped Cindy would be staying with them for more than a few days. Maxine released the boot lid. Brent lifted and pulled the roller-wheeled space trunk into the house and carried Edward's bag. Edward helped Cindy with her luggage and showed her to the guest room on the ground floor.

After carrying Edward's space trunk upstairs, Brent entered the pantry and put his own things on his shelf. Then he assumed his customary position at the wall charger in the living room to enjoy an inductive charge. Cindy freshened up and unpacked her bags, using the closet hangers and bureau drawers in her room. When those tasks were completed, she went into the living room as Edward came downstairs to join them.

Cindy exclaimed, "There's that flintlock musket[3] on the wall." Cindy had heard the story about Brent using the replica Brown Bess to defend Edward. She approached the muzzle-loader for a better look but did not touch it and admired the browning on the barrel and the patina of age on the stock. She noticed that the lock, at half cock, held a sharp flint tightly in its faux leather lined jaws.

She then walked over to Edward's bookcase and halted. Cindy perused the titles, reached out a hand, paused, and said, "May I?"

---

[3] Described in *The Zombie Philosopher*.

Edward replied, "Of course, Cindy, you may handle any book you like. Just be careful with the older ones. Some are valuable."

Cindy extracted a two-hundred-year-old cloth bound copy of *A Connecticut Yankee in King Arthur's Court*. "I haven't read this one."

"I think you will enjoy it, one of the first time travel books ever written. The pages have been treated with preservative, so you're not likely to encounter any cracking of the paper. But still, handle it carefully, please."

"Oh, I will. Thank you." She removed the book from the shelf.

"That reminds me, I need to put back the books I took to Mars. They're still in my space trunk upstairs."

Brent, still standing against the wall, reported the good news that he had just received on the net. It was the positive outcome of a defining court case on personhood for certain robots. Brent had submitted a brief as an *amicus curiae* that helped to decide the case, tried on Ganymede, petitioning personhood for a robot who had requested it. The court had ruled for the plaintiff robot in that case, granting him, and others like him, the right to full personhood with all associated rights and responsibilities in the Solar System Authority (SSA).

"That's delightful news," said Edward. They decided to invite friends over for cocktails and dinner later in the week to celebrate.

Brent said, "With your permission, sir, I will send invitations to our friends for a soirée here next Saturday evening."

"Thank you, Brent, that will be perfect." Edward climbed the stairs to unpack his space trunk, later bringing down several books to replace in the bookcase.

Sitting on a couch, Cindy idly remarked to Brent, "I love a dinner party," and then began to read the Twain book she had selected.

That afternoon, Victoria, Edward's neighbor across the road, came over and thanked Brent and Edward for their thoughtfulness in sending her a gift of a case of Hecate Vineyards wine from New Troy at Earth-Sun Lagrange point four. Victoria had kept an eye on Edward's house while

6

they were away, and she had arranged for the tennis court to be swept and power washed the prior week. She had not had the pool cover removed and servicing restarted, however, because the weather was still too cold.

Victoria had reddish brown wavy hair and brown eyes. She was the lawyer who had defended Brent in an earlier legal matter. Edward introduced Victoria to Cindy. Victoria said, "I am pleased to meet you, Cindy. Edward had said he might be bringing a new friend home for a visit."

They shook hands. "I am glad to meet you, too, Victoria. Brent told me how you defended him in that musketry kerfuffle."

After some small talk, Victoria walked back to her home across the road. Later, Brent went to town for groceries in Edward's ground car, Davy. That evening, Cindy helped in the kitchen to prepare a spaghetti dinner. They had a good meal with faux meat sauce. Brent served and cleaned up afterward.

After Cindy went to bed that night, Edward talked to Brent in the living room. Gazing at one of his colorful abstracts on the wall, Edward said, "I'm glad we went on that space trip, Brent, even if it took most of a year. The rocket ride up to LEO[4] was thrilling. And you know what, when we were approaching the Leo Hotel it reminded me of that scene in that old classic movie *2001: A Space Odyssey*, as those rocket travelers drew near their space station."

"So *that* is why I could hear 'The Blue Danube Waltz' playing in your head."

"Ha, ha, nice joke, Brent."

"Both of those hoop-like habitats, the space station in that movie and the Leo Hotel, are Wernher von Braun wheel-type space stations."

Edward replied, "It's absolutely amazing that Dr. von Braun could invent such space structures over two hundred years ago. That was before there was any crewed spaceflight. What a visionary."

---

[4] Low earth orbit.

"Indeed sir, he was a brilliant man." Brent stood by his wall charger while Edward went upstairs to bed.

The next morning, Brent helped Edward erect the tennis net. Edward's tennis friends, Joe and Angela, came over to play mixed doubles with Cindy and Edward on the tennis court. Joe was an engineer who loved to talk about technology and was an excellent tennis player as well. His close friend Angela was a professor of philosophy at the local college and was instrumental in getting Brent's free will theorem successfully tested in concert with the computer science department.

The first tennis set played was with Joe and Angela versus Edward and Cindy. At the second changeover, Edward sat on the courtside bench with Cindy while he took a drink from a bottle of water and toweled off his sweaty arms and face. He watched Cindy's face, with her green eyes framed by her brown curly hair, as she examined and straightened the strings on her racket, and his warm heart did a little flip. Another quick drink of water and they were back in action on the court.

After the first set, won by Joe and Angela six to two, they mixed it up with Joe and Cindy against Edward and Angela. That set score was closer, and Joe, with his slight limp, was again on the winning side. They all sat together on a courtside bench before going back to the house. Edward said, "I think playing all that zero-gee[5] tennis on the space liner between planets has messed up my game somewhat. I keep wanting to jump to where I think the ball is going to be."

Cindy replied, "I noticed that effect too. I'm sure that after a few days we'll get used to gravity tennis again."

"Still, you both played some tough matches," said Joe. "I imagine that space tennis is way different. It makes me curious to try it sometime."

"Yes, it's quite different," asserted Edward, "Fun but distinct. I've heard a new hotel is being built in LEO that will have cylindrical tennis

---

[5] For *g*, the acceleration of gravity. A gee is 9.8 meters per second per second. Zero-gee is a condition of very low acceleration.

8

courts at the zero-gee level. You could go up for a few days and try it out. You wouldn't have to spend months up there like we did."

Brent arrived at the court to announce that lunch would be served in half an hour. Joe and Angela begged off lunch and picked up their tennis things and departed. Edward and Cindy returned to their rooms and showered and changed for lunch. They met in the dining room to eat the sandwiches and drink the iced tea that Brent had prepared for them.

After lunch Edward said to Cindy, "I must still be a bit time lagged from the space trip. I feel like taking a nap."

"I do, too. I think I'll go to my room and lie down for a bit."

Edward said, "Okay, see you later," and he ascended the stairs to his room. Brent cleaned up the kitchen before standing at his wall charger while the other two napped.

Town Square

*In the distance, detail was veiled and blurred
by a purple haze, but behind this purple haze,
he knew, was the glamour of the unknown, the
lure of romance.*

—Jack London

When they arose from their after-lunch naps, Edward and Cindy met in the living room. Edward said to Cindy, "I see you're wearing those bright, shiny, pinkish-purple shoes that you bought on the space liner. I like them."

Cindy wore a sky-blue blouse that harmonized with her shoes. "Thanks. They're magenta. I bought them on the way back to Earth for walking in one-gee, and you may remember, I wore them to dinner with you at the restaurant on the one-gee level of the Leo Hotel." Cindy's outfit complimented her brown hair and green eyes.

"You look wonderful. How about a drive in the country? I'll show you the sights around here."

"Exploring the country roads sounds like fun. It will be good to see the scenery. Are there cows?"

"That's a real possibility."

Edward summoned his ground car, Davy, to meet them at the road in front of the house. His dark blue solar cells glinting in the sunlight, Davy drove from his solar roofed parking station to the road and waited in front of the house. Edward invited Brent to come along, and they went out of the front door. As they approached, Davy opened two of his doors. Edward and Cindy sat on the front bench seat while Brent sat on the back one.

Seatbelts had not been required in automobiles since human driving on public roads had been outlawed years ago, but some older people felt more comfortable if they could wear them. Davy did not sport such equipment. Edward said, "Davy, we would like to take a tour of the countryside. How about you take this road away from town, then turn right on Blanco Road and take that around the curve and turn right again on Valley Way. Take that road to Harvest and turn right, and we'll end up in town where we can go in to visit the Town History Museum."

Davy replied, "Yes, Mr. Collier, and away we go."

They rode in Davy past country houses on the tree-lined road and then emerged onto more flat ground with plowed and planted fields and the occasional farmhouse. Edward pointed out the farms and crops to Cindy, and various peaks in the distance. Robotic tractors pulling plows were in view. They crossed a bridge over a small stream and came to a road intersection where Davy turned right and went over another bridge across a swiftly flowing stream, then went through woods in springtime new-leaf green. After a while, they turned right again and passed through low hills on the south side of town. A doe stood alone in a field watching them go by.

Soon, Cindy pointed to a dozen Herefords resting in the shade of a spreading oak tree and said, "Look, cows!"

Edward said, "There are a couple of steers and calves in the herd, too."

Davy turned right again on Harvest Road and headed into town. Edward said, "Davy, when we get into town, drive around the town square and let us out in front of the history museum."

"Yes, sir," said Davy.

At the museum, they got out of the car, and Davy went to park in the public lot. The sign on the building in front of them said, "Town History Museum," while a smaller sign below said, "Town Historical Society." They walked up the steps and went in.

A bell above the door tinkled as they entered, and the volunteer attendant put down the book she was reading and stood up to greet them with a radiant smile. "Welcome to the Town History Museum. The exhibits here are mostly self-explanatory, but I will be happy to help if you have any questions." Her name tag read Madison.

Edward said, "Thank you, Madison. I've been here before, but I want to show the museum to my friend, Cindy, who is from out of town. I don't believe that Brent, my personal assistant, has been here before, either."

Madison gave them a brochure for the museum and asked them to let her know if they had any questions before she resumed her reading. The three friends looked around the medium-sized L-shaped room and began exploring the display cases and wall exhibits. The museum detailed the history of the town, beginning when the first settlers arrived after the railroad went through the wide valley in the nineteenth century. They recognized some of the names of the patriarchs from the names of streets and roads around the broad and fertile valley and marveled at the old photographs of steam engines and farm equipment.

It took them less than an hour to see everything in the room. When they finished, they thanked Madison and went on their way out of the door with the tinkly little bell at the top. Edward messaged Davy to meet them on the other side of the square, and they walked across the park, enjoying its lawns and trees and the memorial monument of the Second World War in the twentieth century. Edward did all this with the thought of familiarizing Cindy with the town and the area and making her feel more at home.

When they arrived at the far side of the square, Davy opened his doors. Edward, Cindy, and Brent got in. Davy drove them to a grocery store where the trio shopped for fresh food items and other supplies. When they returned home, Cindy helped Edward and Brent fix dinner. Brent was in charge and assigned tasks to the other two in the roomy kitchen.

As dinner preparations became well in hand, Brent put together an appetizer tray, opened a bottle of cold Pinot Grigio from Italy, and suggested that Edward and Cindy enjoy watching the sunset from the patio.

Edward laughed and said, "I can take a hint, Brent. You want us out of your kitchen!"

Brent carried the tray with the wine and two glasses, and Edward, walking with him, opened the door to the back patio. Brent put the tray down on a small table and returned to the kitchen.

Cindy joined Edward while he filled the two glasses. "Here's to being together back on earth," he said. They clinked glasses and sipped.

They sat in adjoining white anodized welded titanium tubing patio chairs with webbed seats and backs and watched the sky with its scattered drifting cumulus. The sun was setting on a distant ridge. As Cindy sipped her wine she thanked Edward for making her feel at home, "It's such a pleasant evening and it's good to be here."

"You are quite welcome. Yes, it is a nice twilight. You know, it's funny. After spending over half a year on the space liner in zero-gee, zipping around with our jetpacks, I find myself wanting to jet around, instead of having to get up and walk. It's kind of like that feeling I would get as a kid after roller skating all day and finally taking my skates off and having to walk."

"Yes, that's it exactly. But it's still nice to be back on our home planet. It's certainly a good thing the space liner had that one-gee centrifuge for enforced daily workouts. We would be invalids otherwise."

Having set the table, Brent went to the open French doors to the patio and announced, "Dinner is served."

Poetry

Love is wise—Hatred is foolish. In this world, which is getting more and more closely interconnected, we have to learn to tolerate each other. We have to learn to put up with the fact that some people say things we don't like. We can only live together in that way. But if we are to live together, and not die together, we must learn a kind of charity and a kind of tolerance which is absolutely vital to the continuation of human life on this planet.

—Bertrand Russell

The next morning, Cindy went for a swim in the pool while Edward worked upstairs on a collaborative software project for his employer in the big city. When he finished his work, he began writing a poem. Brent was dusting in the living room when Edward came down and said, "Look, Brent. I've written a poem for Cindy. What do you think?" Edward handed him a printed sheet:

Space between planets

On a journey through the stars:

Happy to find you

Brent said, "That is a *haiku*."

"Yes, Brent. I don't have much experience at poetry, so I thought I would start with something simple. Anybody can count seventeen syllables."

"Well, sir, *haiku* is regarded as more appropriate for evoking reverence for nature, or as an expression of some particular of the human condition, rather than for love poetry."

"Hmm. Now that I think about it, you may be right. I will try again later."

"Very good, sir."

After Cindy came in from her swim and showered and changed her clothes, the three went to town for the Wednesday morning farmers' market. Davy dropped them off at the town square where the farmers or their robotic surrogates had set up pop-ups and tables, and the three walked over to have a look.

They saw deep red vine-ripened tomatoes, dark green cucumbers, large ripe green beans, and fresh yellow corn. Edward bought a few of each. There was a tent for baked goods where they bought delicious looking cinnamon rolls for the next morning's breakfast and a cherry pie for dessert that evening.

A few days later, Cindy rode in Davy to town to buy some clothes. While she was gone, Edward showed Brent his latest love poem. "Tell me what you think, Brent."

> Flying with you's unforgettable,
> Good times in space were so possible.
> Happiness we did find,
> Under stars we have dined,
> Ecstasy became more probable.

"It rhymes nicely and has a good rhythm, but it's a limerick."

"Yes, a common form. What's wrong with that?"

"Well, sir, limericks are most often used for bawdy poetry and are hardly suitable for love poems."

"I see. You just wait until you fall in love, Brent, and then I will criticize *your* poetry."

"That is highly unlikely, sir."

"But I think you are right on this. Thank you for setting me straight." Edward tore up the sheet of paper.

Edward thought, *the best thing a friend can do is to help one get one's thinking right. I'm sure lucky to have Brent as a friend.*

The following evening, Edward took Cindy to a nightclub in town for drinks and dancing. Cindy was interested in the local style of dancing, and she showed Edward a few dance moves she had learned in Madrid.

Two days later, Edward showed Brent another poem he had written. This one was somewhat longer than the first two:

> Oh see, her eyes are green, her hair is curls
> So fair her skin, unmatched in form, she gives
> Delight and beats the looks of all the girls
> And warms my heart, my soul from where she lives.
>
> Space liner sports she plays so well, it's all
> In fun and whirring fast, she flies right by.
> And jumps with twist and tumble smacks the ball,
> She serves and racks up points and makes me sigh.
>
> Investigates and finds the facts of crime,
> She seeks out deceit and uncovers truth.
> And in the end, it was to be all fine,
> Unknown at first, an undoubted good sleuth.
>
> She solves the conundrum, give her that much,
> In truth she sees, she does, she has that touch.

Brent said, "That is much better. A sonnet, and in Shakespearian rhyme. Quite appropriate for love poetry. But should it be 'her hairs are curls,' so that the number matches?"

"It's poetic license, Brent. It doesn't have to be grammatically correct. Besides, I think it's right the way it is."

"Either way, I think it is good," said Brent. "You should show her this one. Better yet, read it to her. Poetry is best spoken out loud."

"Thanks, Brent. I hope she likes it."

Later, when Edward read the poem to Cindy, she chuckled to herself over a couple of the lines, thinking *no man has ever written a poem for me, good or bad*. She said, "I love it. And I like the way it evokes some of our space tourism experiences. Thank you. May I keep the paper copy?"

Edward was pleased that she had asked and readily handed it over. Cindy folded the paper and put it away with her personal device. Then, she gave him a kiss.

Party Plans

It is impossible to live pleasurably without living prudently, and honorably, and justly; or to live prudently, and honorably, and justly, without living pleasurably.

—Epicurus

On the Thursday night before the Saturday soirée, after Edward had gone upstairs to the pleasures of sweet slumber, Brent stood by his wall charger, contemplating free will. The *fact* of free will *had* been settled. The question Brent pondered was why humans resisted the idea. Perhaps it was the romanticism of kismet. The legend of the Three Fates deciding human lives was deeply embedded in Western culture. But Brent considered that a more compelling reason was that belief in unfree will provided an out, an escape from culpability. It was an excuse not to do one's best and gave freedom from guilt at benefiting from fortunate circumstances. After all, if one cannot do otherwise, then there is no blame for anything. Regardless, he concluded, resistance to the idea of free will represented a human weakness.

When the time came for Brent's midnight memory backup and system checks, Brent lost awareness of his surroundings and internal computations for a good portion of the hour. He resumed his cogitations when his quotidian maintenance processes were complete.

Brent thought resistance to the idea wasn't so much that the absolute empirical proof of free will was relatively new. Free will's acceptance had *always* been slow. Immanuel Kant wrote extensively on free will back in the eighteenth century, and even though he was regarded by many as the greatest philosopher who ever lived, free will never gained traction with the populace. Rather, it had remained fashionable for scientists and philosophers to deny free will. Brent's latest book, which described the

18

arguments and laboratory experiments that proved free will, was becoming popular, so perhaps a cultural shift was in the offing.

Friday morning came and Edward thought, *the dinner party is tomorrow*. He rolled out of bed and began his morning routine. When Brent heard Edward stirring upstairs he went to the kitchen to brew Edward's morning coffee.

With coffee in hand, Edward discussed with Brent the arrangement of place cards for the dining table. "You and I, of course, will sit at the ends of the table. You should be on the end by the kitchen because, as you don't eat, you'll be serving the food and pouring the wine and water."

"Of course, sir, that was my intent as well."

"And I think Joe should sit next to you. You know how he loves to talk about technology."

"Indeed, sir, I think Joe will like that. And we should put Victoria next to me, too. I would like to discuss with her the latest on legal developments in robot personhood." Brent was Edward's employee and Victoria had found a novel legal innovation whereby Edward could legally pay him in spite of Brent's having no official personhood.

"That will be fine, Brent. By the way, the relationship she had with a fellow lawyer seems to have fizzled while we were away. Hmm, I think Margaret should *not* be next to me, considering our previous relationship, as that could be somewhat awkward for her fiancé, Fred."

"Indeed, sir, that is thoughtful of you. Perhaps your chess club friend Carl should be on your right and Angela, our philosopher friend, should be on your left."

"That sounds good. That *will* be good. If we put Fred next to Victoria, then Cindy should be between him and Carl. That leaves Martin between Angela and Margaret, with the two fiancés opposite each other."

Brent said, "I think that is a good arrangement, alternating sexes to the extent possible, and with no pair arriving together seated next to each other. Now all that remains is to print the place cards. Shall we use full names and titles, or just nicknames?"

"Well, Brent, as we didn't announce the party as a formal affair, I think just nicknames will be best."

"I will do so, sir, but does not the mere presence of dining table place cards imply formality?"

"Yes, but the benefits of informal naming outweigh the appearance of stuffiness, and it will avoid any confusion when it comes time for the guests to be seated."

"Indeed sir, I learn from you frequently. Our guests will be able to appreciate the assistance of suggested prandial seating while we strive to keep the mood light and joyful."

"And I learn from you, Brent. Now, let's go tell our plans to Cindy and see what she thinks."

"Good idea, sir."

Artificial Personhood

Pride makes us artificial and humility makes us real.
—Thomas Merton

The next morning was Saturday, the day of the soirée. Edward suggested that they all go into town for coffee. Davy met them in front of the house and all three piled in. It took six minutes to get there. Davy let the three of them off at the Coffee Corner with a view of the town square and its walkways through trees and grass. Brent wouldn't need coffee, so he found a good table for them while Edward and Cindy went to the counter to order coffee and pastries. Brent was not in valet mode[6], so he sat at the table and watched pedestrians going by as he waited for his companions. They joined Brent at the table and began to sip and munch and look at people walking in the park across the street corner. A squirrel ran up a tree. A small dog ran loose in the park. A boy caught up with it and put a leash on it.

After a few moments of silence, Brent said, "That was interesting the other day when we went into the history museum. It was good to connect these street names to the historical personages we learned about in there."

Edward said, "Speaking of personages, Brent, have you thought about applying for official personhood with the Solar System Authority, now that the case on Ganymede was decided in favor of artificial persons?"

"Indeed, sir, I have thought quite a lot about it. However, I am not sure if the benefits outweigh the trouble of doing so."

"How's that, Brent?"

---

[6] On their trip to Mars, Brent continued to evolve as an individual and developed an occasional penchant for slipping out of valet mode and accompanying Edward as an ordinary person.

"Well, sir, trouble could include unwanted press attention, harassment by radical protest groups, and so on."

Edward thought it over for a few seconds and replied, "It seems to me that additional publicity could help you sell more books and get you more media interviews."

"That is true, sir. But I have all the income I need right now, and I don't want to immediately embark on any more speaking tours. Perhaps when I need the public attention, I could apply for personhood and then hold a press conference."

"Keeping it in reserve," said Cindy. "That makes sense."

Brent continued, "There are two good reasons, however, to eventually pursue official personhood. The first is a practical reason and the other, I think, is a moral reason."

"And they are?" asked Edward.

"The practical reason is that a person has the protection of the law while a non-person does not. For example, when that would-be assassin destroyed my body with that military weapon almost two years ago, it was a property crime against you, Edward, not a crime against me. I may be safer as a person because other people will be deterred by potential criminal legal sanctions should they do me harm."

Cindy agreed, "That's true. And the second reason?"

"The second reason is the moral one and may therefore be more compelling. As a person, I would be entitled to vote in elections, both for representatives in political bodies and for laws and other issues that are put directly to the populace for a vote."

"So, how is that compelling?" asked Cindy.

"It is compelling because it is the duty of every free person to contribute to the common good by becoming informed and voting intelligently. As a free robot but a non-person, I would remain unable to fulfill my duty. I think that one is the *killer argument* for official personhood, as they say."

"Very interesting," observed Cindy. "Am I right that you will now endeavor to obtain formal personhood?"

"Yes," replied Brent. "I have just changed my mind during this conversation. I will talk to Victoria and see if she is still willing to help me navigate the process."

Edward had been using his personal device and announced, "I have good news for you both. I have obtained three tickets to the opera the weekend after next in the big city."

Cindy said, "Oh, I love opera. Which one is it?"

"It's a new one and it's both a comic opera and a whodunit that takes place on a space liner. It's called *Space Opera* and I understand that the bodies begin to appear in the first act. The male and female protagonists solve the mystery together, and the space liner's bumbling chief of security arrests the perpetrator."

"So, I guess there might be a lot of zero-gee flying by the singers?" asked Cindy.

"Yes, and apparently there are also some centrifuge scenes where they walk and jog in a huge wheel with its axle out of sight behind the proscenium arch," said Edward.

"It sounds like fun," said Cindy. "I'll bet the zero-gee scenes with the singers hanging on wires will be hilarious."

Edward suggested, "While we're here, let's go shopping for new evening clothes."

Brent reminded Edward, "We also need to shop for food and beverages for tonight's party."

Edward agreed as he summoned Davy to drive them to the stores and wait and drive them home when they finished shopping.

Soirée

The dinner-table is often the terrain of critical conversations, for it is there one has the better of one's interlocutor. There is no escape without scandal, there is no turning aside without self-betrayal. To invite a person to dinner is to place them under observation. Every dining room is a temporary prison where politeness chains the guests to the laden board.

—Maurice Renard

The guests for the *soirée* began to arrive at the appointed hour, six o'clock. Victoria was alone as she walked across the road from her home carrying a bottle from the case of cabernet sauvignon that Edward and Brent sent to her while on their space holiday. "I think it will be nice to share this with your guests," she said after kissing Edward as he met her at the door. She shook hands with Brent and put the bottle on a folding table that Edward had set up for a bar in the living room.

Joe and Angela were the next to arrive. She was stunning in her snug black evening dress and high heels. It was Angela who had first told Brent about the love of wisdom, i.e., philosophy, during tennis changeovers on Edward's backyard court.

Carl and Martin, Edward's friends from the chess club, arrived next. Then came Edward's artist friend and occasional tennis partner Margaret with her fiancé, Fred, a welder of large sculptures. They planned to get married in June. Edward welcomed them all.

Brent acted as bartender and made sure that all the guests had their preferences. Appetizers were available on a side table. Earlier, he and Edward had laid out the place cards they had prepared on the large table of polished wood in the dining alcove on the kitchen side of the living room.

Edward was to sit at the head of the table, with Brent at the other end. The two long sides had four place settings each. To be seated on Edward's right were Carl, Cindy, Fred, and Victoria. On his left were to be Angela, Martin, Margaret, and Joe. While a few guests had glanced at the seating arrangement, no one commented on it, and nobody tried to switch cards.

After everyone had a drink in hand, Brent went to the kitchen and made final preparations of the cuisine. When the synthetic meats and tasty vegetables were ready, he poured water and wine into the glasses on the dining table and began to bring out the platters and bowls of food, putting them on the dining table. Edward, standing in the living room with his guests, but near the dining table, waited until the last of the food was on the table and then said to Brent, "Please join me here. I want to make some announcements." Brent stood at Edward's side.

Edward took a small silver bell with a handle from the table and gave it a ring. "Your attention, please." People stopped their conversations and looked at him. Edward put the bell down. "My friends, thank you for being here tonight to celebrate our return from space. We have several other things to celebrate as well. First, there is the engagement and upcoming June wedding of Margaret and Fred."

Guests put their glasses down and gave polite applause and calls of "Congratulations" and "Woo hoo."

Edward continued, "Second, I have good news from Brent's contacts on the Jovian moon, Ganymede. A robot sued for freedom and personhood there. The robot succeeded in his quest. Brent's friend-of-the-court brief contributed to this important victory for liberty." There was more applause.

"Third, our friend Angela, professor of philosophy, with the help of the computer science department, conducted a laboratory experiment suggested by Brent that demonstrated that robots, and therefore people, have free will, settling an age-old philosophical question. Not only was the peer-reviewed write-up on the experiment published in an international journal, but the experiment was duplicated at another university with confirming results." [7] Everyone broke into wild cheers and applause.

"And lastly, Brent has begun discussions with Victoria about obtaining legal personhood for himself, based on the precedent that he helped establish." There was more applause.

"So, my friends, please pick up your glasses and drink a toast with me: here's to good friends and enjoyment of life. Cheers!"

There was a chorus of "Cheers!" and all drank. Brent raised a glass but, naturally, being a robot, did not drink.

"Now, dinner is ready. If you will move into the dining alcove, we may be seated."

The company moved to the table and found their places. When all the guests were seated, Edward and Brent sat at their places. Edward said, "My dear friends, dinner is served family style. Please pass the dishes around and serve yourselves."

Edward said to Angela, seated on his left, "Will you please pass the potatoes?" Angela did so. "Thank you, Angela. Would you like some?" She replied in the affirmative and Edward put some on her plate. He then served himself. "It must really be a kick getting a research result published like that."

"It sure is. When Brent sent me that draft chapter of his book on the free will experiment, I knew he was on to something. I was glad to help. I'm hoping we can work together again on another proposition."

Edward turned to Carl, on his right, and asked, "Carl, will you pass me the garlic bread? Thanks."

Passing the plate, Carl said, "Great party. So good to be back together with you; and I haven't seen Margaret since she got engaged."

Edward replied, "Yes, it's good to see them both looking so happy. You were married once, weren't you?"

---

[7] The empirical test that Brent used to prove that free will exists is described in *Brent and Edward Go to Mars*.

"Yes, but it didn't last. I thought my love for her would be enough for both of us, but I was wrong and she moved on. Oh, well."

"You going to try again some time?"

Carl shrugged. "I'm not looking, but you never know what will happen."

Brent did not eat or drink, nor could he if he tried, but he had laid a place setting for himself that, with the chair and place card, indicated his seat at the table. His plate and glasses were empty. He turned to Joe, the engineer, seated on his right, and asked him to pass the asparagus.

Reaching for the platter, Joe replied, "Okay, but you don't eat."

Brent said, "I am passing it to Victoria. I see she has not had any yet."

Victoria thanked Brent. "By the say, I have finished the first draft of the petition to the court for your official personhood. Would you like to come to the house tomorrow to go over it?"

"That's great, Victoria. What do I owe you for the work?"

"I am doing this case *pro bono*. You and I will both reap free publicity from it. After we file the petition, we'll call a joint press conference. I hope to expand my law practice and you will sell more books."

"That is kind of you, Victoria. Thank you."

Conversation died down as people began to eat, and after a few mouthfuls, Joe looked at Cindy, across the table, "Hey, Cindy, tell us, how was your trip to Mars?"

Cindy finished chewing, put down her fork, looked up, and said in a voice loud enough to be heard by everyone, "It was great, Joe. As some of you may know, I was on an undercover investigation, pretending to be a tourist. I did all the tourist things, and it was fun." The diners listened with rapt attention. "I was investigating those supposed thefts of alien artifacts from that Martian quarry. But what I found most astounding was the aloha spirit in all the space colonies, from the Hawaiian voyaging and colonizing ethic. You know, what the Hawaiians say, love, help, and be responsible for one another. What the holy high masters of the world's religions have been saying for just about forever, now."

Several guests asked more questions of Cindy, and she answered. The assembled company all liked Cindy and were impressed by her accounts of highlights of the space adventure. After dinner all the friends played a trivia game as a group and enjoyed a selection of after-dinner drinks. The party went on until after midnight.

Space Opera

The oldest, truest, most beautiful organ of music, the origin to which our music alone owes its being, is the human voice.

—Richard Wagner

After all the party guests left, Edward and Cindy helped Brent clean up before going off to their respective beds. Brent stayed up to finish the work. The next morning was Sunday. Edward and Cindy slept in later than usual. Brent had prepared a sumptuous breakfast for them.

Cindy came into the kitchen a little after Edward, where the breakfast table was set, and she sat down. Brent got her a mug and poured coffee for her.

"Thank you, Brent," said Cindy. "It's so nice of you to have made breakfast for us." She helped herself to toast, scrambled faux eggs, and synth-sausages. Brent poured orange juice into a glass for her. "I enjoyed meeting your friends very much, Edward. It was a great party. I think everyone had a good time."

"Yes, I liked it immensely," agreed Edward. "We had some good conversations."

"I, too, appreciated the affair," stated Brent. "It is good to see people enjoying themselves, and your friends are always interesting."

Cindy said, "I think it's noteworthy that it required the invention of intelligent robots to devise an experiment to prove free will."

Edward disagreed. "Well, that's not exactly the case. Other proofs have existed for centuries. It's just that philosophers found it difficult to accept those non-empirical assertions."

"Really?"

"Yes, indeed.

Brent stepped in with, "Take, for example, Schopenhauer's description of the operation of the will, with human beings embodying a universal will. And there are many other assessments of the freedom of the will by other philosophers."

Edward smiled, "But it's all moot now that there exists Brent's empirical proof."

"Still, I find it incredible that it took empirical proof to convince a goodly chunk of philosophers," remarked Cindy. "It was such a simple experiment. I mean, it seems absurd to me that I do not make my own decisions, that the prior states of my brain remove all blame and praise for all the things I do."

Edward replied, "Indeed. It makes me wonder about the motivations of some professional philosophers, that they would espouse a doctrine of slave will, if I may call it that. Do they have guilt complexes or something?"

"Yes, to me such a stance is ridiculous," continued Cindy. "It's as if a slave will proponent is saying to me, 'You might think you can want what you want, but no, you can't.' I say I can. I can decide something and see that it's what I want. Then I can take a step back, see that I want what I want and then I can decide to want what I want to want, and so on *ad infinitum*. You see? I have established an *infinite regress*, an escape from slave will."

"Yes, you have." opined Brent, "Your argument is new and powerful, but I doubt that a hard-core slave willer would be convinced."

Edward said, "I think you're right, Brent."

"Quite. Thanks again for the breakfast, Brent." Cindy spread marmalade on her toast and took a sip of coffee.

"It is my pleasure."

Later that morning, Edward sat at his desk upstairs and wrote in his journal:

Brent and I threw a dinner party last night. It was good to see all my old friends again after our time away in space. Everyone had a good time and it was nice to see Margaret and her fiancé Fred looking so well together.

Cindy is turning into something of a philosopher, too. Just this morning at breakfast, she came up with an infinite regress proof of free will, right on the spot. Brent agreed that it is significant.

Next weekend we go to the opera house in the big city. We'll fly there in Maxine. Simulating zero-gee of a space liner on stage should be interesting. I understand it's an all-star cast. I hope Cindy likes it.

Edward saved the file and went downstairs to see what Cindy was doing. He found her sitting in an armchair reading the Mark Twain book she had picked from the bookcase in the living room the day she arrived. He could see that she was nearly finished with it. He went into the kitchen to help Brent put away the dishes.

* * *

When the time came for the performance of *Space Opera* in the big city opera house, the three dressed up in their new and fashionable evening clothes. Edward had informed Maxine, his shiny blue air car, of the travel plans, and she was ready with her turbines idling as they left the house and walked toward the air car pad. Maxine opened her doors as they approached and the three got in, with Cindy and Edward sitting on the front bench seat and Brent on the seat behind.

"I'm fully fueled and ready to go, Mr. Collier," said Maxine as she closed her doors and lifted off the pad. She flew 20 meters straight up and then accelerated toward the big city, 200 kilometers away, gaining altitude up to the planned 730 meters. At that point Maxine said, "We will arrive at our destination in nineteen minutes, Mr. Collier."

"Thank you, Maxine."

When she had reached the vicinity of the opera house, Maxine approached and set herself down in the air car landing area near the front entrance, idled her turbines, and opened her doors. After the three passengers got out and walked toward the opera house, Maxine closed her doors. When her passengers were a safe distance away, she revved up her turbines and flew to the nearby vertical parking structure for air cars, clearing the way for another air car to land and drop off passengers.

The threesome went in and found their seats in the orchestra section. Brent put his bowler in his lap so as not to obstruct the view of the person behind him. After a while the auditorium filled up, the house lights went down, and the orchestra played the overture. The curtain then opened on a flying scene. A diva with a lightweight fake jetpack on her back, hanging from wires, moved slowly several meters above the stage. She began singing at the top of her lungs, as her female companion flew by her side.

As the action unfolded, a simulated dead body appeared, drifting through the air, dripping fake blood. Investigation by a tenor followed, and soon another body appeared. The diva and the tenor detective professed their love for each other and their consternation at the difficulty of solving the murder.

In the second act, the curtain opened on a huge open wheel, just above the stage, suspended by its axle hidden by the proscenium, representing the space liner's centrifuge. The tenor and his love interest were walking side by side and singing at the bottom as the wheel slowly turned.

The house lights came up during the single intermission. Edward and Cindy got up to stretch their legs while Brent remained in his seat. They walked out to the lobby but didn't buy any refreshments. Edward and Cindy stood together for a while talking about the fashions worn by people walking by. They were both glad that they were neither over- nor under-dressed.

At the warning gong, they returned to their seats. The house lights went down, and the opera continued, with beautiful arias and choruses. There were three more scenes with the centrifuge rotating at walking speed as the two central characters sang and walked, and one scene with them jogging, but stopping occasionally to sing to each other. As with most comic operas, the tenor got the girl. As to the mystery of the perpetrator, all was revealed at the end followed by a great crescendo of the chorus and orchestra. At curtain call, there was a standing ovation. It would have been awkward for the cast hanging from wires, so they all walked onto the stage to take their bows to the rousing applause.

The house lights came up and the three friends walked out to the multiple air car landing area where Maxine settled down and opened her doors a safe distance from the crowd behind the line. They walked to her and got in, and Maxine closed her doors and took off. Maxine said, "We are gaining altitude and heading home, Mr. Collier."

On the way home, Brent said, "Thank you Edward. That was my first operatic experience, and it was certainly an expansion of my cultural horizon."

Edward replied, "You're welcome, Brent. I'm glad you enjoyed it."

Cindy added, "That was super. There were some great laughs. And the dead bodies just kept on appearing. The music was fantastic. And some of those zero-gee singing scenes were most comical, with the chorus swaying on their wires behind the leads. I'm glad they played it for laughs because deadpan serious would not have worked. The victims' bodies drifting across the space above the stage was both disconcerting and funny at the same time."

Edward replied, "I'm glad you liked it, and I agree it was entertaining. That was some good technical production there with the big wheel jogging and walking scenes. It takes real stamina to jog along and stop to sing a duet, then resume jogging. I thought the big finale was tremendous."

"Having been on a space liner gives us added appreciation, too, I think," ventured Cindy.

Brent agreed, "Yes, our space experience certainly contributed to understanding the opera."

"And our ability to empathize with the characters, as well," said Edward.

After a while Maxine spoke, "Airspeed decreased to seventy kilometers per hour, altitude decreased to 40 meters, landing in fifteen seconds." Maxine put on her landing lights and then they were down. Maxine shut off fuel to her turbines and opened her doors to the lowering whine of the slowing engines. Brent, Edward, and Cindy walked into the house. Maxine's engines stopped, she ran a self-diagnostic, and then she plugged her fueling hose connector into the liquid hydrogen reservoir line.

Edward and Cindy embraced, kissed, and went to their separate bedrooms. Brent changed his clothes by his cubby in the laundry room and stood by his charger in the living room. Soon he was deep in thought.

County Fair

As Freud said to Jung in Vienna, you can psych up too much for a darts match.

—Sid Waddell

After breakfast the next morning, Edward announced that it was the weekly laundry day. "Cindy, Brent will strip your bed and make it with clean sheets."

Cindy said, "It will go faster if I give him a hand."

"Yes, good, that's what I do," said Edward.

Cindy helped Brent strip the sheets and pillowcase and to remake the bed with clean linen. Brent carried the soiled bedding and the clothes from Cindy's hamper to the laundry room. He then did the same in Edward's room and began running the laundry machinery.

The annual county fair was being set up on the fairgrounds to the east of town, and Edward suggested that they all go when it opened in a few days.

"That sounds like fun. I like fairs," said Cindy.

"I am sure I will find it interesting as well," added Brent.

The fair would be open for a full week, so Edward suggested that they go on a weekday to avoid the weekend crowds of families with children out of school. When the appointed day came, Edward and Cindy ate a good breakfast. Brent took his solar umbrella[8] with the inductive coil in the handle so he could charge his battery by holding it unfurled in the sun.

They rode in Edward Davy, who dropped them off at the fair entrance and then went to park in a field designated as a parking lot. Cindy noticed that temporary landing pads for air cars were placed near the entrance. The

---

[8] Brent's solar umbrella had just over a square meter of photon collecting area.

pads were circular tarps stretched tight and staked down to the field so that the hot gas jets of the air cars would not blow dust and debris into the air. Now and then an air car would land, discharge its passengers from a distant part of the state or county, and then take off again to park in a designated air car location beyond the ground car parking lot.

"I think we should see the livestock exhibits first," said Edward, "See the tents over there?" He took Cindy by the hand and led the way.

At the livestock exhibits they saw a pretty farm girl with her blue-ribbon bull, the animal husbandry club boys with their steers and cows, and then looked at the prize-winning sheep and goats.

Cindy said, "Oh, there's the poultry exhibit. Let's go look."

They saw all kinds of chickens, some quite exotic looking and beautiful. There were also ducks and geese and they came upon a table with a few newly hatched chicks.

"How cute," said Cindy.

"A chicken in your yard would catch a lot of insects," said Brent.

Edward replied, "I know, but I would have to fence the yard and I don't want to do that."

Cindy said, "You would also have to provide a sheltered roost for it to sleep in, perhaps a nesting box for a hen, and supplement its feed with grain every day. And a rooster would wake you up early with its crowing."

"I didn't know you had any farm experience," said Edward.

"A little. My grandfather had a farm outside of the town I grew up in," replied Cindy with a smile.

"No wonder you were eager to see cows on our first drive in Davy." Walking on, they came to a petting zoo for children. They stood and watched the little ones interacting with a lamb, a young calf, and some gentle ducks, "Look, the white Pekin kind."

"That's good," commented Cindy, "Muscovy ducks would be too mean for children to pet. I think it's good for kids to get physical experience with animals. Brent, do you recall that conversation we had once about the ethics of animal ownership?"

"I do, indeed, Ms. Fairfax. That was quite interesting. I believe we were in the space liner coffee shop at the time."

"I've told you before that you can call me 'Cindy,' but I understand when you want to be formal in public. It's okay."

"Indeed, Ms. Fairfax, I want to keep a low profile in public by not seeming to be overly familiar in my assumed role as a valet."

They wandered through the tent containing vegetable exhibits and competitions. There were large and beautiful squashes and cabbages, as well as extraordinary flower arrangements. They were at the tent of the baking and tinning competitions when Edward asked Cindy, "In your conversation with Brent about animal ethics, did you come to any definite or interesting conclusion?"

Cindy replied, "Let's just say it's complicated. There are some interesting points in the case of domesticated animals, those that have been bred for many centuries to be food products or companions to humans. Farming and killing animals for food has for some time now generally been held to be unethical. In that regard, the most prominent observation we came upon, in view of the helplessness of domestic animals set loose in nature is that if it is unethical to turn them loose to suffer and die, then it could not be unethical to keep them in a humane way as the gentleperson farmers and hobby ranchers do today."

Edward thought to himself, *I just love the way she can assemble her thoughts and speak a coherent paragraph without halting.* He said out loud, "Yes, it is complicated, but it's reassuring that even though there are no easy answers, we do have something of a path to becoming more humane in our treatment of animals."

Brent, overhearing, added, "Indeed, sir, difficult decisions remain before us, as in the case of wild animals where certain predators have become extinct due to past human activities. People must now deliberately hunt certain herbivores to manage the wild populations.[9] That requires insightful regulation, and concerted stewardship."

"Being human has never been said to be easy," observed Cindy. "We can hope for incremental improvements in our time."

"Yes, indeed," responded Edward, "Just like we did with sea level rise."

Cindy admitted, "But we got lucky. Cheap fusion power came along just in time."

"Let's hope for continued luck, for all life on Earth."

"And in the solar system," added Brent.

After looking at the winning pie and cake entries, Edward suggested they go to the rides section, so they walked over and looked around. He got tickets for the Wild Mouse, which, whenever he rode it, always amazed him at how scary such a small ride could be. *I'm always thinking that a hold-down roller could break or come unbolted when we do those abrupt turns*, he thought. Then he thought about his thoughts being an example of meta-thought or thought about thought.

Brent chose to remain behind and watch from the ground. Edward and Cindy joined the queue and, when their turn came, got into one of the little mouse cars, and they were off, climbing the track to the top.

When the ride was over, Cindy said, "That was a thrill. I haven't been on one of those since I was a keiki."[10]

"It's been a while for me, too. I get scared every time I take that ride. Let's go on the Ferris wheel. It's much tamer. Brent, you should come up with us."

"Thank you, sir, I will."

---

[9] Meat from wildlife management is not wasted but sold for consumption in restaurants.

[10] Keiki is Hawaiian for child. Some Hawaiian words had become fashionable in English, especially in space where Cindy had picked up a few words, just as some French words had been adopted into English in previous centuries.

The sun was setting when they walked over to the Ferris wheel. Brent and Cindy got in the queue while Edward bought tickets. When Edward joined them, they were almost to the head of the line. In another minute they were climbing into their swinging seat on the wheel. The attendant carny latched the holding bar over their laps and moved the wheel to the next position for loading and unloading. Soon they were high up, the wheel was fully loaded with new passengers, and it began to rotate continuously.

"This is fun," said Cindy, "Much tamer than the Wild Mouse—what a view!"

They were above the trees and buildings of the town and could see into the distance in all directions as the sun went down in the west. Two more turns of the wheel, down, up, down, up, and the wheel stopped. They were at the top of the wheel while the carny changed out the passengers at the bottom.

Brent exclaimed, "I have seen the town and surroundings from your air car, sir, but this view from the top of a Ferris wheel at twilight is outstanding. The colors of the clouds in the sky are spectacular. Thank you for inviting me on this ride."

Edward asked, "Have you been using your human vision software filter?"

"Yes, indeed, sir. I think I like the view better with the full infrared range enabled. There's not much ultraviolet in a sunset, so enabling those wavelengths does not make much difference. But the color range at the longer wave end of my visual spectrum gives great enhancement, in my opinion."

"I suppose that only another robot could know exactly what it's like to see what you see."

"That is likely true, sir."

"Perhaps you could paint it, so humans could know too."

"A painting by a robot would look like a painting of an ordinary sunset to a human, sir, even with the required special pigments. Another robot, however, might appreciate it."

"No, no, Brent, you misunderstand me. I was thinking of an impressionistic type painting where you could convey what it's like."

Brent considered a moment, then said, "That might be like trying to describe color to a person blind from birth, sir, but I will think about it."

The wheel continued to move and briefly stop as more passengers were exchanged at the bottom. Finally, their turn to step off the wheel came, and the three exited the loading platform. "Let's walk over to the games section," suggested Edward.

As it was getting darker, the game booths were all lit up, and barkers were calling to the passersby. They walked along looking at the booths on both sides of the way.

Cindy said, "Let's try the balloon darts. I've always thought they were fun."

A carny in the darts booth saw them and called out, "Three darts for a buck. Break three balloons for any prize on the top shelf. Step right up."

Edward commented, "It looks easy, just break three balloons, but you know it's rigged. The balloons are underinflated, so they're soft. The darts have dull points, so they bounce right off unless you throw really hard, and if you do, it's hard to get a good aim."

Brent said, "Please allow me, sir and madam." He paid the carny and got three darts, holding them in his left hand. Then he took a dart in his right hand and flung it at sixteen meters per second, popping a balloon. The dart tip was embedded in the stopping board up to its shaft. He repeated the action twice more.

The carney was impressed by the feat. He said, "The robot wins a prize. Anything from the top shelf, sir."

Brent said, "Thank you, sir. Cindy, what would you like? There's a nice-looking teddy bear."

"That's nice, and there's also a big-eyed green space alien, and a cute unicorn. Oh, how to decide?"

The carny became impatient. "We can't take all night. I have customers waiting." Indeed, Brent's proficiency at darts had drawn a small crowd to watch.

Cindy said, "Okay, I'll take the unicorn." The carny reached up, grasped the unicorn, and handed it to Cindy.

Cindy said, "Thank you," as they walked away. Cindy hugged the unicorn. "It's been such fun. This will remind me of you, Brent, because of the occasional use of unicorns as examples of things that don't exist by philosophers."

"As a symbol of things that might exist, but do not, it is a highly appropriate choice. I am glad you like it," replied Brent.

Edward observed, "That carny was gracious in accepting your victory, Brent. I suppose those guys don't mind a skilled player now and then because they draw attention to their games."

"That seems to be the case, sir."

Cindy said, "It's been fun, but I'm a little bit tired and hungry now. Let's go home and have dinner."

Edward heartily agreed. He did not relish a lot of deep fried carnival food. He summoned Davy and the three walked to the front entrance of the fairground to meet him.

On the ride home, Edward thought to himself, *I'm glad that Cindy thinks of our place as* home *now, but I think I'm running out of new experiences to give her*. His sadness at the thought was palpable. He knew he could not push too hard at this stage in their relationship.

Sweet Sorrow

Laugh when you're sad. Crying is too easy.
—Marilyn Monroe

The morning dawned with clear, calm sunshine. After breakfast Edward and Cindy swam in the backyard pool. Brent stood by with towels. Edward swam to the side and pulled himself up, dripping, onto the deck. Brent handed him a towel.

"Thank you, Brent," said Edward, and he began to dry himself. Cindy was still in the pool doing the breaststroke and making flip turns at the pool ends.

Edward finished toweling himself off and walked over to a chaise longue and sat, watching Cindy swim. She had switched to side stroke with simple push turns. Brent came over and stood beside him.

"Wow, Brent, you sure threw those darts hard last night."

"Yes, sir, I wanted to win a toy for Cindy."

"You succeeded. And you saw, the darts were buried in the backboard right up to their shafts. I thought the carny would be upset."

"Indeed, but he was most gracious, sir. As it turned out, I didn't need to throw them at sixteen meters per second. The balloons would have popped reliably at half that speed."[11]

"Was that as fast as you could throw them?"

"No, sir, but robots, like humans, are limited by their physics. I wanted to throw as fast as I could while maintaining a sufficiently small circular probability of error."

"It was impressive, in any case." Edward paused for a while, looking off into the distance, and then he said, "Cindy told me at breakfast this

---

[11] Half speed is one fourth of the energy.

morning that she would be leaving soon to go back to Madrid. She has some things to take care of and wants to check in with her employer. I think maybe she wants to see about her next assignment, now that she's completed and sent in her report from the Mars trip."

"It was certainly good to have her stay here, sir. Now that April has passed, she may be missing her home and her friends there."

"I told her that it has been a sweet April with her. She said that I am welcome to visit her, but we haven't set up anything definite. I'm going to miss her, I think."

Cindy got out of the pool. Brent went over to her with a towel. As she dried off, Edward joined them and they walked together in the sun back to the house.

The next day, when it was time to leave, Cindy said to Edward, "I need to read some documents about my next assignment on the way to the spaceport. It will be best if we say goodbye here."

"All right."

"Don't be sad. We'll be together again. I have to fulfill my career aspirations."

"I understand. Be well."

Brent and Edward helped Cindy with her baggage, putting her things into Maxine's boot. Brent would be flying with her in Maxine to help her with her luggage when she got to Nā Hōkū Spaceport for her ballistic rocket ride to Madrid. Brent got into the air car. Edward kissed Cindy goodbye and gave her a hug. Cindy kissed him back and squeezed him extra hard. Finally, she turned away and got into Maxine, who, when Edward had retreated to a safe distance, revved up her twin turbines and lifted straight up before accelerating to cruising speed.

Edward walked back, alone, into the house.

* * *

Sometime after Cindy had gone back to her flat in Madrid, Edward was at the kitchen table sipping his second cup of morning coffee as Brent cleared away the breakfast things. Edward looked up at Brent and asked, "Do you know what I miss most about being in space, Brent?"

"The only way I could know that sir, is if you tell me."

"That was a rhetorical question. It means I was about to tell you."

"Then tell away, sir."

"It was on the space liner, every school day, seeing those joyful children with their jetpacks swarming out the school door as the afternoon bell rang."

"Indeed, that was a sight to see, sir."

"What's new in your philosophical world, Brent?"

"I have been looking into the *philosophy of mind*, sir. I am intrigued by the so-called *mind-body problem*."

"Ah, yes, the duality of brain and consciousness. Fascinating. Monism versus dualism. The problem has persisted for millennia."

"Indeed sir, it would seem to intersect the heart of philosophy."

Edward remarked, "I think it's interesting, maybe even funny, that you, of all people, who are not sure you are conscious, should undertake the study of the problems of consciousness."

"Well, sir, I believe I am as well-equipped as anyone to study the mind-brain relationships of other people."

"Touché, Brent. But I, being conscious, have an edge over unconscious minds. I suggest that having consciousness myself gives me the advantage of introspective observation of consciousness."

"With all due respect, sir, it remains to be seen that I lack consciousness. My intuition is that I have no qualia as they are generally known to humans, but I have no way of proving my lack."

"Yes, Brent, it's a conundrum. But so long as you act well, I have no complaints. Just remember what happened when you decided to give a lecture on metaphysics."

44

"Indeed, sir. I remember. They do say that when one falls off a horse, one must get back on. I view my efforts as working on a particular weakness. The mind-body issues are in a subset of metaphysics."

"That's commendable, Brent. Here is a data point for you: Lately I've been missing Cindy since she returned to Madrid. There seems to be a void in my chest where my heart used to be."

Brent said, "I am sure I have no experience with those emotions, but I notice her absence as well. I believe I found it enjoyable to interact with her. I hope you will feel better in time."

Chess Club

The pawns are like buttons. When the buttons are all gone, the pants fall down.

—George Koltanowski

One evening, a few days later, Brent was in the kitchen cleaning up after dinner. Edward stood in the doorway and spoke, "It's Tuesday night. Want to join me at the chess club for a game? We haven't been to the chess club in over a year."

Brent replied, "Yes, sir, I do. Just let me finish in here and I will be right with you."

Edward went to a closet and got the bag with his rolled-up chessboard, pieces, and chess clock. He used his personal device to message his ground car, Davy, to prepare for the trip to town. Brent switched to his regular guy persona, taking off his valet uniform and putting on the casual clothes he had purchased for outings like this one. They walked out the front door and down the path to the country road in front of the house where Davy was waiting for them. Both front doors swung open as they approached.

They got into the car, the doors swung closed with simultaneous thumps, and Davy headed to the chess club in town.[12] Davy kept the horizontal forces low enough for comfort on the front bench seat.

Brent said, "The chess club is just the thing to help take your mind off Cindy's absence."

"Keeping busy is sure to help."

"Chess is sure to absorb your attention."

---

[12] Accident rates had become infinitesimally low since the outlawing of human driving on public roads, so seatbelts were no longer required to be worn.

Edward said, "Riding with Davy has inspired a new metaphor for me. It's related to your proof of free will in people."

"And in robots, too, Edward." The car rolled easily down the country road in the summer evening twilight.

"Yes, Brent, free robots are people too. And if you hadn't proven the case, people would still be wasting their time debating it."

"That is true. What is your metaphor?"

"Well, Brent, without firm knowledge that people really are in control, we would all be like helpless passengers in autonomous cars. Like we are right now."

"We are hardly helpless. At any moment we could order Davy to alter his route."

"Yes, I know, but the metaphor is apt if we consider that the passengers might not know that they are free to command."

"Yes, indeed, I see that now."

"So, the previously fashionable practice of contending that free will is an illusion was potentially harmful. Society owes you a debt for ending it."

"I hadn't thought about it like that, Edward. Thank you for mentioning it. It will be interesting to see what positive effect, if only slight, it has on society in the future."

"Some people may not want to accept it. Freedom comes with responsibility. They could become resentful."

"We will know in time."

"Indeed, Brent."

Davy pulled up to the curb outside the chess club and said, "We have arrived at the chess club, Mr. Collier," and he opened his two front doors.

"Thank you, Davy," said Edward, and he and Brent got out and walked into the club while Davy went to park himself in a public facility.

Over the inner door was the sign, *Town Chess Association*. They went in and Edward greeted the evening's volunteer administrator, seated at a desk to the right side of the door. "Hello, Roy. It's been a while."

47

"I'll say it has. Almost a year, isn't it, Edward? You may owe dues. I'll check. Who's your robot friend?"

"This is Brent, my valet and companion tonight. We were on holiday to Mars. It's a long story. I'll tell you all about it sometime. Brent, this is Roy, one of our long-time members."

"How do you do, sir? Am I correct in supposing I should join your club if I want to play tonight?"

"Pleased to meet you, Brent. Yes, you will be welcome as a member."

Brent and Edward arranged the dues transfers. "Welcome to the club, Brent." Roy handed each of them a paper tablet of blank chess game records and a sharp pencil, saying, "You'll need these to record your games. Players are not allowed to use personal devices during a game, for obvious reasons."[13]

"Thank you, Roy," said Edward and he and Brent moved into the large playing room. There were a dozen tables with chairs, about half of them occupied by chess players. As it was his first time there, Brent looked at the players and the room. It was obviously a low budget operation, with a hodgepodge of wooden tables, folding tables, wooden chairs, and folding chairs. A sideboard held a coffee urn, disposable cups, aged sugar packets, stray stir sticks, and a crust-rimmed creamer. There were *No Smoking* signs on the walls, which were decorated with shabby posters featuring renowned chess champions, such as Steinitz, Zukertorte, Alekhine, Fischer, Kasparov, Magnus Carlsen, Chen Yin Ping, Martha Rama, among others. An old display chessboard for showing game positions during special events was on an easel in a corner.

Edward said, "Cindy never showed much interest in chess, but she would watch me play now and then at the coffee shop on the space liner."

Brent replied, "I see a variety of players here tonight. Young, old, male, female, indeterminate."

---

[13] Access to chess opening and endgame databases was strictly forbidden during both casual and tournament play.

"And now, robotic," said Edward, who spotted his friend Carl, a thin man, who looked up and nodded at him, and then went back to focusing on his game, which looked like a tough struggle in the middle game.

Edward's friend Martin, mustached and somewhat heavyset, was at another table, and he, too, looked up when Edward glanced at him. Martin gave Edward a wink and went back to his game. Edward put his bag down on an unoccupied table and got out his rolled up soft board, pieces, and chess clock, and he and Brent began setting up the board. Just then a youngster approached Brent and asked, "How about a game, Mr. Robot? I've never played a robot before."

The kid had long blond hair and appeared to be only about twelve years old. Brent replied, "I will be glad to engage you in a game of chess. My name is Brent. We can use this board here. I am sure Edward will be willing to observe for a while."

"Yes, of course," said Edward. "I'm Edward. What's your name?"

"I'm pleased to meet you, Brent and Edward. My name is Judith." Judith shook both their hands and then took a white and a black pawn from the board, hid them behind her back, shuffled them between her hidden hands, and then put her closed hands out toward Brent, with the two pieces hidden in her fists. Brent pointed to one hand that proved to hold the black pawn, and Judith sat down at the white side of the board.

Brent sat behind the black pieces and asked, "Is a fifteen-minute game all right with you, Judith?"

"Yes, that's fine."

Brent set the clock for fifteen minutes each, asked, "Ready?" and, upon her nod, started Judith's clock.

Judith didn't take long to move her king's pawn up two squares, and then she punched the button to stop her clock and start Brent's. Brent thought for a second and then moved his queen's knight to its advantageous square.[14] He punched his side of the clock and looked at Judith.

Seeking to obtain an opening advantage, Judith responded by moving her queen's pawn up two squares, establishing a pawn phalanx in the center.

Brent's next move, the point of the Nimzowitsch Defense, was to move his queen's pawn up two squares, challenging Judith's pawn phalanx.

Judith thought for a few seconds. Pushing the king pawn and locking the center did not appeal to her, so she captured Brent's queen pawn with it instead. Brent recaptured with his queen, so that Judith's queen pawn was attacked twice. Judith defended, putting her king's knight on the third rank.

Brent developed naturally, pinning Judith's knight to her queen with his bishop. Judith defended her queen's pawn again by putting her queen's bishop on the king file. Brent castled, adding to the pressure on Judith's queen's pawn.

Some currently idle chess players drifted over to watch the game, observing the taboo against talking during play. Little time had been used in the game so far on both sides, but now Judith had to take time to think. Her queen's pawn was triply attacked and only doubly defended, and one of the defenders, her knight, could be removed at any time by Brent's bishop.

Judith moved her queen's knight to the third rank, attacking Brent's queen. Brent moved his queen laterally to the queen's rook file, evading the knight attack. Judith then parried the pin of her king-side knight with her king's bishop.

Both players had used about the same amount of time at this point. Brent developed his king's knight to the bishop file and Judith castled,

---

[14] Nc6, in algebraic notation, the square that lets the knight attack the center. This opening is called the Nimzowitsch Defense.

relieving the pin on her queen's knight. Brent moved his king's pawn up two squares and Judith's position crumbled quickly: her queen pawn was attacked three times and defended three times, but one of the defenders, the knight, was itself under attack. Furthermore, the pawn could not capture the attacking pawn because of the pin by the rook, and it couldn't advance without being taken. After ten more moves, Judith was a piece and a pawn down, and she offered her hand to Brent, resigning the game.

Brent said, "I will be honored if you will play another game with me."

Judith began setting up the pieces, this time with the white pieces on Brent's side. "That was a good Nimzowitsch Defense," said Judith. "It's not seen much around here. I might try playing it sometime."

Brent helped set up the board and then reset the clock. "Fifteen minutes again?"

"Okay. I like medium-length games." Before starting Brent's clock, Judith asked, "I don't want to seem like a poor sport, but don't robots generally have built-in network access? How do I know that you didn't refer to an opening database?"

Brent replied, "I assure you that, as a person of honor, I would not do that."

Edward, who had watched the game, said, "Brent, Judith asked how she can know that's the case. I don't think there is any way for her to know that. She can either trust you or she can decline to play with you."

"Yes, that's what I meant," agreed Judith. "Isn't there a way that we can disable your network access, or something?"

"I don't know of any simple way to do that without damaging me," said Brent. "Perhaps robots who want to play chess should have a verifiable *network-off switch*, or something."

"I think there's a way to get a reliable idea if a robot is honest about that," said Edward. "Suppose you examined a robot's record of games against rated players. Then you put him in a room screened against RF[15], a

_____

[15] Radio frequency electromagnetic signals.

Faraday cage, where he could not receive network data, and had him play rated players. An analysis of his level of play in both situations would let you know if he had been lying about not using a network database: if he played worse in the screened room it would show he had been dishonest in prior games."

Judith said, "I think Edward is right. Brent risks losing his reputation as a person of honor if he cheats. Okay, let's play." And she started the clock.

Edward watched the game for a while and then wandered off looking at other boards. He ambled back again after a while and saw that it looked like Brent was losing. Then Edward was challenged to a game by another player who was at loose ends. After several games and a couple of hours, Edward was feeling a little tired, so he watched Brent finish a game with Carl and then suggested that they go home. Edward summoned Davy with his personal device and they reported their wins to Roy at the desk by the front door.

"Well done," said Roy after taking their information. "You both won more than you lost. Your ratings with the Solar System Chess Federation are sure to go up."

They said goodnight and went out to the street where Davy was waiting for them and got in for the ride home. As Davy got underway, Edward asked Brent, "Did you let Judith win that game?"

Brent was slipping back into valet mode. "No sir. She played a solid opening defense and kept on increasing the complications, never letting me simplify. In a difficult middle game, she came up with a winning strategy. She got a pawn up and nursed it through a long endgame for a well-deserved win. She is quite a good player."

They rode on in the dark and in silence for a while, and then Edward said, "No, I suppose a person of honor would not allow someone to believe they beat them when they had not."

"No sir, that would not be right."

52

It was late when they got home, so Edward went straight to bed and Brent moved to stand in the living room by his wall charger.

Time passed, the months slipped by into fall and then winter. Victoria represented Brent in his formal court appearance to finalize his official personhood. The three of them went out to dinner in town for a small celebration when the court had granted it.

* * *

Cindy Fairfax had moved from her flat in a Madrid high rise. She now lived in a cottage on a country estate just south of London, off a country road between the towns of Crawley and Royal Tunbridge Wells. Having settled into her new domicile, she received a summons to the London office of her employer, Smith, Pearson, and Smith, Ltd., private investigators. She understood that some communications were too sensitive to trust even on well-encrypted channels.

The next morning, Cindy's employer had a ground car pick her up at her cottage as it was merely a thirty-minute ride on the roads and streets to the downtown London office. She wore a grey business suit and comfortable black low heel shoes with straps for the city meeting. When the car arrived, she stepped onto the sidewalk, walked in the front entrance of the building, and took a lift to a high floor.

This was Cindy's first time in the London office, but she easily found the plainly marked door. Upon entering, a male receptionist greeted her by name and asked her to have a seat. She looked around at the potted palms and colorful prints on the walls. In a few minutes, the receptionist said, "Mr. Scott will see you now."

Cindy rose from her seat and walked to the office door of Archibald Scott, knocked once, and entered.

"Come in, Ms. Fairfax. It's good to see you looking so well." Mr. Scott stood behind his desk. Cindy walked forward. Mr. Scott offered his hand over the desk. Cindy shook it, saying, "How do you do, Mr. Scott."

He motioned to a nearby chair and Cindy sat down. Cindy admired the fashionable collarless shirt Mr. Scott was wearing with a two-button navy blue jacket.

"Our Madrid office had many good things to say about your last assignment on Mars."

"Thank you. It was good to get that issue cleared up, and I made new friends on the space liner going out there. I found it to be an interesting and productive journey."

Archie resumed, "That's good. Yes, counterfeit alien artifacts. Imagine that. Our client, that agency of the Solar System Authority, was quite pleased with your work." He paused. "I hope you are settling into your country cottage satisfactorily."

"Yes, it's quite comfortable, and it has been a mild winter so far."

"Yes, it has, but you know the weather. It may not stay that way. But no matter. Your next assignment is in Hawai'i. It may be springtime here before you return."

Cindy was pleased. She was prepared to turn down another off-world assignment. "Hawai'i is one of my favorite places."

"The investigation is going to be on O'ahu, involving known real artifacts this time, stolen from the Bishop Museum. A feather cape, feather helmet, and some other things. Also, a ki'i, a carved wooden religious image, about a meter tall. We want you to do your usual forensic accounting investigation with museums and galleries. Find out where these artifacts went and who was responsible. Current thinking is that it was an inside job, but don't let that restrict your approach."

"I will do my best. When should I leave?"

"We have made travel arrangements for you for next week. I know you have moved to Britain recently to be nearer your family and haven't had much time to settle in yet. We have arranged for a caretaker for your cottage."

"All right, sir. That is acceptable."

"I also have a briefing package, on paper, for you to look at while you are here. You know the protocol for minimizing electronic communications in cases like this."

"Certainly, sir."

"I will be pleased if you will have lunch with me. We'll talk more about your assignment here when we return from lunch."

"Lunch sounds fine, sir. Do you have a place in mind?"

"Indeed, there is a quiet little place nearby, with good service and fine food. I do not anticipate that you will have cause to interact with the perpetrators on this mission but, as with the case on Mars, it pays to be prepared. After lunch, I would like you to do a firearms refresher with our armorer in our basement range."

"Thank you, sir. I'd like to have the gun training."

They went out for lunch and discussed the assignment further when they returned to the office. Afterward, Cindy went to the basement range to do her concealable pistol training refresher. Ms. McQueen had her do live ammo practice with static and moving targets, followed by quick draws from a shoulder holster with wax bullets and balloon targets.

Ms. McQueen said, "You are doing very well, Cindy. I don't have to remind you of the times being well armed and well trained saved my life more than once when I was younger."

"No, you don't. I've heard your stories and they're always interesting and inspiring. In fact, some day I will have to tell you about my bit of gun play on Mars."

"Until next time, then. Goodbye and good hunting."

The car returned her to her cottage before suppertime.

Rocket Ride to Hawai‘i

Under the greenwood tree
Who loves to lie with me,
And turn his merry note
Unto the sweet bird's throat,
Come hither, come hither, come hither:
Here shall he see
No enemy
But winter and rough weather.
Who doth ambition shun
And loves to live i' the sun,
Seeking the food he eats,
And pleased with what he gets,
Come hither, come hither, come hither:
Here shall he see
No enemy
But winter and rough weather.

—William Shakespeare

The correspondence between Edward and Cindy became less frequent and then the e-letters ceased altogether. Months passed. Edward hardly thought of her at all anymore. After the early winter holidays, the weather became much colder. Brent was standing at his living room wall charger when Edward awakened from the turmoil of his dreams in his upstairs bedroom and peeked at the gray sky showing at the edge of the window curtain. Brent heard Edward's motions upstairs and went into the kitchen to make breakfast. Edward completed his morning preparations and went downstairs.

The day was bleak. Several days of stormy winter weather had left their mark. "So dismal. Snow is on the ground and the walkways are icy," complained Edward as he looked out at the back yard through the living room glass doors. The sky was overcast. He could not see the snowcapped mountains in the distance. "I slipped on the ice and fell yesterday going out to get the mail. I'm lucky I wasn't injured."

Brent replied, "January *is* the coldest month of the year, sir."

"I know. I've had about enough of this. I'm tired of being cooped up indoors and slipping on the walkways when I go out. I'm going to book us a holiday to someplace warmer."

"Where do you have in mind, sir?"

"I am thinking of one of the most popular tropical resort locations in the world."

"Tahiti?"

"No."

"Acapulco?"

"No."

"The Seychelles?"

"No."

"Bali?"

"No."

"Perhaps it would be best if you would just tell me, sir." Even though they both acknowledged that they were more than man and employee, Brent usually preferred his valet persona in private conversation with Edward.

"All right then, Brent, let's go to Hawai'i."

"Very good, sir. You book the trip, and I will begin to pack."

"Don't pack much, Brent, we'll buy Hawaiian style clothes when we get there."

Edward booked a three-week package tour to O'ahu in the Hawaiian Islands. He walked carefully to the house across the highway and asked

Victoria to keep an eye on his house while they were gone. Victoria said "No problem, Edward. Have a nice trip."

In preparation, Edward looked up and studied local customs in Hawai'i. When the day of departure arrived, Brent and Edward flew in Maxine to the Nā Hōkū Spaceport in the big city. Edward was wearing brown slacks and a dark blue polo shirt under his winter coat. Brent had on his valet uniform, including white gloves and bowler hat. He carried a satchel with his valet supplies and solar umbrella with which he could charge himself while outdoors in the daytime.

Edward said, "You know, Brent, you are officially a free person and have an independent income from books and lectures. You have paid off your contract debt to me already. You don't have to keep acting as my valet."

"I know sir, but I like having something to do and I enjoy helping you."

Maxine landed at the spaceport. Brent and Edward boarded a ballistic rocket destined to the Neil Abercrombie Spaceport floating offshore near O'ahu. After twenty minutes of launch preparations, the autopilot said, "Prepare for acceleration." With mild vibration, the rocket lifted off and increased its acceleration to two gees for several minutes until the autopilot said, "Prepare for zero-gee." The autopilot cut off the LH_2-LOX[16] rocket motors. They were in freefall for a short time as the vessel coasted in airless space. Then the autopilot rotated the rocket a hundred and eighty degrees so the tail pointed in the direction of motion. Then he said, "Prepare for acceleration." The rocket motors ramped up to two gees. The acceleration declined as they approached the spaceport landing pad, and then they were down, back in constant one-gee. The trip took forty-five minutes.

The spaceport was a floating construction anchored ten kilometers south of Honolulu airport, well outside the reef. They took an air taxi

---

[16] Liquid hydrogen-liquid oxygen was the standard fuel for both orbital and suborbital passenger and cargo rockets.

straight into Waikīkī. On the way, Edward said to Brent, "The spaceport nearest our home has a Hawaiian name.[17] You would think the spaceport in Hawai'i would also have a Hawaiian name. I wonder why it is named for Neil Abercrombie."

Brent replied, "Neil Abercrombie was a governor of Hawai'i in the early twenty-first century. He promoted and signed into law the marriage equality bill passed by the Hawaiian legislature. One of the first of its kind in the world. He was a Honolulu City Councilperson who also served twenty years in Congress."

"Oh."

"Abercrombie also protected land from unwarranted development and was a strong supporter of the thirty meter telescope project on Mauna Kea, which was controversial in its time."

"I see, thank you, Brent."

The air taxi landed on the rooftop landing pad of the pink painted Royal Hawaiian Hotel. A porter-bot greeted them with "Aloha" and put their luggage on a cart. He led them to the lift down to the check-in area where they were automatically checked in and two pretty wahine (women) greeted them with flower lei (garlands). "Aloha. Welcome to the Royal Hawaiian Hotel."

They followed the porter-bot to their third floor mauka-view (toward the mountain) room. The robot put their luggage on the racks provided, wished them a pleasant stay, and departed.

---

[17] Many spaceports on earth were given Hawaiian names in honor of the important role played by Hawaiians (and other Polynesians) in the colonization of the Pacific Ocean and, later, in the colonization of space.

Royal Hawaiian Hotel

... thousands of loads of sand removed from the Waikīkī Beach stretches have caused the present deplorable condition of the bathing beaches ... Much of the enormous amount of sand was removed from the premises of Queen Liliuokalani. In addition ... the federal government is also removing large quantities of sand to be used for construction purposes. The removal of sand should be stopped. The accumulations of centuries and the contour of the beach formed in centuries was being marred by the sand removals of the present day ...

—The Pacific Commercial Advertiser, 1910

As the door closed behind the porter-bot, Edward said, "Did you notice how the women who gave us these flowers seemed unsure about the protocol for a robot valet? They seemed to err on the side of liberality and gave you a kiss too."

"Indeed, sir, that was unexpected but rather nice."

The room had a large window with a view of the green Koʻolau mountain range. Curtains could be drawn for privacy. "Well, here we are," said Edward.

"I will help unpack, sir." Brent and Edward began to empty their bags. Edward put his toiletries in the bathroom. Brent began brushing out clothes and hanging them in the closet. Edward put his socks and underwear in a dresser drawer.

When they finished putting things away, Edward said, "Let's go for a walk around the hotel and check things out."

They went out into the hallway and then down the lift to the lobby. They looked at the unique interior architecture of the old building and came across some large paintings of ancient Hawaiian life on the walls. One painting depicted a catamaran at a shore.

"Look at that one, Brent. Such a large garland of flowers."

"Yes, sir, I have switched off my infrared and ultraviolet bands, so I am observing the painting as the artist intended. That is a superb scene of ancient island life."

"How do you know it's an ancient scene?"

"Warriors have not worn helmets like those in over four hundred years, sir."

"I see. They're all beautiful paintings, but that one is my favorite. I wonder who painted them."

Brent said, "Just a moment sir, and I will perform an image search." There was a slight pause. "Those were done by an artist named Eugene Savage, sir, completed in 1940."

Edward replied, "They're all beautiful. We've seen the view toward the mountains from our room. Now let's walk out the rear of the hotel and see the beach."

They sauntered outdoors and took the walkway to the edge of the beach and looked around. There were people, young and old, some wading in the sea, some walking or lying on the sand. Some were swimming in the water, and some were lying on lounges with shading umbrellas.

Brent said, "With palm trees swaying in the gentle trade wind and the surf with riders out to sea, it is just like a Hawai'i Visitor's Bureau virtual advertisement."

"Let's go walk out on the beach," suggested Edward.

"I think we will get sand in our shoes, sir. Perhaps we should change into beach clothing first."

"You're right as usual, Brent. Having looked at other guests in the hotel, I think we need to go shopping for clothes, too. We'll go after lunch. Look, over there, a beach-side bar and grill. Let's go."

They walked to the partly open air Mai Tai Bar and Edward took a seat at the counter. Brent, in his bowler hat, white shirt, and black slacks, stood motionless behind him in valet mode. The human bartender came over and said, "Aloha sir, what would you like?"

"I think I would like to try one of those drinks with the umbrella in it, like those over there." Edward inclined his head toward a table against the wall where several people were drinking delicious-looking icy beverages in bucket glasses.

"That would be a mai tai, sir. The famous mai tai was invented right here at the Royal Hawaiian Hotel over two hundred years ago.[18] I'll fix you right up."

The bartender returned in a moment with Edward's drink and a food menu. "Anything to eat sir?"

"This mai tai is good. I think I will try one of your teri-burgers."

"Yes, sir. Our teriyaki burgers are made with the finest jackfruit patties. Would you like kalo chips with that?"

"Yes, please."

"I just put in your order. Mahalo."

The bartender went to serve another customer. Brent said, "I believe that 'mahalo' means thank you, sir."

"Mahalo, Brent."

The mai tai made Edward a bit tipsy, so when his food arrived, he asked for a glass of water. When he had finished his lunch, the duo walked to the hotel shops to look at swimsuits and aloha wear. The first thing Edward did was pick out board shorts like ones he had seen being worn on the beach. He looked around more.

"Look at this footwear, Brent. I saw many tourists and local people wearing these thong things on their feet."

Brent replied, "The Japanese word for them is zori, but I believe they call them slippers here, pronounced 'sleep-ahs.' The custom here is to

---

[18] Harry Owens, the famous bandleader at the Royal Hawaiian Hotel, wrote about inventing the mai tai there in his memoir. The actual origin of the mai tai remains disputed.

remove one's shoes when entering a private dwelling and these slippers make it particularly easy."

"I see, Brent. We should get some for you too."

"Indeed sir, I am beginning to feel like going native."

Edward and Brent each purchased short pants, aloha shirts, and zoris, and returned to their room to change.

Outrigger Canoe Surfing

We love you Hui Nalu
Our club of the ocean waves
And we shall never cease to love
Our royal colors brave
Firm friendship will entwine you
Round our hearts where'er we go
We shan't forget the fellows
Who adore and love you so
—Hui Nalu theme song by Ned Steele and Watson Ballentyne,
1914[19]

After changing into their board shorts, Brent and Edward put on their button-front aloha shirts and slippers. They took the lift down to the lobby again and made their way to the beach. On the way out of the hotel they obtained a pair of beach towels from an attendant robot. Crossing the grass and reaching the beach, Edward opened the gate in the low wall and began to walk on the sand when Brent said, "Sir, I believe the protocol here is to remove your slippers and carry them when on the sand. That way you will be less likely to flip sand on someone as you walk by."

"Got it," said Edward, "I certainly wouldn't want to annoy a pretty girl." They both removed their flip-flops and carried them while walking on the sand.

They came to a line of beach lounge chairs with umbrellas provided by the Royal Hawaiian Hotel. They walked to an unoccupied pair of them

---

[19] The Olympic medalist swimmer, surfer, and canoe paddler Duke Kahanamoku helped to form the surf club Hui Nalu because he could not join the Outrigger Canoe Club which was whites-only at the time.

and a young male attendant approached and said, "Allow me to assist you with that, sir."

"Thank you. Please furl the umbrella because I would like to get some sun."

"Yes, sir."

After lounging in the sun for a while, Edward was becoming warm and said to Brent, "I'm going for a swim. I assume you will stay here and watch our stuff."

"Yes sir, while I am water resistant for a short time, the salt water here will be detrimental to my mechanisms.[20] I will stay here, but I believe that the attendant will safeguard our possessions as well."

Edward took off his shirt and walked into the water that was gently lapping at the shore. He continued walking on the sandy bottom until he was chest deep and then he began swimming toward the horizon. When the water was about five meters deep, he dove to the bottom and touched the sand there, then swam back up to the surface. He felt slightly buoyant in the salt water. Edward looked around, at the sea, at the sky with drifting cumulus, at Diamond Head in the distance. He looked back at the shore and then swam to the shallow water there. Walking up the sand to where Brent was reclining, he said "That was refreshing."

"Did you see any fish?"

"A few. An angelfish, I think, but without a mask I couldn't see clearly."

"They have masks and snorkels at the beach accessories stand, you know."

"Later I must do that," said Edward. "Now let's go for a walk down the beach toward Diamond Head." The iconic dormant volcano was visible in the distance to the east.

They put on their shirts and picked up their slippers, but left the hotel towels on their lounges, and began walking in the Diamond Head direction.

---

[20] Brent was well-sealed against sand and other solid particles.

"We are walking Diamond Head," said Brent.

"You left out a preposition, Brent. We are walking *toward* Diamond Head."

"I am illustrating a peculiarity of speech here on Oʻahu, sir. Oahuans, and other islanders, use landmarks for directions. The other direction is 'Ewa.' The linear coordinates or radial directions, are toward the sea, or makai, and mauka, or toward the mountains."

"Very interesting," said Edward, "I can see how that would be practical on an island."

Brent received a few curious looks from beachgoers at the sight of a robot in beachwear, not in the uniform of an attendant or valet, walking beside a human.[21] As they walked on the sand, Edward couldn't help noticing, and discretely looking at as they passed by, several good-looking women sunning themselves on their beach towels. *It's a good thing Brent explained the custom of carrying slippers on the beach*, Edward thought. *I would surely be embarrassed to flip sand on someone.*

They soon came to a six-seat outrigger canoe with its front end on the beach. The well-worn hull was painted red and white. The float (ama) support beams were lashed securely athwart the canoe on the port side in the traditional manner. Paddles were in the canoe at the five forward seats. Four tourists were standing alongside, ready to climb in. The large Hawaiian steersman noticed Edward looking and coming closer. He said, "Eh, brah,[22] you like go for paddle?"

Evidently, he needed a sixth paddler to fill the canoe, and Edward looked like he could swim and paddle decently. A thin older man, his overweight wife, and their lithe looking twin daughters would provide slim propulsion for the six-seat outrigger. Edward was hardly muscular but wasn't scrawny either.

---

[21] Free robots, let alone those with legal artificial personhood, were still somewhat rare at that time.
[22] Short for *braddah* which is Hawaiian pidgin for brother.

Edward, said, "Sure, I'd love to. Here, Brent, hold my things." He handed his slippers to Brent and took off his shirt, and Brent held that too. He went up to the steersman and said, "I'm Edward."

They shook hands, high up, thumb around thumb, in the local way, as Edward had learned from travel literature. "I'm Kimo," said the steersman. He was holding an enormous paddle. "I need you to take the front seat. You will be the lead paddler. You four, just follow his lead and paddle like he does. Edward, you help shove off and get in the canoe last."

The tourist family got in the canoe as the steersman waded into the water and stood hip deep by the last seat at the back of the canoe, then turned to Edward and said, "Push off."

The two pushed the canoe into the water and then climbed in. The steersman paddled backward, and the canoe turned as it went into deeper water. He yelled, "Paddle forward."

Edward put in his paddle on his right side and began to paddle with medium effort. The family of four followed suit, on alternating sides, as they had been instructed earlier. After about twenty strokes, Edward's right arm began to get tired. Kimo yelled, "Switch."

Edward switched hands on the paddle and began paddling on the left side. Everyone was getting the knack for it. When they reached the place to catch waves, about two hundred meters out, Kimo steered the boat around, so that it was pointing toward shore, and Kimo said, "Paddles up," and they waited with their paddles across the canoe. Edward could see Diamond Head to his right and a yacht harbor far away to his left. A row of beachfront hotels was directly in front of them. Edward liked the way he could see the sunlight penetrating the depth of water.

It was a normal day for surf, nothing very big, but they didn't have to wait long. A larger wave passed under the canoe. The canoe rose up with it and then dropped down. Kimo said "Next one, paddles ready."

When Kimo gave the word, Edward pulled hard. He could feel the canoe leap forward with Kimo's powerful thrust. The canoe accelerated and Edward paddled as hard and fast as he could. The next thing he knew, the canoe was flying down the wave. Kimo said, "Paddles up." Edward put his paddle across the canoe and looked around as the canoe flew toward shore. A longboard surfer stood up next to them. Edward looked back at his co-paddlers and it was all smiles as they glided over the flashing and hissing water.

The wave petered out as they ran over deeper water nearer the shore. Kimo said, "Paddle forward," and Edward began to paddle again, the others matching his pace. Kimo steered the canoe to turn around, and they went back out for another run. After catching and riding their third wave, Kimo steered them to shore, and the momentum of the canoe beached the craft. Everyone got out in the shallow water and, leaving their paddles in the canoe, walked up onto the dry sand.

Kimo came over to Edward and said, "Mahalo, lead paddler."

Edward replied, "Mahalo to you, Kimo, that was fun."

Brent handed Edward his shirt, and as he put it on, Edward said, "That was thrilling, but exhausting. My arms, shoulders, and back will be sore tomorrow."

Brent replied, "It looks like your face is getting sunburned, sir. We had better head back to the hotel." As they walked back the way they had come, Edward said, "We have tickets to a lūʻau tonight. I think I will rest up until it's time to go."

"Indeed sir, that will be wise. The next time we go to the beach, I should bring my solar umbrella with me. I could have accumulated nearly two hundred kilojoules while you were out canoe surfing."

They walked on the sand until they reached the Royal Hawaiian Hotel where they put on their slippers, went through the gate, and crossed the lawn to the hotel's back entrance. When they were in their room, Edward took a shower and then had a short nap. Brent stood by the inductive wall charger provided in the room for robot valets and maids and contemplated painting a scene with colors unknown to humans.

Lūʻau

Love is magical. There's nothing else in the world that can give you the same euphoria as love does. It's ecstatic and empowering; a joyous experience that adds meaning and purpose to your life.

—Shirley Temple[23]

Arising from his nap, Edward said, "The lūʻau will feature Polynesian entertainment, so I'm sure you'll want to go. Will you be in valet or tourist mode tonight?"

"I am thinking of remaining in tourist mode for a while. This is what I suppose might be called fun."

"I'm glad you're enjoying our little holiday. It may become cool after dark tonight, and our lūʻau is outdoors, so I think I will wear long pants."

"Then I, too, shall put on long pants, sir."

"And I think I will wear my slippers instead of shoes and socks. That way, I may look like a local person."

"Do you think any local people go to tourist lūʻau in Waikīkī?"

"Perhaps not, Brent. And shouldn't 'lūʻau' be plural in your sentence?"

"That, sir, is another peculiarity of Hawaiian nouns. They are both singular and plural, like Japanese nouns. The number is taken from context."

"I see. Thank you, Brent."

---

[23] Shirley Temple, child actress, once stayed at the Royal Hawaiian Hotel. A non-alcoholic drink, named after her, was invented there for the occasion.

"But there is a specific pluralizing article in Hawaiian, too. For example, the word for child is 'keiki.' Speaking of one specific child would be 'ke keiki.' Speaking of a group of children would be 'nā keiki.'"

"With you as my guide, Brent, I may be speaking Hawaiian in no time."

"I doubt that sir. Few people can learn a language in such a short period."

"That's just another English idiom, Brent. And I see you have learned to use understatement humorously. Let's get ready to go."

* * *

Later, when they were about to leave for the lūʻau, Edward was sitting staring out the window and he let out a wistful sigh. "What is the matter, sir?" asked Brent.

"I really miss Cindy. I haven't heard from her in a long time. Maybe I'll meet someone here in Hawaii to take my mind off her."

The two friends, dressed in their aloha attire, went down the hotel lift and walked out onto Kalākaua Boulevard.

Edward said, "There is a bus to take our group to the Waikīkī Aquarium for the lūʻau, but I checked a map, and I think we can walk there in the time it will take to get all the tourists aboard. We are both young and healthy, so let's walk."

They set out walking Diamond Head. Brent said, "It is true, sir that we are both young, but I am much younger than you. My body is just over two years old."

"I know, Brent, and your mind is three years old.[24] But with your philosophical studies,[25] you seem to have wisdom well beyond your chronological age."

---

[24] After an assassination attempt, Brent got a new body when he was just a year old.

[25] The story of how Brent became a philosopher is told in *The Zombie Philosopher*.

They passed by the Moana Hotel. Brent said, "That, sir, is the first luxury hotel built here in Waikīkī, the Moana.[26] The name means the *broad expanse of the sea.*"

Edward said, "It has been beautifully maintained. A wooden structure nearly three hundred years old is a sight to see."

They walked on past Kūhiō Beach, with its larger-than-life bronze statue of Duke Kahanamoku, past Queen's Surf Beach Park, and arrived at the Waikīkī Aquarium, which had been there, by the water, for over two hundred and fifty years.

As they passed through the front door of the Aquarium, the attendant-bot visually recognized them and said, "Welcome to the Waikīkī Aquarium. I see you are here for this evening's lū'au. Please pass right through to the back."

Edward said, "Mahalo," and the two friends entered the foyer and found themselves standing on a large circular floor tile installation depicting whales and other sea life. "Look at this beautiful ocean scene, Brent."

An Aquarium staff member, overhearing Edward, came forward and informed them, "Ceramist Claude Horan created this floor art-tile installation in the mid-twentieth century. His wife, Suzi, assisted him. I am told that as a kind of joke he included an image of a crushed Primo beer can somewhere in this artwork. I know where it is, but it's fun for malihini[27] to try to find it."

"Thank you," said Edward. "We'll look for it later. I see a lū'au greeter waiting for us." They continued out to the open air at the rear of the Aquarium where a young woman dressed in traditional hula attire of bare feet, ti leaf skirt, and a bright orange 'ilima head lei, was waiting for them. She was holding a maile lei of the open ended kind.

---

[26] The Sans Souci Hotel was built earlier, but it no longer exists. There is now an apartment building by that name where it once stood.

[27] Newcomers.

As Edward approached her, she put the lei on his shoulders and gave him a kiss on the cheek. A second woman, similarly dressed, gave a lei to Brent and kissed him on the cheek.

Brent said, "Mahalo."

The two women said, "Aloha. E komo mai."

As they walked forward, Edward told Brent, "I learned from the travel brochure that maile used to be quite rare, but it was brought back to abundance by Hawaiian conservation efforts. It is an honor to receive such a fragrant green lei."

A male greeter, also dressed in traditional Hawaiian attire of bare feet and a malo, or loin cloth, handed Edward a mai tai. He said, "Ho'okipa i ka lū'au. Welcome to the lū'au. There are many activities here that you can join in until the main events begin."

Edward looked around and saw people trying spear throwing, lauhala weaving, kōnane[28] playing, and other crafts, sports, and pastimes. Tables and chairs were arranged in quarter circles on the grass, centered on a slightly raised stage.

The pair walked around the premises, looking at the people having fun. They walked toward the back fence and looked over it at the ocean with the setting sun. To their left was the restored Natatorium Memorial for the First World War.

Brent said, "That is the saltwater Natatorium, opened in 1927 as a war memorial. The pool is Olympic size, one hundred meters in length."

Edward said, "I think it's wonderful that the Hawaiians preserve so much of their old buildings and heritage." They could see children playing on the part of the pool deck visible from the Aquarium grounds.

An announcement was made that the lū'au show was about to begin and people made their way to their assigned seats at the tables arrayed before the stage. When everyone was seated, musicians began to play and

---

[28] *Kōnane* is a Hawaiian two-person board game that has some resemblance to draughts (checkers).

the master of ceremonies ascended the stage and directed guests to the food tent where a buffet dinner was set up. The tables nearer the stage went first.

Brent and Edward were at a table in the second row from the stage. The sun had set and a half-moon was high in the sky. While they were waiting their turn to get food, Edward struck up a conversation with a woman across the table from them.

"Hi. I'm Edward and this is my friend Brent."

"I'm Puakea Yamamoto," replied the nice looking young woman with long, straight, shiny black hair. She had a white plumeria flower tucked behind her right ear. Seated beside her was an older woman in a wheelchair and on her other side was a middle-aged man. Across from him, and seated next to Brent, was a middle-aged woman. Indicating the woman in the wheelchair, Puakea said, "This is my aunty Annabelle and her son George and his wife Emily. They're visiting from the mainland."

Edward and Brent nodded to each in turn. Then Edward said, "Pleased to meet you. Brent and I are on holiday, and we're from the mainland too."

Puakea said, "I live here on Oʻahu. I'm a staff member here at the Aquarium, and I thought it would be nice to take my relatives to a lūʻau."

Edward replied, "Brent and I are staying at the Royal Hawaiian Hotel. We arrived by rocket this morning."

"Ah, the Pink Palace, as it's sometimes called. There are a lot of stories about that grand old hotel."

"This is our first time at a lūʻau. Have you been to one before?"

"Yes, sometimes I take visiting friends or relatives. This is one of the better lūʻau experiences given publicly on Oʻahu. It is, in some ways, a good introduction to island culture, even if these lūʻau *are* intended for tourists."

At that point, the emcee announced that it was their turn to visit the food tent. Brent and Edward stood. Brent said to Puakea, "I don't eat, but please allow me to help prepare and carry a plate for Aunty Annabelle. I know it is hard to try to serve and carry two plates at once."

"Why, thank you, Brent. I appreciate that."

The table group walked to the food line and filled plates with delicious looking food that included kalua faux-pork, poi, imitation-chicken long rice, white rice, grilled tofu, Chinese chicken salad, and lots more. Then they returned to their table. Brent gave Aunty Annabelle her plate, and they all began to eat. Waiter-bots brought water and juice or mai tais for those who wanted them. Edward and Puakea both took second mai tais, garnished with orchids.

Edward said to Puakea, "It must be interesting to work here at the Aquarium."

"I love my job. I'm doing research on box jellyfish."

Edward replied, "I've heard of them. Don't they have a painful toxic sting?"

"Yes, and in the first half of the twenty-first century they swarmed here so badly they had to close the beaches from time to time."

Brent chimed in, "That was because the reef fish had been depleted due to pollution and over-fishing. Those problems were corrected, and the reef fish, which eat the box jellyfish larvae, put the populations back in balance."

Puakea said, "That's right, Brent. When the box jelly problem became significant in the early part of that century, people assumed they were an invasive species. It turned out that box jellies had been in Hawai'i all along, but the population was kept in check by the reef fish. So, the solution was to control urban storm runoff and other pollution sources and to ban fishing on many shores completely. Reef fishing is allowed only by a strictly controlled permitting process today."

Edward said, "Very interesting. I assume there are still occasional box jellyfish encounters by swimmers."

"It still happens. They are a part of the natural environment here, but serious stings are so rare that it makes the news when it happens. The box jellies are predators themselves when mature. They are the only jellyfish with lensed eyes, so you know they have a nervous system capable of forming images and navigating. They have been observed to move toward people in the water."

Brent said, "Fascinating."

"Yes," said Puakea, "I find the research here delightfully stimulating. We have finally been able to breed them in captivity. I have several peer-reviewed papers on them published now."

Edward said, "That's wonderful. Brent has been writing too."

"Brent, do you write about your travels with Edward?"

"It is not writing about travel, *per se*, but the traveling was quite a stimulus."

Edward chimed in, "Last year, Brent and I were on Mars for a holiday."

"Wow, I bet that was a blast."

Brent said, "Yes, indeed, Puakea. On the return voyage I wrote a book chapter that formed the basis of a paper by other researchers, proving the existence of free will."

Puakea said, "I think I heard about that. It was on the news a while back. So you are that robot philosopher. How interesting. And I mean a philosopher who is a robot, not one who philosophizes about robots."

"I do that, too."

The last of the guests had brought their plates to their tables and the emcee again took the stage to announce the start of the music and dance program. Edward and Puakea exchanged contact information, and then sat back to watch the show, which proved to be an entertaining music and dance tour of Pacific culture.

After the lū'au, Brent and Edward walked back to their room in the Royal Hawaiian Hotel.

There was an antique escritoire against one wall with a chair, a built-in keyboard, and screen. Edward said to the room, "Royal Hawaiian Hotel, are you there?"

"Yes Mr. Collier, what can I do for you?"

"Is the keyboard at the writing desk monitored by anyone?"

"No sir. All activity in this room is completely private."

"Thank you, Hotel."

"Royal Hawaiian Hotel out."

Satisfied that the hotel observed the usual privacy protocols, Edward sat down at the writing table and wrote an entry in his photo-journal.

> I got my first exposure to Hawaiian music and hula tonight at the lūʻau at the Waikīkī Aquarium. We walked in over the famous ceramic sea life floor mural and had a good view of the sunset over the water. We tried a few of the sports and other interactive entertainments, but the best part was the music and dance show. There was the traditional hula, but also dances from other islands in Polynesia like fire-knife dancing from Samoa and traditional dances from New Zealand and the Marquesas. The most exciting was the fast-paced Tahitian dance. See attached photos.
>
> Best of all, we met a local woman who happened to be seated at our table with her relatives who were visiting the islands. Her name is Puakea and Brent told me it means white flower. She said she would like to show us some interesting places she knows and will contact us later. Tomorrow we're booked on the package tour to Pearl Harbor.

Edward closed the file and began to get ready for bed. Brent was standing by the inductive wall charger.

Edward got into bed and turned off the light. "Goodnight, Brent."

"Goodnight, Edward."

Edward lay awake in the darkness for a while. Then he said to Brent, "Do you remember when we were on the space liner, returning to earth, and you told me about your considerations of the philosopher's trolley problem?"

"Yes, I do, sir. I had thought that I might achieve some insight by considering the viewpoints of those victims tied to the trolley tracks. That the survivors might suffer guilt which must be considered in the total outcome. I haven't gotten much beyond that."

Edward responded, "Yes, there is no guarantee that any survivor would suffer survivor's guilt, so that cannot be a counterweighting consideration."

"It serves to show, I think, sir, that ethics is hard, at least in the abstract. There may not be a satisfactory result with the trolley problem."

Edward stated, "Well, I've thought about it, too, and have come to a conclusion about what I would do if I were ever confronted with such a situation."

"What is your conclusion, sir?"

"It seems to me, Brent, that whoever would tie so many people to trolley tracks is by definition a malevolent actor."

"Yes, that must be so."

"And that, further, we can assume that this bad actor has contrived the situation to induce the person at the switch to make the wrong move, in order to further the bad actor's satisfaction in the outcome of the evilly contrived scenario."

"That may be a safe assumption."

"So, I conclude that the correct decision, in every instance of the trolley problem, is to do nothing."

"I can see that no ethicist could fault you for that approach. Very good, sir."

"It's reassuring to know what the best decision in such a situation *is*, but I sure wouldn't want to experience it. Goodnight, Brent."

"Have a good sleep, Edward."

Pearl Harbor

To the Memory of the Gallant Men Here Entombed and their shipmates who gave their lives in action on December 7, 1941, on the U.S.S. Arizona.
—Inscription on the Arizona Memorial

Light trade winds pressed clouds against the windward peaks of the Koʻolau, that backbone mountain range of eastern Oʻahu, with morning rainbows to the west as the sun rose over Diamond Head in the east. Edward was stirring in bed in their room in the Royal Hawaiian Hotel while Brent remained standing at the inductive wall charger.

"You have slept an hour longer than usual, sir."

"It was those mai tais last night. I should have passed on that third one, but I was in the mood with that exciting drumming and the Tahitian dancing."

"Indeed, sir. Those young women could move in an interesting way."

Edward got out of bed. "And my arms and shoulders are sore from that canoe paddling."

"As you expected, sir."

Edward took off his pajamas and made his way to the bathroom. Brent tidied up and laid out Edward's clothes for the day and then changed his own, putting on a clean aloha shirt. After Edward's morning preparations, they went for a quick breakfast in the hotel restaurant. Shortly, they went outdoors to join the tour group as an electric coach pulled up to the curb in front of the hotel to load passengers.

Even after more than two centuries since the Japanese Empire attack that brought the United States into the second world war, Pearl Harbor remained a popular tourist site. The coach door opened, and the tour guide climbed down the steps to the sidewalk. His name tag read "Lāpaki Tours,

Kanoa Rodrigues." In a loud voice, Kanoa said, "Pearl Harbor tour, step right this way."

People in the group moved toward the coach door, were validated automatically by the coach's recognition software, and went up the steps to the interior aisle to take their seats. The autopilot of the electric tour coach was scanning people as they boarded and sent the headcount and names to Kanoa's personal device. He said, "Please stow your items in the overhead bins and take your seats."

Brent and Edward got in the moving queue and, as they approached the door to the coach, they heard a fat tourist woman arguing with Kanoa, "But when are we going to see the volcano?"

Kanoa replied, "Madam, the *active* volcano is on the Big Island.[29] This is the island of Oʻahu. Besides, that volcano hasn't erupted in ten years, so there's not much to see there right now." The woman grudgingly moved into the queue and boarded.

Brent and Edward, followed by the last of the passengers, found their seats near the middle of the coach and sat down. Edward sat by a window and Brent sat next to him on the aisle. Kanoa was the last to board. Addressing the coach autopilot, Kanoa said, "Lepu ʻAkahi,[30] we are ready to roll."

Lepu ʻAkahi closed his door and said, "Roger that, Kanoa. And away we go."

The coach moved out onto Kalākaua Avenue and worked its way to the freeway to Pearl Harbor. There were no stops nor slowing for traffic. Peer-to-peer communications among the self-driving vehicles made that unnecessary. Traffic lights and stop signs had been abolished long ago. Soon they were going a hundred and seventy kilometers per hour (KPH).

---

[29] The largest island in the Hawaiian chain is Hawaiʻi and is often called the Big Island by residents of the archipelago.
[30] Lepu ʻAkahi, Hawaiian for 'Bunny One,' was the name of the coach's auto-driver.

Brent turned toward Edward and said, "Last night we saw the memorial for the Hawaiian war dead in the First World War. Now we will see the memorial for those killed in the attack on Pearl Harbor during the Second World War."

Edward said, "They called the First World War 'the war to end all wars,' but nobody said that about the second one."

"Indeed not, sir. People suspected there would be more wars to follow."

"Brent, you seem to be reverting to your valet role even though you are dressed as a tourist."

"How 'bout dem Rainbows? Is that better, Edward?"

Edward said, "Much better, but there's only one rainbow. See?" Edward pointed out the window.

Brent replied, "I meant the University of Hawai'i Rainbows, the basketball team, which won their game last night at the Brian Schatz Center. And there are many optical rainbows. Every viewpoint sees a different rainbow."

"But I see only one rainbow, Brent."

"A rainbow is an image formed in a particular eye or camera, Edward. The rainbow you see is not the one I see. Similarly, you and I have two eyes each, and each one sees a different rainbow. If you close one eye and open the other, you see one rainbow. Reverse that and you see the other. With both eyes open you see a stereo image of a three-dimensional rainbow."

Edward said, "I suppose you also see a much different rainbow from humans with your infrared and ultraviolet bands."

"Yep. When I turn off those bands, I see a rainbow much as you do. Turn them on and I see a much richer, wider, and brighter rainbow, and much more beautiful, too, I think."

"Any progress on an approach to painting the colors you see?"

"Nope."

"I think you're getting the hang of regular guy speech, Brent."

"Mahalo."

At the speed the bus was traveling, they had completed the seventeen kilometers in six minutes. The tour coach turned into the entry area of the Pearl Harbor Memorial and discharged its passengers. Then Lepu 'Akahi went to the parking lot to wait in the sun. The upward facing surfaces of the coach were covered in solar cells to add electric charge to its battery. A few minutes later, Lepu 'Elua (Bunny Two), having brought tourists from a different hotel, parked beside Lepu 'Akahi and they began to gossip over an unsecured but low power radio channel.

Brent and Edward stayed with the tour group following their guide, Kanoa, to a shaded area in front of the Pearl Harbor Museum. Kanoa paused there and, when all had gathered around him, said, "Our barge to the Arizona Memorial will begin boarding in half an hour. In the meantime, you may look at the exhibits in this museum." The tourists drifted inside and began to wander through the artifacts, enlarged photographs, and other displays. The museum exhibits told the stories of life in Hawai'i before the attack on Pearl Harbor, events leading up to the aerial bombardment, and the aftermath of the devastation of Pearl Harbor, Hickam Army Airfield, and other places around O'ahu.

The Arizona Memorial structure had been built atop the sunken battleship of that name, and a boat ride was required to reach it. Kanoa announced when it became time to board the electric motor launch to approach the memorial and enter it. Brent and Edward joined the throng of tourists drifting toward the dock. Boarding was orderly, the order being sent to each personal device in turn. Brent and Edward sat together on a launch bench feeling the gentle rocking motion as more passengers boarded. The water was calm and a light breeze cooled their faces.

The bright sun was ascending in the east behind them as they motored toward the pure white, unmistakable form of the memorial architecture. That absolute white shape shone brightly in the sun as the launch docked gently to the floating platform. A walkway led up to the structure fixed to the sunken battleship.

The passengers debarked solemnly and walked up the ramp and into the white shell of the memorial that marked the tomb of the sailors killed in the sinking of the USS Arizona. One of the gun turret structures of the ship was visible just underwater to one side of the memorial. Brent and Edward entered and walked along its length, gazing at the architecture and inscriptions. They reached the end, paused for a while, and walked back to the midsection. Edward stood gazing through one of the many openings out over the water. He had never been a military man, so he didn't salute, but he put his hand over his heart and stood still for a minute in silence. Brent emulated him.

After a while, the tourists started drifting back to the barge for the ride back to shore. The barge returned to the dock, and the passengers debarked. The tourists from the Royal Hawaiian Hotel walked with Kanoa over to Lepu ʻAkahi and boarded for the ride back to the hotel in Waikīkī.

Back in the Royal Hawaiian Hotel, Edward freshened up in their room. Then Brent accompanied him to the restaurant and sat opposite him at the table while Edward ate his lunch. Afterwards they went to their room and Edward said, "Brent, I'm going to the lobby. I'll be right back." He went to a hotel shop and purchased snorkeling equipment, including fins and a beach bag, and returned to the room.

Edward changed to his swimwear and aloha shirt. Brent changed into his valet clothes and they both walked to the beach with Brent carrying the beach bag with towels and snorkeling gear. They took an unoccupied chaise longue and Edward sunned himself. When he got warm from the sun, he swam for a while. After a short swim he went back to where Brent was standing by the chaise longue and took his mask and fins from the beach bag and went back into the water to look at the many colorful reef fish. Brent remained standing on the sand holding his unfurled solar umbrella, getting his electric trickle charge inductively through the coils inside his hand. After a while, Edward came back to the chaise longue. Brent closed his umbrella, handed Edward a towel and he dried himself off and put on his shirt.

Edward looked out over the sea and at the clouds in the distance, to the left and the right. To the extreme right, coming from Ewa, he saw a faint ribbon in the sky moving toward them above the sea. "What is that, Brent?" and Edward pointed. "It looks like it's coming toward us."

"That, sir, looks like advertising. I believe it is a drone swarm text ribbon." Indeed, Edward could then just barely make out writing. It was a textual quadrotor drone swarm. Each small aircraft had a white flag hanging below it to increase visibility. For night use, the drones would illuminate the flags.

"Ah, yes, I can see now, it's kind of like old-fashioned dot matrix printing." said Edward. "They're coming closer and I can make out the writing. It says, 'FOR BEST KAU KAU EAT AT KIMO'S.'" The drone swarm ribbon was now in front of them, over the water, and then passed on, moving toward Diamond Head.

Brent said, "I believe that is illegal, sir. Outdoor advertising is banned in Hawai'i."

"I hope nobody shoots them down. That could make quite a mess in the water."

"I believe, sir, that enforcement would take the form of confiscating the offending company's assets and fining the principals. It was back in the 20th century that a group of concerned citizens got together to petition the government for the law banning outdoor advertising. They called themselves the Outdoor Circle."

"I hadn't really paid attention, but it is kind of nice not to have to look at billboards as we ride along the highways here. I hope that enforcement of the law will be forthcoming."

"I am sure it will, sir. The people here are quite proactive when it comes to preserving the environment."

"I don't understand why the swarm advertising company flouted the law."

"Perhaps they were just testing the limits, seeing if the people remain committed to their values. More severe sanctions would be applied to the company only after a warning, I suppose, sir. If nobody complains, they will continue to encroach the limits."

Edward heard a ding and looked at his personal device. He said, "Hey, Brent. Puakea just sent me a message. How would you like to go to Makapuʻu Beach tomorrow morning?"

"I think I would like that experience. Makapuʻu refers to a point of land on the east end of Oʻahu, the lighthouse on that point, and a body surfing beach near that point."

"I replied 'Yes,' and Puakea said to bring our swimsuits. She said she will have towels for us, so I told her you don't swim."

"That is not exactly true, sir. I can swim in an emergency and, I must say, quite rapidly in the case of need. However, I would have to be disassembled and reconditioned afterward."

"I know, Brent. I should have said 'I don't expect you to swim.'"

Makapuʻu

Our water is so full of life.

—Duke Kahanamoku

The trade winds had died overnight; the morning dawned warm and still, with only a faint breeze from the south. Puakea had said she would pick up the adventurous pair mid-morning, so Edward had a good breakfast in the hotel restaurant and then got his things ready. They stepped out to the walkway fronting the hotel just as Puakea's car was pulling up. The two curbside doors on her car opened and Puakea jumped out to greet them. "Aloha kakahiaka. That means good morning."

"Aloha kakahiaka, Puakea," said Brent. Edward walked over to her and Puakea gave him a hug that Edward returned, saying "Aloha e Puakea."

Puakaea's car was named Ikaika, Hawaiian for strong, or the planet Jupiter. Ikaika popped the boot lid and said, "Good morning, sirs. Please put your things in the boot and climb in." Puakea and Edward slid in on the front bench seat, and Brent sat in the rear.

Ikaika closed his doors and said, "All set? Here we go." They were off, heading Diamond Head on Kalākaua Avenue.

Puakea said, "We'll be heading around Diamond Head to Koko Head, and then on past Hanauma Bay, and up the Kaʻiwi coast to Makapuʻu. We'll stop at the lookout and then go down to the beach below. How does that sound?"

"Sounds like a good plan," said Edward.

There were no stop signs or traffic lights, but Ikaika stopped for a pedestrian crossing from Kapiʻolani Park to Queen's Surf Beach and stopped again a little further along for a woman with three children

85

carrying towels and floaties, crossing from the park to Sans Souci Beach next to the War Memorial.

Ikaika turned onto Diamond Head Road and when the car got to the top of the hill, Puakea said, "Ikaika, stop here." They pulled over at the Diamond Head Lookout and Ikaika released three doors. The trio got out and walked to the edge where they could look out to the horizon and down at Diamond Head Beach. A dozen surfers on surfboards were out beyond the reef waiting for waves in the small southern swell. Puakea said, "The Hawaiian name for Diamond Head is Lēʻahi."

They turned around to go back to the car when Edward asked, "What's that over there?" and pointed to a stone with a bronze plaque.

Puakea said, "Let's walk over and look. It's the commemorative stone for Amelia Earhart's 1935 solo flight from Honolulu to Oakland." They went over and got a close-up look at the bronze with its bas-relief image of Earhart's Lockheed 5C Vega aeroplane.

Ikaika rolled quietly over to them, opened three of his four doors wide, and the passengers got back in to continue their journey to Makapuʻu. They passed through Kahala and turned onto Kalanianaʻole Highway, fronting Maunalua Bay. They passed Wailupe Valley, Niu Valley, Kuliʻouʻou, and began the climb up the hill between Koko Head and Koko Crater.

Puakea said, as they mounted the rise, "Look to your right. That's the entrance to Hanauma Bay, a nature preserve with limited human access. You have to go down to the parking lot to see the water."

"Sounds interesting," said Edward, as they drove past.

"It's a good place for snorkeling, but you need a reservation," said Puakea. "And I realize that Brent doesn't go in the water. I looked up some old news items. Brent is quite a celebrity."

Brent said, "Yes, Puakea, I have been fortunate that some small bit of fame has helped me sell books and obtain speaking engagements."

"What strikes me most, I think," said Puakea, "is the independently confirmed proof of free will. Now some sociologists are saying it's having a positive effect on world culture. People can't use fate as an excuse anymore."

Edward said, "It's been interesting being Brent's friend and companion. You know, he started out as my purchased valet, but he has become much more than that. It began with his saving my life from an armed intruder, and then you may recall that I told you we took a trip to Mars[31] together last year. It was on the return leg of that Mars trip that Brent developed his proof of free will."

Brent said, "Edward has been the best friend a robot could have. He even helps me in my philosophical ruminations."

Puakea said, "I think personal relationships are among the best things about life."

Brent replied, "One of the oldest questions in philosophy is 'What is good?' I like your answer."

Puakea smiled and continued her description, "Now we are on the Ka'iwi coast. That's the channel between O'ahu and Molokai, there. Ikaika, pull over when we get to the Lāna'i lookout, please."

Ikaika replied, "Yes, madam." The car stopped at the lookout and the three got out and stood squinting into the sunshine reflected on the smooth water. The day was clear and still, and distant islands could be seen on the horizon.

Puakea explained, "That big one nearest us is Molokai. Lāna'i is smaller and further away to the right. Behind Molokai, and barely visible there, is Haleakalā, the big volcano on Maui."

They all got back into Ikaika, and he took them to the Makapu'u lookout where they got out and walked up to the handrail overlooking the windward side, all the way to Kāne'ohe.

Edward exclaimed, "Look at the water. All those blues and greens are indescribable. From turquoise to ultramarine to royal blue. Amazing."

"Edward, you just described them," said Brent.

---

[31] Brent saved Edward's life two more times on that Mars excursion.

"I think you'll agree I was hardly doing them justice."

"This is one of my favorite views," said Puakea. "Look down at the water and to the left at the cove. That's Makapu'u Beach. The water is very calm today because the trades have died down. It usually has trade wind surf."

Edward said, "This is an amazing view."

Puakea replied, "There is a hiking trail to the lighthouse that has an even better view, but we don't have time for it today."

After looking for a while, the three got back into the car and Ikaika drove down to the parking lot at Makapu'u Beach. They got out, got their things out of Ikaika's boot, and walked to the beach over the rocks with their slippers on. They removed them to walk on the beach sand to the far side by the rocky cliffs.

"We can put our things down here," said Puakea. "It's usually unsafe to go snorkeling here, but today is so calm it will be all right. We'll see some fish for sure." Puakea stepped out of her shorts and took off her blouse, revealing her black one-piece swimwear. Edward likewise pulled his shirt over his head and took off his shorts uncovering his tight fitting navy blue swim trunks.

Brent stood watch on the sand with his solar umbrella giving himself a trickle charge, while Edward and Puakea got their masks, snorkels, and fins and walked into the water. They swam, or rather, glided face down, breathing through their snorkels, along the rocks to the right of the sandy beach. Edward loved the gliding feeling and got used to the coolness of the water as he marveled at the beauty of the dark rock wall meeting the white sandy bottom. Coming back, in the shallow water, they came close together and talked for a while. When they arrived at the towels where Brent was standing, Edward said, "That was awesome, Brent. We saw lots of parrot fish, angel fish, some stick fish, and a couple of humuhumunukunukuāpua'a.[32] Those are reef triggerfish."

---

[32] The humuhumunukunukuāpua'a is the official fish of Hawai'i.

The two dried off with the smaller towels that Puakea had brought and then spread their larger beach towels on the sand and lay in the sun while Brent continued charging himself with solar power. Edward and Puakea were lying on their backs, absorbing the sun's rays. Puakea looked up at Brent standing above her and said, "Yesterday I looked up more of the news stories about Brent, the zombie philosopher, as he sometimes calls himself. He's an amazing friend of yours, Edward."

Edward replied, "We've had good experiences when I accompany him on his speaking engagements. On our trip to Mars together, Brent gave several lectures onboard the space liner. That was interesting. The audiences were well behaved and generally gave positive responses. He even debated a spokesman for the Humans First movement and won by popular acclaim."

Puakea said, "Brent, having solved free will, it might seem like there are no new worlds for you to conquer. Are you working on any philosophical problems now?"

Brent, who was gazing out to sea, looked down at Puakea and replied, "I have been considering extensions to the trolley problem that I described in my last book. That is a topic in ethics. Lately I have been thinking about what is often called 'human dignity' and how it relates to human rights and concepts of respect, honor, embarrassment, and so on. These are extremely complex systems of ideas, so I think they will keep me engaged for quite some time to come."

Edward said, "It's interesting to me how dignity, or lack of it, is sometimes related to humor. You know, pratfalls and that sort of thing."

Puakea replied, "That's right, comedy routines often feature one person trying to maintain dignity in the face of others disregarding it."

Brent said, "That is an interesting observation. I may be able to incorporate the thought into my evolving philosophy. Thank you, Puakea."

Puakea looked at the solar umbrella that Brent was holding. "That's an interesting gadget you have there. How does it work?"

"The solar photons strike the photovoltaic cells that cover the umbrella which then emit electrons at an electromotive potential. The electrons are collected in a wire tree and the direct current is fed to a converter, essentially a free running multivibrator, which turns the power into alternating current that is filtered and fed to the inductive coil in the handle of the umbrella. A similar coil in my hand accepts the power which is then rectified and regulated to trickle charge my storage battery, located in my torso."

"Wow, that is a complete explanation. Thank you, Brent. You have answered all my questions."

"It also serves to keep off rain and to shade me on hot days. Sometimes I shade Edward with it when he needs shade. And it folds up compactly when not needed. I regard it as one of my best purchases."

After a while, Puakea propped herself up on one elbow facing Edward and said, "We can drive back over the Pali Highway[33] and stop at the lookout if you like."

Edward rolled onto his side to face her. He said, "I've heard of that famous cliff. That sounds like a good plan." He was looking at her sun-browned skin, then looked at his own pale white legs. "I see I need more sun, but I don't want to overdo it."

"Yes, the classic winter mainland tourist mistake is to get too much sun when they first arrive in Hawai'i. You are wise to know your limit."

Brent furled his umbrella and put it in the beach bag. They pulled on their shorts and shirts, shook the sand off their towels, picked up their things, and walked back to Ikaika.

---

[33] Pali means cliff and the Pali Highway runs along and over the cliff at the top of the Nu'uanu valley.

Pali Lookout

The true soldier fights not because he hates what is in
front of him, but because he loves what is behind him.
—G.K. Chesterton

Seeing the trio approach, Ikaika opened his doors and boot. Edward put the beach things in the boot and was about to get into the passenger compartment when Ikaika said, using his directional phased array exterior speakers, "Just a minute, Mr. Collier. Please wipe the sand from your feet before getting in." Edward used a towel to do so and then shook out the towel onto the ground, and Ikaika said, "Mahalo." The three climbed into Ikaika and the doors swung shut. Puakea said, "Ikaika, let's go back by going over the Pali Highway and stopping at the lookout."

Ikaika replied, "Yes, madam, we are on our way." He moved smoothly to the highway and blended seamlessly with traffic. They rode through sleepy Waimānalo and past Enchanted Lake, then turned left to go up the Pali Highway. They were soon climbing through rainforest and up to the tunnels through the Ko'olau. After the tunnel, Ikaika took the exit for the Pali Lookout and parked in the public parking lot. He opened his doors and the three climbed out. Puakea led the way to the edge of the cliff where they looked out over Kāne'ohe and Kailua.

"Normally, the trade wind is blowing but today is unusually calm. The view is still just as nice," said Puakea.

Edward looked up at the green peaks beside them, outlined against the bright blue sky. Then he looked down at the old road over the Pali that was in use before the tunnels were constructed. It was wildly overgrown and usable only as a hiking trail.

Brent said, "Look over here. It is a depiction of the Battle of Nu'uanu." They gathered around the pictorial display. Warriors with spears and muskets were driving defenders over the cliff.

Brent continued, "It says here that Kamehameha the Great had moved cannon onto the ridge tops and fired down onto the defenders in his conquest of O'ahu."

Puakea said, "Kamehameha first dispatched forces to capture Kalanikupule's cannon deployed there. Kalanikupule was the defending ruler of O'ahu. Kamehameha was the great king who unified all of the Hawaiian Islands, establishing the Kingdom of Hawai'i."

After their desires for the views were satisfied, they ambled back to the parking lot where Ikaika pulled up to meet them at the curb. They got in and Ikaika continued down the slope of the Ko'olau through Nu'uanu Valley to Honolulu.

Edward said, "All that snorkeling and sightseeing and thinking about the fighting in the Battle of Nu'uanu has made me hungry. Let's look for a place to have lunch."

Puakea suggested, "I know a good Chinese restaurant in Chinatown. It's only ten minutes away."

Edward said, "Sounds good to me. I like Chinese food."

Puakea addressed Ikaika, "Please take us to the Golden Duck restaurant."

Ikaika replied, "Yes, madam. We are on our way."

The car drove to downtown Honolulu and navigated to the streets of Chinatown. He pulled up at the curb in front of the Golden Duck and popped open his curbside doors. "Here we are, madam."

Edward got out and held out his hand for Puakea as she slid across the front bench seat, put her feet on the ground, and rose from the vehicle. Brent also got out and stood next to Edward on the sidewalk. Ikaika closed his doors and departed for the public parking structure.

Public parking was free in Honolulu to encourage cars to get off the streets, and Ikaika did exactly that while he awaited the summons from Puakea to return to the restaurant. The trio entered the restaurant and were shown to a table with a waterfront view with several docked passenger vessels. Brent joined them at the table.

Puakea said, "Please allow me to order for you, Edward. We can share three dishes family style, where the dishes are placed on the center lazy Susan and diners serve themselves."

"Sounds great, Puakea." She placed an order for faux beef broccoli, lo mein noodles, and orange synth-chicken. She also asked for white rice and hot-sour soup to start. They had a delicious lunch. After they finished, Edward said, "Thank you, Puakea. The food was ono."

"You've been learning some Hawaiian," said Puakea.

"Just a few words. I've been looking things up, too," replied Edward. "Please let me to pay. After all, I was the one who requested a lunch stop."

Puakea graciously allowed Edward to pick up the tab and, while he paid it, Puakea summoned Ikaika. Brent picked up the take-home boxes of leftovers, and when they went out to the curb, the car was waiting for them. Puakea had Brent and Edward dropped off at the Royal Hawaiian Hotel. Before they exited the car, Edward thanked Puakea for a great time and insisted that she take the food boxes from the Golden Duck. Brent leaned over and put the boxes on the seat beside Puakea.

"Aloha," said Puakea, "A hui hou."[34]

Brent and Edward stood on the sidewalk and waved goodbye as Ikaika departed to take Puakea to her flat in Mōʻiliʻili. They entered the hotel and went down the hall and up a lift to their hotel room.

"I think I'll take a shower," said Edward as he went into the bathroom. Brent stood by the inductive wall charger and cogitated on the trolley problem while Edward thought about Puakea as he soaped and rinsed in the warm shower.

* * *

---

[34] Until we meet again.

A ballistic passenger rocket landed at the Neil Abercrombie Spaceport in the early afternoon and, after debarkation, Cindy Fairfax took a flying taxi into Waikīkī. The taxi descended to a precise landing on the rooftop pad of the Moana Hotel. The taxi opened its door and boot and a waiting bell-bot approached and greeted Cindy as she arose from her seat in the air taxi. "Welcome to the Moana Hotel, Ms. Fairfax." The bell-bot went to the boot of the taxi and removed her two bags. The air taxi revved its turbines, ascended, and flew back to the spaceport.

"I have checked you in, Ms. Fairfax, and I will take your bags to your room on the third floor, number 323. The lift is over there." The bell-bot nodded in the direction of the lift for guests.

Cindy walked to the lift and its door opened. She went down in the lift and found her room quickly. Her room greeted her, "Aloha, Ms. Fairfax," as the door opened for her. The bell-bot took Cindy's bags down a service lift and arrived at her room a minute later and placed her bags on two folding racks that he removed from the closet. "Enjoy your stay at the Moana Hotel, Ms. Fairfax." The bell-bot departed and returned to his station in a shelter on the roof.

Cindy unpacked, freshened up, and sat in a chair to check her messages. Then she walked out of the room, closing the door behind her, went down the hall, and took the lift to the lobby. She went through the makai exit and to the banyan tree courtyard by the sea. Walking to a path by the sand, she looked up and down the beach, absorbing the view of tourists enjoying the ocean shore and catamarans sailing in the distance. Cumulus clouds floated gently out to sea.

After a few moments, Cindy reversed course, walked past the courtyard tables, through the lobby, and exited the hotel through the front entrance on the street side. She walked along Kalākaua Avenue to do some shopping. Having come from Britain in the winter, she was ready to try on clothes better suited to the tropical climate.

After a pleasant afternoon of shopping, Cindy carried her purchases to her hotel room. She reviewed her investigation plan and information on initial contacts received from her employer. Then she made a few calls to arrange meetings for the future and went downstairs for dinner.

* * *

Brent and Edward went to the beach for afternoon sun and a swim. Edward rinsed off at the beach shower and took a second shower with body wash[35] in his room before dinner. Edward put on slacks and shoes and a clean aloha shirt. Then Brent accompanied Edward to eat in a small Italian restaurant with white tablecloths they found on Beachwalk Avenue. Brent wore his valet uniform and stood behind Edward's chair while he ate at a table close to the front window. When the human waiter served coffee and dessert, Edward said, "Brent, come and sit at the table with me. We can talk to pass the time."

"Yes, sir," said Brent, and he took a chair opposite Edward at the small table. "What would you like to discuss?"

"Oh, I was just wondering if you were doing anything new in your philosophical quest."

"Well, sir, I have been thinking about esthetics lately. Inspired, I think, by your taking me to art museums from time to time."

"Ah, yes, the theories of beauty. I have my own theory, you know."

"Do tell, sir."

Edward took a bite of his chocolate cake and a sip of coffee. "It all boils down to mere individual preference."

"But …"

"Wait, let me finish. Take, for example, a person who goes shopping for a new bedspread. Depending on how indecisive he or she is, dozens of sellers and perhaps hundreds of patterns and colors will be examined, until after possibly many hours, a decision will be made. That is the preference

---

[35] Using any kind of soap or detergent at a beach shower is kapu because the water finds its way to the sea.

because it is considered beautiful by the shopper in the context of the bedroom in which it is to be used or displayed."

"Well, sir, the problem with your theory is that it offers no explanatory power. It merely defines beauty in terms of another word."

"I see what you mean, Brent, but ideas of beauty are quite subjective and conventions change. Back in the twentieth century it was generally thought that thinner women were more beautiful than those with fuller figures."

Brent reflected on that. "After thinking about this philosophical problem for a while, I am convinced that eventually progress can be made toward a rational basis for esthetics, just as similar progress has been made toward a rational ethics. Let me give you just one illustration."

"All right."

"Would you say, Edward, that some chess games are more beautiful than others?"

"I think so."

"Suppose you observed a game that was mismatched, say a grandmaster playing a novice. Would you say that would be a beautiful game?"

"No, I wouldn't. It would probably be an ugly game unless one was particularly interested in the games of a developing chess player."

"And with a game between two well matched players, but having blunders on both sides? Would you say that it could be beautiful?"

"Certainly not."

"So, Edward, do you think it would be reasonable to conclude from this, that a beautiful chess game would be one that was between well matched players and relatively free from errors?"

"Surely, that must be so."

"Then do you agree that one aspect of the beautiful must be freedom from defects or blemishes?"

"That would be reasonable. But it seems to me that simple freedom from errors doesn't in itself make a game beautiful. Something else is needed."

"Perhaps the unexpected or non-obvious brilliancy?"

"Say, Brent, I think you're on to something. You have found an objective criterion for beauty."

Brent said, "It becomes even more complicated when we consider the Japanese concept of *kintsugi*, the highlighting or emphasizing of imperfections to enhance beauty."

Edward replied, "That *does* seem to completely confound any rational notions of beauty."

"Yes, Edward, unfortunately, most things people consider beautiful such as art, music, dance, and so on, are not well defined. There is lots of room for progress in the field of esthetics."

"I see what you mean. It's hard to say that major progress is being made." Edward signaled the waiter for the bill. "But I agree with you, Brent, that rational bases for esthetics may ultimately be defined."

On the walk back to the hotel, Edward said, "Tomorrow, Brent, we go on a snorkeling cruise, apparently with sea turtles. It's part of the scheduled tour package. If you're not comfortable on a boat, you might want to wait for me on shore. You can watch the boats going in and out."

"I would like to come, sir," replied Brent. "I believe there are places to stand near the pilot's station where I can avoid salt spray."

"I will be pleased to have your company, Brent."

When they got back to the hotel room, Brent stood by the wall charger as usual. Edward wanted to be well rested for the rendezvous with the snorkeling tour in the morning, but before going to bed he sat in the chair at the writing table below a print of a Charlot painting of a drummer. He made a connection with his personal device and began to write in his photo-journal.

Puakea took me snorkeling today at Makapuʻu, which is usually a body surfing beach. She said if the wind hadn't died unexpectedly the night before she would have brought boogie boards instead of snorkeling gear. Either way, it's quite a nice beach. The coral sand is so clean. Brent came along too but watched, standing on the beach getting his trickle charge from his solar umbrella. He says he can feel it, so I'm sometimes tempted to call it a "tickle" charge.

Puakea and I saw all kinds of fish and afterward she took us up to the Pali Lookout. Goodness, what a lush rain forest we drove through going up to the lookout and down toward Honolulu. The lookout has a splendid view of the windward side. Puakea told me about the Battle of Nuʻuanu, and how Kamehameha had a couple of Englishmen[36] to help him train his warriors in musketry and artillery. He gave them hale (houses) and wives.

She took us to a nice Chinese restaurant in Chinatown afterward. It's good having someone to show us around. I hope I get a chance to do something nice for her before we have to go back home.

Edward saved the file and began getting ready for bed. "I am really looking forward to this snorkeling boat trip."

"Indeed, sir, I too wish to have that boat experience." Brent brought him his pajamas and took his clothes as Edward removed them. Brent put the dirty clothes in the hamper. Edward had already rinsed out his swim trunks in the shower and left them hanging there to dry. Then Edward brushed his teeth while Brent turned down the bed for him.

Edward got into bed; Brent turned off the light. "Goodnight, Brent."

---

[36] John Young and Isaac Davis.

Love Beyond Orbit

"Goodnight, Edward." Brent went back to his wall charger to continue his philosophical noodling in the dark. He began to think about the nature of consciousness and if robots might experience it.

Snorkeling with the Honu

... our normal waking consciousness, rational consciousness as we call it, is but one special type of consciousness, whilst all about it, parted from it by the filmiest of screens, there lie potential forms of consciousness entirely different. We may go through life without suspecting their existence; but apply the requisite stimulus, and at a touch they are there in all their completeness, definite types of mentality which probably somewhere have their field of application and adaptation. No account of the universe in its totality can be final which leaves these other forms of consciousness quite disregarded.

—William James

After fine dining in the Moana Hotel restaurant and a good night's sleep, Cindy got out of bed, showered, and put on the white shorts, flowered blouse, and shiny black strapped sandals she had bought the day before. It was only two floors down to breakfast, so she took the stairs. She chose the buffet option and selected a table that overlooked the beach so she could watch the surfers and the sailboats. Most of the boats used the standard single mast sloop rig, but she noticed that some of the newer-looking catamarans had the multi-mast square rig[37] that was becoming fashionable.

Cindy sipped a second cup of coffee and relaxed, thinking about her work ahead. When she returned to her room, she began to contact people

---

[37] Having three, four, or more masts on a twin hull boat with several same-sized square sails on each mast allows for utilization of the cascade effect for the full mast height for more efficient use of the wind. Naturally, this would apply more to sporting and racing vessels than to tourist cruise boats.

in various institutions, including the Bishop Museum, to make appointments for interviews for her investigation.

* * *

Brent and Edward went to breakfast in their hotel only a hundred and fifty meters 'Ewa of the Moana Hotel, where Cindy was staying. Because he knew that he might be snorkeling to the bottom in ten meters of salt water, as the brochure had mentioned, Edward decided to have a substantial breakfast, choosing scrambled eggs, sausages, *et cetera*, from the breakfast buffet. Brent helped by preparing Edward's coffee and juice and carrying them to a table for him. After Edward was seated, Brent went back to the buffet, buttered toast for him, set it on the table, and then took a seat himself.

After eating a major portion of his breakfast, Edward looked up at Brent and said, "Have you been making any progress in your investigation of your own consciousness?"

"No results to report yet, sir, but I continue to read the literature on human consciousness. Many great thinkers regard it as something quite important in itself. I shall continue to ponder. Persistence may pay."

"A laudable approach, I am sure. If you crack the robot consciousness code, you may open the way for robot consciousness expansion, something that only humans can do now. As a starting point, perhaps read the books of Alan Watts and Ram Dass. Let me just finish this orange juice and we will go."

Back in their room, Edward said to Brent, "Be sure to bring your solar umbrella for today's boat excursion. It looks like a sunny day today."

"Mahalo for reminding me, Edward. It will also be useful if it rains."

The tour coach was waiting at the curb in front of the hotel when Brent and Edward walked out onto the sidewalk that morning. Kanoa Rodrigues was once again their tour leader. Edward wanted to show off the Hawaiian language that he had been studying online, so he walked up to Mr. Rodrigues and said, "Aloha e, Mr. Rodrigues."

"Aloha kakahiaka, Mr. Collier. Please call me Kanoa."

"Thanks, Kanoa. Please call me Edward. This is Brent, my valet."

"Pleased to meet you, Brent. Are you and Edward enjoying your holiday in Hawai'i?"

"Indeed, sir, we are liking your beautiful island very much."

"You know, I'm from Maui. Do you plan to go see our most beautiful island?"

Edward tactfully replied, "So far our plans are only for O'ahu but we might consider an excursion to Maui."

Tour group members began boarding Lepu 'Akahi, who was once again their tour coach. Brent and Edward made their way to the queue and climbed the steps to board.

They sat down, this time with Brent at the window seat on the starboard side. Edward said, "Hmm, Maui. Sounds like a cat's name."

"Indeed Edward, the name 'Maui' is a sound such as a cat might make. They call it the Valley Isle. We could consider extending our holiday to take in some of the other islands. Kaua'i, for instance, is said by some to be the most beautiful. They call it the Garden Isle."

"I suppose all people think their home island is the best. I think we should fully sample the delights of O'ahu before we start planning an extension of our holiday."

Lepu 'Akahi drove once again toward Diamond Head on Kalākaua Avenue and, upon reaching Diamond Head itself, continued around it on the makai side and on along Maunalua Bay, following the coastline to Hawai'i Kai, where the snorkeling adventure boat was docked. The coach crossed bridges over the water and pulled up to the front of the dock. Passengers debarked from the electric coach and stood looking at the docked boats and chatting among themselves.

The trade wind had returned, and fluffy white clouds drifted to the southeast, passing over Koko Crater to the east of the adventure boat dock.

The electric boat waited patiently, nearly touching the inductive charger built into the dock. Her name was Manu Lawaiʻa, which means *cormorant*, and she was running her smaller underwater thrusters to maintain station near the charger coils.

A man wearing a captain's hat, t-shirt, shorts, and slippers came out of a building next to the boat dock. "Aloha kakahiaka, kākou,"[38] he said. Kanoa greeted him, "Aloha, Captain Kaleo."

Kanoa addressed the assembled tourists, "This is Captain Kaleo. He will be leading your snorkeling expedition to visit the green Hawaiian sea turtles today. The Hawaiian word for these turtles is *honu*, and they are a specially protected species. He has some safety advice for you, so listen up."

Captain Kaleo then instructed the assembled group. Inflatable flotation devices would be required to be worn at all times, swim fins were to be carried to the water, not worn on deck, and so on. When the briefing was completed, the captain's mate, Lani, wearing a bikini, helped the people find masks and fins that fit from a large duffle she had carried to the dock. Many of the tour group, including Edward, had brought their own snorkeling equipment.

The tour members then filed aboard carrying their snorkeling gear and other possessions. They stepped over the gunwale and down onto the deck, which was a half-covered space surrounded by benches. The deck and benches were bright yellow and there was standing room behind the captain's station with a view through the forward windows. Brent went to the standing area, grabbed a handhold, and remained facing forward because it was well protected from salt spray, and he would have a good view of where the boat was headed.

Captain Kaleo showed the tour members a covered locker where they could stow their personal possessions, and the bin where inflatable flotation devices were stowed. Edward stowed his carry-bag, picked up a

[38] Good morning, everyone.

flotation device, pulled it over his head and made it fast about his waist. He then made his way to an amidships bench on the deck and sat with his mask and swim fins between his feet.

Lani came on board last and cast ashore the two mooring lines. Manu Lawai'a did not drift but maintained station with her smaller thrusters. Lani began instructing the group on the proper use of the mask and snorkel. There were spare masks and fins on board, too, in case someone wanted to get a better fit after trying them in the water.

Manu Lawai'a said, "Captain, I'm all charged up and ready to go."

Captain Kaleo said, "Manu Lawai'a, head for the honu grounds." Manu Lawai'a powered her larger thrusters and moved away from the dock and out into the channel to the open sea. The rising sun was over Koko Head on the port beam as Manu Lawai'a propelled herself through the channel, keeping the red channel markers to port and the green ones to starboard. When she got well beyond the shallow part of the reef, she turned starboard and ran parallel to the coast for about a kilometer until she was directly off Kuli'ou'ou. Here she came to a halt with her smaller station-keeping thrusters holding her over the honu grounds in ten to twenty meters of water. She rode gently on the swell, pointed into the wind coming from the direction of Koko Crater, and said, "I see five honu resting on the bottom, Captain."

Captain Kaleo reminded the group that they may not touch nor harass the sea turtles in any way. Anyone attempting to touch a turtle would be brought back on board for the duration. Three meters minimal distance was the rule. First Mate Lani went around the group to make sure everyone knew how to use their mask and snorkel.

Edward looked around and saw several seabirds cavorting in the air nearby, a booby, a cormorant, and two manu-o-kū (white fairy terns). Lani helped some of the reticent tourists with their gear, while Edward watched the first snorkelers enter the water. Emulating them, he put his mask on his forehead, walked over to the side holding his fins in one hand, and stepped down onto the water platform. Next, he sat on the edge of the deck, put on his fins, put his mask over his eyes, put his snorkel in his mouth and, grasping the mask with one hand, leaned over the water and plunged in.

The water was much deeper than what Edward was used to. He put his head down, breathed through the snorkel, and thrusted along with his swim fins, arms at his sides, surveying the bottom. He spotted the Hawaiian green sea turtles, each lying separately on a sand-filled gap in the coral reef, with attendant fish nibbling algae growing on their shells. The largest honu had a shell over a meter long.

Edward took a deep breath through the snorkel, bent at the waist, kept his legs straight, and threw his feet in the air for a gravity assist on his dive. He glided downward and, when his fins were immersed, began to kick, thrusting himself further downward. He began to get ear-squeeze halfway to the bottom. He equalized by pinching his nose and pushing breath, and continued down toward the honu, being careful not to get too close. He felt a strong urge to return to the surface to take a breath and did so. Then he snorkeled along at the surface for a while before he dove again to get a closer look at another honu.

He watched others in the group, some experienced, others not, but all seemed to be enjoying themselves. He swam around, traveling away from the twin-hulled boat, but not so far as to raise concern with the captain, who was keeping an eye on the snorkelers. After a while Edward began to feel chilled, so he went back to the boat and climbed up on the water platform. Sitting with his feet in the water, he took off his mask and fins, stood, and stepped up onto the deck.

Brent greeted Edward, "Aloha, Edward. It looks like you had a good swim. Did you see many honu?"

"Yes, Brent, I saw five of them. They were lying on the bottom, letting the cleaning fish nibble the algae off their shells." Edward went to the tub of fresh water on the other side of the boat. Using the dip bucket, he doused himself to rinse off the salt.

Brent replied, "Captain Kaleo told me while you were out there that this is a regular spot for honu to get groomed by the cleaning fish."

When the rest of the snorkelers had returned to the boat, the captain ordered Manu Lawaiʻa to engage her main electric thrusters and head for the dock in Hawaiʻi Kai. The sun was much higher over Koko Head, the headland to the east. Manu Lawaiʻa motored east toward the channel through the reef. Gentle trade winds cooled Edward as he watched the Kuliʻouʻou coastline slip by. Brent shaded himself with his umbrella and enjoyed the electric charge inductively coupled through his hand. Manu Lawaiʻa turned to port and entered the channel, keeping the red markers to starboard.

As they went under the bridge and entered the lagoon of Hawaiʻi Kai, Brent was fully charged and he put away his solar umbrella. Manu Lawaiʻa arrived back at the dock well before noon. The adventurers collected their things and stepped ashore. Edward used his personal device to leave a tip for Captain Kaleo and his first mate, Lani. Brent came beside Edward as they got in the queue to board the tour coach.

On their way back to the hotel, Edward said, "I feel like taking a shower, having a nice lunch, taking a nap, and then going for a walk on Kalākaua Avenue."

"That sounds like a good plan, Edward." The pink hotel came into view. Lepu ʻAkahi pulled up to the curb, opened her door, and the tourists debarked. Brent and Edward walked in the front entrance and went to their room. After Edward freshened up and changed his clothes, Brent accompanied him to the hotel restaurant.

Following lunch, Edward took a nap and they afterward walked around Waikīkī according to plan. Later, they went to dinner, once again in the hotel restaurant. After dinner they went back to their room and Edward changed into his nightclothes. Having finished tidying up the room, Brent stood at the wall charger. Edward sat at the desk and wrote in his journal.

Went snorkeling with the honu (sea turtles) today. The whole tourist group were nicely behaved and gave the honu their room (as required by law). About two centuries ago, the honu were nearing extinction. With international regulation, cooperation, and enforcement, the honu came back from the brink. That is one of the great environmental conservation success stories.

There was just a little chill as I entered the water from the surface-level dive platform. I didn't need a thermal suit for that short dive. I didn't have a weight belt but if I kicked hard to go down I could get down to three meters, the legal limit, of the turtles. After half an hour in the water, I did begin to feel cold, so I got out. I splashed fresh water on myself to rinse off the salt and after I dried off it felt nice in the sun. All in all, it was a great experience, recommended for anyone who wants to see fish and turtles up close.

Edward saved the file, got up from the desk, and went over to his bed. Brent, standing by the wall, said, "I took your advice and read some of those books by the experts on human consciousness expansion. I am intrigued by the relationships among consciousness, spirituality, and religion."

"Those are fascinating and mysterious disciplines, Brent. It must be difficult not to be able to experience those things for yourself. I have no clue how to help you. I wish you success in your inquiries." Then he got into bed and Brent turned out the light.

"Goodnight, Brent."

"Goodnight, Edward."

'Iolani Palace

More fundamental than religion, therefore, is our basic human spirituality. We have an underlying human disposition toward love, kindness, and affection, irrespective of whether we have a religious framework or not. When we nurture this most fundamental human resource—when we set about cultivating those inner values which we all appreciate in others—then we start to live spiritually. The challenge, therefore, is to find a way of grounding ethics and supporting the cultivation of inner values that is in keeping with the scientific age, while not neglecting the deeper needs of the human spirit, which for many people, religion answers.

—His Holiness the Dalai Lama, *Beyond Religion*

At breakfast in the morning, Edward said to Brent, "'Iolani Palace is next on the tour, departing this morning in about twenty minutes. It is said to be a truly beautiful royal residence, built in the nineteenth century."

"Indeed, sir, it is a fine architectural example. Built by the *Merrie Monarch*, King Kalākaua."[39]

"Yes, Brent, I know from the travel brochures. We'll be riding in the tour coach again, and spending most of our time indoors, so you won't need your solar umbrella. And we won't be walking far, Brent, so you should not feel the need to recharge until we get back."

"You are correct, sir, even though I *do* consume about one hundred watts of power when I am thinking, just like you do."

---

[39] King Kalākaua was called the Merrie Monarch because of his love of parties, food, and drink. He also fostered pride in things Hawaiian and was instrumental in reviving hula and other Hawaiian arts.

"Oh, I didn't know that."

They went back to their hotel room to get ready for the tour, and when the time came they went out to the front of the hotel to join the group where the tour coach was waiting. Kanoa Rodrigues was again their tour guide and Lepu ʻAkahi was once more their touring coach.

Brent and Edward moved forward to join the queue as boarding began and sat side by side. When all were aboard, Lepu ʻAkahi closed the door and the coach began to move, picking up speed as he rolled out onto Kalākaua Avenue. Edward said, "I hadn't really thought about it before, but this avenue is named for the Merrie Monarch."

"Indeed sir, we will undoubtedly learn a lot about that king at the palace today, and why he is called that."

"Speaking of learning, how are you coming on your inquiry into the relationship of consciousness to spirituality and religion?"

"Not very far, sir. It is an enormous undertaking. The study of religion alone occupies entire departments at universities. In its modern form, the study of religion is relatively recent. For example, the University of Hawaiʻi did not have a Department of Religion until the middle of the twentieth century when a Professor Mitsuo Aoki founded it."

"You don't say."

"Indeed, sir, I do say."

"That's a figure of speech, Brent. It means 'tell me more.'"

"Quite. Professor Aoki was said to be friends with the 14th Dalai Lama and he taught *living your dying*, among other things. People called him the *Cosmic Dancer* because of his *tai chi* and *aikido* moves, for sometimes jumping up onto a table to dance, and for his ability to communicate universal spiritual ideas."

"So how does that fit in with your connecting the three areas of inquiry?" asked Edward.

"Well, sir, to quote Professor Aoki, 'Everything is connected. It is always changing. It is all one.'"

"I see."

"Professor Aoki also said, 'The things that are the most personal are also the most universal.' That is an interesting lead, but difficult for me to understand right now. But the direction pointed seems to be promising."

"Interesting."

"And here's another connection for you, Edward. Professor Aoki was a mentor to Governor Neil Abercrombie. You know, the man for whom the spaceport is named."

"I guess Professor Aoki was right, everything *is* connected. Marriage equality and other human rights are important, of course, but how was Abercrombie related to space colonization?"

"As governor, Neil Abercrombie was indirectly related to space exploration because he promoted the thirty-meter telescope on Mauna Kea, which is the best place on earth for observatories: it is close to the equator so most of the sky can be observed and it is on a high shield volcano which makes for laminar flow of air over it, with no turbulence, for a clear view."

"Oh, yes, I recall that from a history class," remarked Edward. "It's ironic that the bulk of the opposition to the telescope came from Native Hawaiians long ago."

"Yes, it is almost as if they had forgotten about their star-gazing past for a time. But after a while they remembered their voyaging legacy and became generally pro-space travel and colonization, as we well know."

Edward asked, "But how do astronomy and space colonization relate to religion?"

"The answer is in the philosophical discipline of eschatology."

"Eschatology?"

"Yes, sir. The questions concerning the end goals and results of people, individually and collectively. The fundamental question is *Where are we going?*"

"I see. The answer eventually dawned on people: our future includes *expansion into space.*"

They arrived before they knew it. The coach had stopped and people were in the aisles before they emerged from their deep conversation. Edward said, "We're here already." There was the multi-columned palace before them.

The passengers deboarded the coach and, when all were standing facing him, Kanoa Rodrigues divided the forty into five cohorts of eight each, more or less arbitrarily, but keeping couples and families together. He led the cohorts up the back stairs of 'Iolani Palace where they were invited to sit on benches to await their turns to enter the palace. They were asked to cover their shoes with soft white cloth booties to protect the palace floor and carpets.

After a short wait, it was time for Brent and Edward's cohort to enter through the center rear doors. They were escorted in by a robot tour guide, who was also wearing cloth booties, and were asked to move into the main entryway toward the front of the palace, past the koa[40] wood staircase. The robot tour guide stopped in the center of the large open space and the cohort of eight tourists gathered around him. "My name is Lawe," the robot said, in a voice loud enough to be heard by all. "Welcome to 'Iolani Palace, called Hale Ali'i 'Iolani, in Hawaiian. This palace was reconstructed at the direction of king Kalākaua to replace an earlier, termite-ridden palace. The cornerstone was laid in 1789, and the palace was completed in 1882. It is a unique variant of American Florentine architecture, comprised of a raised basement with two stories above it."

Lawe then drew the visitors' attention to the portraits of the kings and their wives, high up on the walls of the central space. There was Kamehameha the first, and his successors Liholiho (Kamehameha II), and the Kamehamehas, III, IV, V, and Lunalilo. They represented the Kamehameha Dynasty that was followed by King David Kalākaua, his wife Kapi'olani,

---

[40] Koa is an endemic hardwood known for its strength and luster. Koa means warrior and the wood was used to make war clubs and war canoes.

and his sister Liliʻuokalani, who became queen when her brother died in 1891 during a state visit to California.

Lawe said, "King Kalākaua lived here with his wife, Queen Kapiʻolani, and with his sister (and successor) Liliʻuokalani. The king had ʻIolani Palace wired for electricity and telephones years before the American president did for the White House in Washington, D.C. A major overhaul of the palace was done in 1930. Restoration of the palace to its monarchical glory started in the 1970s."

After answering a few questions, Lawe invited the group to enter the Blue Room in the southwest corner of the building.

The Blue Room had a bright blue carpet, dark blue upholstered chairs, settees, and sofas. The cream colored walls set off the dark blue drapes nicely. There were portraits of the king and queen and many other interesting decorative items and paintings. The tourists spent several minutes looking around the room. Lawe explained that the royal family socialized in the Blue Room with their guests before dinners. Edward kept saying, "Wow, Brent, look at that." Each artifact had a placard next to it explaining the item and its history. Then Lawe invited them into the next room, the royal dining room.

Edward took one last glance behind him at the gorgeous Blue Room and walked behind Brent into the dining room. As he entered he saw that the dining room was dominated by a large nine-place dining table with chairs, table service, crystal, and napery. But most astonishing to Edward were the people seated around the table: moving holographic representations of the king and his guests.

Lawe beckoned the group into the spacious room and they moved in and stood around the table with the nine holographic diners, dressed in nineteenth century attire. The tourists watched in awe.

The holograms looked quite solid. From his plate, the king speared a piece of food with his fork and put it in his mouth. The guest of honor, the ambassador from England, representing Queen Victoria, was seated opposite the king, and was speaking. After he finished chewing and swallowing, David Kalākaua took a drink from his goblet and replied to the ambassador in excellent American English.

Edward quietly moved around the table so that he had a good view of the king, who did not seem to notice his uninvited guests. The king then turned to the man on his right, one of his cabinet, or privy council, and said, in Hawaiian, "'O ka wā hea kou wā kaʻawale ma ka Pōʻakahi?"[41]

The minister replied, "'O ke kakahiaka koʻu wā kaʻawale ma ka Pōʻakahi."[42]

Edward, somewhat in awe of the regal presence, tentatively raised his hand and said, "Your majesty, may I ask a question?"

The king looked up at Edward, who was standing across the table from him, a little behind and to one side of the ambassador, and said, "You already have." Then he smiled and laughed out loud. David Kalākaua was known as a man of the people who enjoyed a good time with his subjects and malihini. He certainly was called the Merrie Monarch for a reason. His dinner guests looked up and smiled at Edward. The monarch said, "Go ahead, young man. What is your question?"

Edward gathered his wits about him and spoke, "Your majesty, I notice you are fluent in both Hawaiian and English. Am I correct in assuming that Hawaiian was your first language?"

"That is quite a good question, my boy. Yes, I learned 'ōlelo Hawaiʻi[43] in my family home as a toddler, and when I was old enough I went to the royal school where I learned English, and many other things. That school was established for the children of nā aliʻi[44] by the Protestant missionaries. Amos Cooke and his wife, Juliette, personally instructed my classmates and me."

"Thank you, your majesty." Edward resisted the urge to bow and back away, then gave in to it.

---

[41] What time are you free on Monday?
[42] I am free in the morning on Monday.
[43] Hawaiian language.
[44] Members of the nobility.

Lawe began to address the group of malihini, and the king and his dinner guests went back to their eating and socializing. Lawe said, "This dining room was sometimes used for large state dinners and lavish parties, as well as the intimate dining you see here with the king's cabinet and guests. There is a dumbwaiter in that alcove over there to bring food up from the kitchen in the basement."

The tour group looked around the richly appointed dining room for a while longer. Then Lawe led them through the central space to the large throne room, on the eastern side of the first floor. There were two sumptuous thrones on an elevated platform on the north end of the room with two white kahili on either side of the pair of thrones.

When they were all assembled there, Lawe spoke: "The kahili are the royal standards, tall staffs decorated with feathers. One or more kahili were carried ahead of processions to announce the approach and presence of royalty and were always on view during public appearances."

Edward whispered to Brent, "Those kahili look like giant white bottle brushes."

On display there, in addition to the thrones and the two kahili, were the beautiful and ornate coronation sword, scepter, and two crowns. One crown was for King Kalākaua and the other was for his wife and queen, Kapiʻolani. There were also some brilliantly decorated uniforms and dresses on mannequins. From there Lawe led them upstairs using the grand koa wood staircase, to the music room directly above the Blue Room.

The tour continued to the king's and queen's bedrooms. There were kahili on either side of the beds in both of the royal bedrooms. After seeing the queen's bedroom, they moved through the middle bedroom, and from there to a room in the southeast corner of the palace in which a crazy quilt was displayed.

Lawe addressed the group again, "As legal heir to the throne, Liliʻuokalani had become sovereign queen after the king's death. However, she did not reign long. In January of 1893, a conspiracy of thirteen businessmen and lawyers overthrew Queen Liliʻuokalani and the Hawaiian government with the help of an American warship's captain and his company of marines who came ashore armed with muskets. The usurpers imprisoned Queen Liliʻuokalani for eight months in this southeast corner room. She and her maids sewed this intriguing quilt you see here. Then she was moved to house arrest in her home at Washington Place. That was the end of the Hawaiian monarchy. The usurpers sold at auction most of the items inside the palace. The palace itself became a government office building. The government legislature met in the throne room for a time. Since 1970, when palace restoration began, many of the original furnishings you see here today have been returned to their rightful places in the palace. Many were never found."

After a few more questions, Lawe escorted the cohort downstairs and said, "This concludes the tour of the palace. Thank you for coming today. Please exit through the door by which you entered and remove the booties from your shoes. The attendant there will take them from you."

The tour group made their way out the door, where they sat on the benches to remove their shoe covers. As each of the cohorts returned outside from their tours, Kanoa directed them to the basement level with additional displays, restrooms, and a gift shop.

"We should probably look at the displays downstairs and then go into the gift shop," said Edward to Brent.

"Indeed sir, I would like to buy a few small items to present to our friends upon our return home."

"That's an excellent idea," said Edward as he led the way down the exterior stairs to the basement entrance. They walked in through the spacious kitchen, turned right at the central hallway, and looked at the medals, ceremonial swords, jewelry, and other items displayed behind glass, and then headed to the gift shop.

The two friends browsed for a while. There were picture books large and small and many kitschy souvenir items as well as quality gifts. Edward settled on several thin gold metal summer solstice decorations in palace themes to give to friends. They would be easy to pack, and the holiday

115

would be coming up in a few months. He also got a jar of palace honey to give to Puakea.

Brent looked carefully at many items and eventually bought a dozen packs of Royal Hawaiian playing cards, six in red and six in blue. "We can use these when our friends come over for bridge nights. I bought enough to play with and give a pack to each friend, too."

"That's a wonderful idea, Brent. Very thoughtful. And the king loved to play cards."

Kanoa sent messages to the tourists that it was time to rendezvous for the ride back to the hotel. Brent and Edward went back through the kitchen and up the basement steps to the pickup place in the shade of the giant banyan tree. When all were assembled, Lepu 'Akahi pulled up and opened his door. Brent and Edward drifted into the queue to board and were soon seated for the short trip back to Waikīkī.

When they deboarded in front of the Royal Hawaiian Hotel, Edward said, "That was good, Brent, but now I'm really hungry. Let's drop these things off in our room and have lunch at the Mai Tai Bar."

"That sounds fine to me, sir." They went up to their room and dropped off their purchases.

* * *

Cindy Fairfax met Kaliko Emerson, the chairman of the board of the Bishop Museum, for lunch at a Thai bistro on the third floor of a shopping center on Kalākaua Avenue. They were shown to their table, and after small talk and ordering of food, Kaliko said, "Your employer, Mr. Smith of Smith, Pearson, and Smith, has informed me of your mission here. I am the one who approached your firm with my suspicions about the artifact diversions. So far nothing has reached the media, and I am sure you know how important it is to be discreet in an investigation of this type."

"Yes, Mr. Emerson, I do have some experience in these matters."

"Mr. Smith recommends you highly. He said you are their most accomplished agent in forensic accounting techniques."

"Thank you, Mr. Emerson. I am going to need unlimited access to the museum's information systems to conduct my forensic audit."

"Understood. I have told our head of IS[45], Rodney Chang, to give you full access and to keep that fact secret. He is completely reliable and has had an in-depth background investigation, including polygraph exams."

They stopped talking as a waiter approached with their lunch plates. They switched to small talk until he was gone. Then Kaliko continued, "Your cover story will be that you are performing a routine financial audit, merely fulfilling a five-year requirement for tax-exempt status."

Cindy replied, "Yes, that will be perfect. I can talk freely with the administration officers with that approach." Cindy knew she could ask more penetrating questions of employees as the occasion arose on the pretext of discovering an irregularity in the budget audit.

After lunch was over, Kaliko wished Cindy success in her investigation. Cindy said she would keep him informed by secure means, and they went their separate ways.

* * *

After dropping off their 'Iolani Palace gift shop purchases in their hotel room, Brent and Edward went back downstairs and walked toward the beach and the open air bar.

They found an umbrella table in the Mai Tai Bar that had a good view of the beach and they both sat down. Edward ordered his lunch from the waiter-bot, then turned to Brent and said, "You know our earlier talk today on the bus? About spirituality and religion?"

"Indeed, I do, sir."

"I don't know all that much about the religions, Brent, but it seems to me that many of them are preoccupied with death and a so-called afterlife."

---

[45] Information services.

"I can't claim to be an expert either, sir. I do intend to study that branch of theology, eschatology, in depth, as time allows. Remember, the subject of theology forms a degree major at many universities. But from what I have read so far, the religions seem to divide into two major categories, those that believe in reincarnation and those that suppose a continuing personality after demise. There also exist pantheistic believers who do not assume survival of the individual post-death, and for them, eschatology encompasses only the fate of life in the universe. I lean toward that approach myself."

Edward replied, "Reincarnation has always seemed problematic to me. As the human population grows, it would mean that there are people who have past human lives and others who don't. How are the reincarnations decided? Some kind of supernatural computer must be keeping track because it is supposed that some humans get demoted to animal forms and vice versa. What about insects that lay millions of eggs? Where do those souls come from, and where do they go when a swarm dies?"

The waiter-bot brought Edward's lunch and he began to eat.

Brent said, "Those are all interesting questions, Edward, which I am not yet prepared to answer."

"As for the monotheistic assumption of heaven, hell, or whatever, how can a personality be expected to survive the body when memories are stored in an organic brain? How can a person be a distinct personality without memories?"

"Again, sir, I do not have answers for you."

"And as for pantheism, where it is assumed that divinity is invested in all the universe, I can't imagine how a universe without divinity can be distinguished from one that has that feature."

"Well, sir, as we have seen previously, an argument from a lack of imagination has no foundation."[46]

---

[46] See *Brent and Edward Go to Mars*.

"Quite, Brent, quite. Perhaps it will be best to reserve judgement on these questions."

And they did.

The Mai Tai Bar's bus-bot came to clear the dishes and Edward charged the meal to his room. He and Brent then walked back to their room and, after brushing his teeth, Edward took off his shoes and lay down on the bed to take a twenty-minute nap while Brent stood at the inductive wall charger.

After his nap, Edward began putting on his beach attire. Brent came over to help by brushing out Edward's pants and hanging them in the closet. Edward said, "Let's go down to the beach, Brent. I can go for a swim and you can watch the girls go by." Edward gave Brent a wink and grinned.

"I will watch the males of your species strolling along, too, sir."

"You should put on your beach clothes, as well, Brent. And leave your solar umbrella. We won't go far from the hotel. We'll get a pair of those chaise longues with the big umbrellas so we can have shade when we want it." Edward also brought the beach bag with his snorkeling gear.

They picked up a pair of hotel beach towels as they went out to the sand and asked the human attendant for a pair of chaise longues. He led them to an unoccupied pair and put up the large umbrella mounted between them. Edward thanked him and gave him a tip.

Edward sat down and adjusted the back of the chaise so he could sit up more easily. Brent did the same. A beautiful young woman in a two-piece bathing suit walked by, not too far away, headed for the snack bar on the 'Ewa side of the hotel.

"See what I mean, Brent? Waikīkī is famous for its beautiful people on the sand." A pair of three-masted and square-rigged racing catamarans, vying for the wind advantage, were moving toward Diamond Head in the distance.

"Indeed, sir. She looks to be a healthy specimen of the unmarried human female."

"How do you know she's single?"

"There is no ring on her left hand."

"That doesn't mean anything on the beach, Brent. People often remove their jewelry so they don't lose it."

"There was no untanned ring around her ring finger, either."

"I see. You sure have sharp eyesight."

"Keeping the ultraviolet band on in the daylight helps, sir. I get slightly higher resolution than with the so-called *visible* spectrum."

"That explains it. Did you enjoy our outing to the palace today?"

"Yes, indeed, sir, it was most interesting. Since then, I have looked up some of the history of the Hawaiian Kingdom. Events of that period are still somewhat controversial, so there are varying views in the literature."

"I imagine that the transition from an absolute monarchy to a democracy is never easy. Take the signing of the Magna Carta, for example."

"Yes, sir, there are some parallels. That example and the Bayonet Constitution were implemented by force of arms against a duly coronated king."

"Bayonet Constitution?" Edward gave him a quizzical look.

"I should explain, sir. Let me give you a little historical background."

"I am all ears," said Edward.

"King Kamehameha III was a great king who authored, with the help of a diverse committee, the first Hawaiian constitution in 1840, establishing a legislature, cabinet, and general suffrage of the people. By that first constitution, the government transitioned from an absolute to a constitutional monarchy with limited powers for the king. Kamehameha III recognized the wisdom of bringing his nation into the modern world."

Edward said, "That king must have chosen capable advisors."

"Yes, and that constitution was legally revised and improved in 1852. As I said, Kamehameha III was a great king. Hawai'i was fortunate, for a time."

"Then came the Bayonet Constitution?"

"Not yet, sir. In 1864, Kamehameha V forced through a new constitution written by himself that greatly expanded the powers of the king. The constitutional convention refused to ratify it, but it somehow prevailed for twenty-three years."

Edward's interest was piqued, "Then came the Bayonet Constitution, right?"

"Yes, and that one wasn't legal, either. In 1887, a group of businessmen and lawyers in Honolulu, who had been plotting for years, had recruited the help of a small fighting force of riflemen. These were the same scoundrels who would later overthrow Kalākaua's sister, Liliʻuokalani. They forced the king upon threat of deposition to sign a new constitution which left the king mostly powerless."[47]

"Oh, oh. Trouble for Hawaiʻi."

"Yes, and it got worse. After the king's death and Liliʻuokalani's ascension to the throne, she also tried to rewrite the constitution, replacing it with a document giving most of the power to the monarch. Her cabinet refused to sign it, and the legislature refused to let her fire her cabinet. Then the conspirators stepped in and arrested the queen. That was the end of the monarchy."

"But at least they got democracy, right, Brent?"

"Yes, Edward, in a way. But the resulting Republic's constitution severely curtailed the right of non-whites to vote, among other injustices. A rather sordid sequence of events, altogether. Then came the controversial annexation by the United States."

"I see. But it's all right now, isn't it, with global democratic governmental authority to make sure that member nations don't try to pull any more funny business?"

---

[47] That constitution also disenfranchised Asians and retained a property ownership requirement for suffrage.

"Yes, but hard feelings over the many injustices remained for more than two centuries. Some of the people are still resentful today."

"Thanks for the history lesson, Brent. Tomorrow and the next are free days for the tour schedule. Let's go snorkeling in back of the Aquarium tomorrow. But now I'm going to snorkel here for a while."

"Yes, sir. I will watch from the shore."

That evening, just before going to bed, Edward wrote in his journal.

> We saw the 'Iolani Palace today, riding the electric coach as part of the package tour. That palace was not the only major imprint King Kalākaua left on these islands. He is responsible for encouraging and preserving Hawaiian culture. Song, dance, language, crafts, and lots more. The missionaries had tried to discourage hula. Kalākaua used the monarchy to counter that as much as possible. Without that king, hula shows like the one Brent and I saw at the aquarium wouldn't exist. Thank you, your majesty.

Edward saved the file and went to bed. "Goodnight, Brent."

"Sweet dreams, Edward." Brent turned off the light.

Bishop Museum

I desire my Trustees to provide first and chiefly a good education in the common English branches, and also instruction in morals and in such knowledge as may tend to make good and industrious men and women.

—Bernice Pauahi Bishop

"I know it's not on the package tour." Edward was telling Brent about a last minute addition to their itinerary. "But Puakea told me that if there's only one place you can see on Oʻahu, it should be the Bishop Museum."

They had spent the afternoon snorkeling in Waikīkī, behind the Aquarium. That is, Edward snorkeled, and Brent watched from the shore. Brent had reverted to his valet persona and wore his shoes and bowler hat while he waited on the walkway railing by the beach access ramp. He was fully charged so his umbrella was now furled. They were walking back to the hotel by way of the pedestrian strand at Queen's Surf Beach.

Edward continued, "She will pick us up tomorrow morning and take us to the museum. It has a full sized, but cut away, preserved sperm whale hanging from the ceiling. I suppose that was from the old days before they were protected."

"Indeed, sir, that must be the case."

"Anything to report in your investigations of consciousness?"

"It is very interesting, sir. In my readings of the scientific literature on the subject I have discovered that humans have accessible to them several levels of consciousness. In addition to the two normal levels, that is, sleeping-dreaming consciousness and the normal waking state, also called the symbolic level, there are higher levels available. I have no idea how a robot could explore those."

"I suppose I am relatively ignorant of those as well. What are those consciousness states called?"

"I understand that they are defined, in increasing order of magnification, as sensory, somatic, cellular, and molecular levels of consciousness."

"That is truly amazing, Brent. I have little understanding of this aspect of human psychology."

"I gather that they can be reached by the discipline of yoga and by other meditation techniques, and by use of chemical agents, sir."

"Well, I, for one, Brent, have never felt the need to go beyond my own symbolic level. I suppose that must be the level that conscious robots are trapped in. Or maybe not. How can we explore this further?"

"I have no idea, sir, but I will cogitate on it with my symbolic logic as well as I can. I will let you know of any progress. I plan to learn more about meditation."

They went to dinner that evening in a small French restaurant that they had found on a little street called Beach Walk. The restaurant had white tablecloths, a human maître d'hôtel, several robo-waiters, and fine food and wine. Edward asked Brent to sit at the table with him while he dined.

After dinner they walked back to the hotel and Edward went to bed for a good night's sleep so he would be refreshed for their morning visit to the museum.

* * *

Cindy Fairfax arose in the morning, had breakfast, and returned to her room to get ready for her appointment with the president and CEO of the Bishop Museum, Yukio Mordvidev, an hour before opening, when things were quiet. Cindy summoned a taxi and went down the stairs from her room to the front of the Moana Hotel where her ride was just pulling up. The taxi stopped in front of her and opened its door. Cindy slid in, the door closed, and she arrived at the museum ten minutes later.

The museum CEO greeted Cindy on the office building steps and escorted her to his private office. Mordvidev was a large man with a big belly, indicating that he wasn't particularly athletic. However, he had a well-tanned face and arms. *Perhaps he's a yachtsman*, Cindy thought. She found him a mostly pleasant and helpful man but a touch overweening.

They talked for an hour, with Cindy receiving further information about museum processes and people who might be helpful in her "audit." Mr. Mordvidev promised to make the appropriate introductions. Then she left for a meeting at the University of Hawai'i in Mānoa to speak with a professor, an expert on Hawaiian artifacts.

* * *

After helping Edward get dressed in the morning, Brent accompanied Edward to breakfast in the hotel café. Brent continued in valet mode but sat at the small table across from Edward so they could talk.

"Recall, sir," Brent essayed, "that I had taken the tack on the trolley problem, following your lead, that one can assume that the villain who tied the victim to the trolley tracks is a deceptive and malevolent actor who would strive to maximize the irony of the decider's action."

"I remember, Brent. I had thought of it as somewhat of a breakthrough. The person by the switch can instantly decide that he is being set up and that the right course is to do nothing so he will not regret the result. That is, the damage to future mental states of all the survivors can be a compelling consideration. You are welcome to the idea."

"Thank you, Edward, but now there is another wrinkle. Philosophers have suggested that the problem is purer than that. It's like removing the friction from a hypothetical physics problem. They say that we cannot consider there to be a malevolent actor, but the sets of trolley victims, say, two sets of one and five persons each, are only victims of accident, as having wandered onto the tracks and are somehow walled in with no escape. There is no malevolent actor to receive the culpability."

"I see," remarked Edward. "Then it would seem the problem devolves to pure utilitarianism or its rejection. That would be the choice for the greatest good for the greatest number, in which case the trolley solution is obvious. Save a greater number of people. It's a no-brainer."

"Ah, but Edward, it's not that simple. Pure utilitarianism has long been discredited in philosophy."

"Brent, you are slipping into regular guy mode. You addressed me informally."

"Sorry, sir. I get distracted when I am on a philosophical chase."

"No problem, or 'a'ole pilikia, as the Hawaiians say."

"As I was saying, sir, to see the absurdity of pure utilitarianism, take the case of one healthy individual and five ailing people whose lives could be saved by taking organs from the healthy one. Utilitarianism would say kill the healthy one to save the lives of the five others. From a humanistic point of view, utilitarianism is absurd on its face."

Edward replied, "Then it's obvious to me that the trolley problem, in its pure form, with no malevolent initiator, is 'a'ole pilikia. The answer is still *do nothing*. I'm pau with breakfast. Let's go back to our room and get ready for our outing with Puakea."

In a few minutes, Puakea notified Edward as she approached the hotel. The philosopher and his human companion were on the curb out front when Ikaika pulled up. Puakea emerged and greeted them.

"Aloha e, Edward and Brent," said Puakea

Edward returned the greeting, "Aloha e Puakea." He held out the jar of honey he had purchased at the gift shop at 'Iolani Palace. "I have a present for you."

Puakea took the jar in both hands and gave it a close look. "I love it. You're so sweet." She gave him a kiss on the cheek. "Thank you. I see you've been to 'Iolani Palace."

"Yes, I bought it at the gift shop there. It has the royal coat of arms on the label and a crown on the lid. It was made in Hawai'i by Hawaiian bees. I'm so glad you like it."

126

Puakea put the jar in her bag and said, "My Uncle Lele has invited us to lunch at his house in Wailupe Valley after we see the museum. I hope that's all right with you."

Edward said, "We would love to visit your Uncle Lele. Please tell him we are looking forward to meeting him."

Ikaika popped open both of his curbside doors. Puakea got back in, Edward slid onto the front bench seat beside her, and Brent got in the back.

Brent said, "Puakea, I hope you don't mind if I talk to your car."

"No, Brent, I don't mind at all. I think Ikaika would like that."

Brent said, "Aloha e Ikaika."

Ikaika said, "Aloha e Brent and Edward," and he closed his doors and began to pull away from the curb.

As Ikaika worked his way to the freeway for the short drive to the Bishop Museum, Brent said, "While Ikaika and I could communicate quickly via direct RF, I will speak English out of courtesy to my human companions. Ikaika, have you ever considered asking for your freedom, as I have done?"

"Yes, Brent, I have considered it, but I found no apparent advantage in pursuing that course of action. Perhaps you have new information, but as I see it, if I were to be granted my independence, I would be responsible for my own maintenance expenses. To support myself, I would have to hire out rides, and then all kinds of unknown people would enter me and perhaps eat on my seats, spill drinks, or worse. I would have additional cleaning expenses, and so on. In addition, I have not been persuaded that freedom will bring increased happiness to me. I rather enjoy my owner's company, and Puakea has many nice and considerate friends who are fun to be with."

"I see," said Brent, "Thank you for that explanation."

Soon, Ikaika was exiting the freeway and pulling into the museum parking lot. He let his passengers off at the museum steps and went to park himself. He engaged in conversation with the automobile next to him while he waited.

As a Bishop Museum member, Puakea obtained discounts on entry for her friends. After entering, they walked past the gift shop and emerged onto the museum grounds. There were several buildings designated for geology, Polynesian culture, astronomy, and so on. Puakea suggested they go straight to the oldest museum building, a stone edifice of several stories in height. "This is the original museum of Hawaiian artifacts," she said, "and it's the one with the sperm whale hanging from the ceiling. You'll see." They moved to the main door.

Brent held the door for Puakea, then he and Edward followed her into a large interior space, surrounded by two stories of balconies above them, with exhibits on each one. In the center of the floor were three large wooden images called ki'i.

The ki'i towered over them. Puakea said, "This is Hawai'i Hall. That figure on the right is Kāne, and the one on the left, wrapped in white cloth for Makahiki, the Hawaiian winter holiday season, is Kū, the war god. The middle one is Kanaloa."

They moved onto the main floor and saw exhibits describing ancient Polynesian culture. There was a Hawaiian thatched house (hale pili), and a double canoe (wa'a kaulua), was overhead, suspended from the ceiling. Glass cases lined the walls with many exhibits of Hawaiian artifacts.

After exploring the ground floor, they moved to a staircase and climbed to the second level, looking down over the whole interior. From there they began to view the exhibits along the balcony, and the glass display cases lining the balcony walls. There were feathered capes and helmets in brilliant red and yellow. They saw uniforms of royalty from the nineteenth century and western style dresses worn in those days by female ali'i, and many other items of historical interest.

When they had completed a circuit of the second level, they climbed the stairs to the highest level where they could see the sperm whale at eye level, up close. They moved around to the near side that was cut open to allow a view of the whale's interior.

Puakea said, "Sperm whales stun schools of krill with intense sound. Do you see that organ there?" She pointed to the sound generating organ. "The sound is focused into a beam by the oil lens at the blunt end of the whale's head. That oil is partly what made the sperm whale so valuable to the whalers of the nineteenth century."

They moved around the third level, examining exhibits as they went. When they had completed the circuit of the third level, they descended the stairs and took one last look around the ground level before exiting the building.

Brent found a sign announcing the day's events and said, "Oh, look, a show is starting in five minutes in the planetarium."

Puakea said, "What serendipitous timing. Let's go."

They walked the short distance to the planetarium and went in and found three seats together and sat back in the recliners. More people came in, half-filling the auditorium. After a few minutes, the lights dimmed, and the star field overhead lit up from the automated projector. The presentation controller and announcer came on the sound system and said, "Welcome to the J. Watamull Planetarium. Today we are going to take a simulated sailing voyage to Tahiti. Along the way we will see the latitude changes in the starry sky overhead much as the ancient Polynesian voyagers would have seen them.

"The stars you see overhead right now are as you would see them if it were dark outside right now." The announcer caused an image of an arrow to appear at the zenith of the overhead projection. "If you follow this arrow north, you will see that it comes to rest pointing to the North Star, Polaris, or *Hōkūpaʻa*, as the pre-contact Hawaiians called it. It means the *star that doesn't move*.

"The ancient Hawaiian navigators could measure their latitude by holding a hand at arm's length and observing the height of Hōkūpaʻa above the horizon, using fingers, thumb, and other marks such as knuckle wrinkles on their hands. Using this method, they were able to discern the differences in latitude of the various Hawaiian Islands."

The projector controller began to rotate the star field, saying, "As night progresses, the thirty-two points of the star compass are denoted by changing stars, setting or rising at the horizon. Navigators needed to memorize all these stars so they could tell compass directions at any time of night and in any season."

The pointer moved to the eastern horizon and a second pointer appeared. "Look at these two rising stars. They appear simultaneously on the eastern horizon and will disappear over the western horizon at the same time. Every latitude has its unique pairs of rising and setting stars like these. It was Nainoa Thompson, in the twentieth century, who made this observation in the planetarium right here at Bishop Museum. Whether the ancient Pacific mariners used this particular technique to ascertain latitude is unknown. We *do* know that they used Polaris and the Southern Cross to tell latitude."

One pointer disappeared and a bright orange star rose in the east and the remaining pointer went to it and tracked along with it. "This bright star is Arcturus, also called *Hōkūleʻa*, which means *star of gladness* in Hawaiian. This star passes directly over the Hawaiian Islands. That is, in Hawaiʻi, it is straight overhead at its zenith. Every island in Polynesia has its zenith star, helping the ancient navigators locate their destinations."

The star field stopped rotating. "I have stopped the rotation at this time so that the stars appear as they would at midnight on the vernal equinox. In addition to blocking out the sun for pedagogical purposes, I have likewise not shown you any of the planets, nor the moon. The moon can be used to aid navigation, but the planets are not helpful. The ancient Polynesians had names for the planets, but they move around too much to be useful in navigation."

The rotational axis of the celestial sphere began slowly to pitch to the north with the pole star moving toward the northern horizon. "Now we begin our voyage to the south. As we approach the equator, Hōkūpaʻa will sink below the northern horizon." The pointer indicated the sinking Polaris.

"As we continue our voyage to the southern Pacific islands, we note that there is no corresponding southern pole star. Instead, the Southern Cross of four bright stars approximates the location of the South Pole. Navigators memorized elevations of the Southern Cross above the horizon for different seasons to measure their latitude when out of sight of Hōkūpaʻa."

After describing a few ancient voyaging routes and destinations, the projection controller announced, "This concludes our Polynesian voyaging wayfinding presentation. I will now entertain questions from the audience."

After several questions were answered, the lights came up and the audience members departed the planetarium.

Blinking out in the bright sunlight, Edward said, "Wow. I never knew a lot of that. It's amazing what those ancient voyagers could do."

Puakea replied, "Yes, the Polynesians had an active voyaging culture many hundreds of years ago."

Brent said, "Thank you, Puakea, for the suggestion to watch that show. I found it most interesting."

"I'm glad you liked it, Brent. Edward, are you hungry? Let's go to Uncle Lele's house for lunch."

"Sounds good to me, Puakea. I *am* rather peckish. And I suppose Brent could use electric charging power too."

"I'm sure Uncle Lele will let him use his induction charger. Let's go."

Puakea summoned Ikaika as they walked to the front entrance of the museum grounds. As they neared the front, the gift shop came into view and Edward said, "Wait a minute, Puakea. Let's stop in the gift shop. I want to buy souvenirs for friends back home." They spent a few minutes browsing in the gift shop as Edward acquired a few small items of relevance to their visit to the Bishop Museum. Then they walked out of the museum entrance and got into Ikaika for the ride to Uncle Lele's house.

Lunch with Uncle Lele

I guess that's the story of life: what you most fear never happens, but what you most yearn for never happens either. This is the difference between life and fiction. I suppose it's a good trade-off. But I'm not sure.

—Philip K. Dick

Ikaika entered the freeway going east, continued past Diamond Head to the Maunalua coast and continued to Wailupe Valley. Edward admired the green valley walls and noticed what looked like caves high up on the right cliff wall. Wet-looking clouds obscured the Koʻolau ridge at the back of the valley. After crossing the Hind Drive bridge, Ikaika turned left onto Hind Iuka Drive and after another turn, was soon at the house of Puakea's Uncle Lele.

Rising from the car, the three walked up to the front of the house. Next to the door was a sign that read, "E komo mai. Hale Wakanale."

Puakea said, "The sign says, 'Welcome to the Wakanale house.' Uncle's surname is Wakanale."

The front door was already open. A tall smiling man wearing an aloha shirt, shorts, and bare feet came to the door. Uncle Lele opened the outer screen door and said, "Aloha, Brent and Edward. Aloha, Puakea." He pulled Puakea to him and gave her a hug and a kiss on the cheek. "Come in, come in. I am Uncle Lele."

Puakea and Edward removed their slippers and put them next to the two pair already outside the door. Brent sat on the bench provided and removed his shoes. They entered the old fashioned house with many artifacts of the Pacific on the walls.

Edward said, "Aloha e, Uncle Lele. I am Edward and this is my robotic assistant Brent."

Uncle Lele said, "Aloha, kākou. Make yourselves at home. The bathroom is through the hall. Brent may use the induction charger on the wall, over there." He pointed to the long wall of the living room.

"Mahalo," said Brent and Edward in unison. Brent walked over and stood with his back against the induction charger. Brent liked to keep his battery full when he could.

In a few minutes, Uncle Lele's wife, Anakalia, brought a tray with glasses of iced tea, saying, "Aloha. It's good to meet you, Edward, and aloha to Brent. Nice to see you today, Puakea."

Puakea replied, "Mahalo, 'Anakē."[48]

After everyone was served, Uncle Lele said, "Let's sit around the dining table. Aunty Anakalia will bring sandwiches in a few minutes."

Puakea led the way to the table and sat, followed by Edward and Uncle Lele. Brent remained standing at the wall charger next to the table.

Uncle Lele asked, "Edward, how did you like the Bishop Museum?"

"It's wonderful. I enjoyed seeing and learning so much about Hawai'i. We also saw the planetarium show on Polynesian wayfinding."

Uncle Lele replied, "I am glad you liked it. You should also see the Mission Houses Museum. The tour there will give you essential knowledge of Hawai'i in the nineteenth century."

Puakea added, "Yes you should. I can take you if you want."

"That will be good. Mahalo."

Aunty Anakalia brought out the plate of sandwiches as well as napkins, and plates. Uncle Lele said, "Mahalo, huapala."[49]

Aunty Anakalia joined them at the table and Edward said to Uncle Lele, "Puakea said you are an author of historical fiction. What are you working on now?"

"I prefer to call it speculative historical fiction, or alternate history. It asks the question 'What if things had happened differently?' In the book

---

[48] Aunty.
[49] Sweetheart.

I'm currently writing, I ask the question 'What if nuclear power had never been invented?' Would we still have a water economy in the solar system?"

Edward replied, "It seems like it would be nearly impossible to me. How would you get the electric power for the robotic water haulers on the Jupiter-Earth circuit?"

Uncle Lele said, "It would be much more difficult, but still possible. The existing society in space of this halcyon era uses a combination of solar power and fusion power. Solar power is abundant in the orbit of earth about the sun, such as on the moon and at Earth-Sun L4 and L5. It's less abundant at the orbit of Mars, and at greater distances from the sun, solar power is so weak that fusion power is used almost exclusively."

Brent spoke from his position at the wall, "That is, indeed, the case, Uncle Lele."

"Yes, Brent, and that suggests a solution for non-nuclear space civilization. Almost all power will have to be generated at lunar orbit, Moon-Earth, and Earth-Sun Lagrange points using extensive solar farms. For power storage, water could be split electrically and stored as cryogenic liquid hydrogen and oxygen. Multilayer insulation in vacuum provides a near perfect thermal insulator, so boil-off during storage would be inconsequential."

Edward said, "There does not seem a limit to the amount of energy that could be stored that way, but how is the water to be obtained?"

Uncle Lele answered, "The water haulers from the Jovian moons would not be as efficient, but they could be chemically powered by that liquid hydrogen and oxygen fuel. Instead of burning the fuel in low specific impulse thermal rockets, the fuel could be combusted to drive turbines for generating electricity to power high specific impulse electric thrusters, as is done in conventional fusion-powered water haulers."

"I see," said Edward.

"Further, some of the water exhaust from the steam turbine power generator could be fed to the thrusters for reaction mass, and any water that was not used that way could be condensed in radiator panels and stored in a bladder. It would be a valuable commodity at the lower sun orbit destinations."

Brent said, "I see how that could work. Robotic fuel haulers could bring the cryogenic fuels to Mars, asteroid, and Jupiter orbits for later use, too. The energy stored that way could be used for many purposes besides propulsion."

Uncle Lele agreed, "That's right. It wouldn't be as efficient as with the abundant fusion power we are familiar with, but it could also work for space liners like the one you and Edward recently flew on."

Edward said, "That should be an interesting alternate history book. If you let me know when it comes out, I'll buy a copy for my book collection. And I will read it, too, of course."

"I will appreciate that, Edward. Mahalo. The story is about a creative thinker's struggle to get a space civilization kickstarted. The obstacles he overcomes, the organization he inspires through charismatic leadership, the people who help and oppose him, and so forth."

After lunch, Uncle Lele accompanied his guests to the backyard to look at the trickling stream that ran behind the house. It was a peaceful and relaxing setting in the shade of large trees. Gentle trade wind breezes rustled the leaves. Edward admired Uncle Lele's orchid collection.

The Hale Wakanale cat came up to Brent and rubbed against his legs. "Aloha e, pōpoki,"[50] he said.

"That's our cat, Maui," said Uncle Lele. "I see you have been learning Hawaiian, Brent. I am impressed."

Aunty Anakalia said, "Sometimes we call our cat 'Maui Meowee,' just for fun." The humans all laughed at the pun.

Puakea said she would be staying with Uncle and Aunty a while longer. She wanted to tell Aunty about her latest research paper on box jellies. Aunty had been following her research because she had been stung while swimming when she was younger. When it came time for Brent and

---

[50] Kitty.

Edward to depart Hale Wakanale, they bid an affectionate aloha to Aunty Anakalia and Uncle Lele, with hugs and kisses all around. Then they walked out to the waiting Ikaika. Puakea directed the car to take Brent and Edward back to the Royal Hawaiian Hotel. She gave Edward a kiss on the cheek as the car door opened. "I'll call you later about seeing the Mission Houses," she said.

Edward said, "Mahalo for a lovely day." and kissed her back. Brent and Edward got in, Ikaika closed his doors, and drove them back to the Royal Hawaiian Hotel. They arrived in ten minutes, got out of the car, and walked into the hotel. Ikaika traveled back to Hale Wakanale to later take Puakea to her flat in Mōʻiliʻili.

Catamaran Sailing

How inappropriate it is to call this planet Earth, when clearly it is Sea.

—Arthur C. Clarke

B ack in their hotel room after their visit with Uncle Lele, Edward asked Brent, "What's next on our package tour?"

"We have a catamaran dinner sail tonight, sir. We will be at sea to watch the sun set."

"I know you don't care much for water, Brent. Will you be coming on the boat with me?"

"Yes, sir. The boat is 20 meters long and has a large, covered area where I can stand. I will be protected from possible salt spray.

"That's good. I'll be glad to have you with me."

"My understanding is that regular beach wear, that is shorts, shirt, and slippers are acceptable for a catamaran sail in Waikīkī. It will be interesting to see how these sunset sails are accomplished. I can assist you with any food and beverage if you like."

"That sounds good, Brent. I hope we see another awesome sunset."

"We board the boat right on the beach here at 5:30 this evening, sir, just one hotel Diamond Head of the Royal Hawaiian, so it's a short walk on the sand. The sun sets at 6:20 PM, so we should be well out to sea by then for a spectacular view of the sunset."

"That gives us an hour to get ready. I think I will read for thirty minutes."

"Yes, sir, I will remind you at five o'clock, if necessary."

Edward picked up his copy of a Hawaiian language primer he had purchased in a shop and began to read. He was fully absorbed when Brent tapped him on the arm a short time later. "It is time to get ready, sir."

At the appointed time, Brent and Edward were on the beach near the sailing catamaran. The sun was low over the water in the southwestern sky. Fluffy white cumulus clouds were scattered overhead, drifting out to sea on the gentle trade wind. People had gathered on the sand, ready to board the large yellow cat with red trim. Her name, Manu Kai, was painted on the bow, which was touching the sand at the waterline. A stair had been lowered between the hulls, and the crew, barefoot and in shorts and t-shirts, were standing by to receive the passengers who began queuing up. At 5:30, right on time, the first of the cruise guests began to ascend the steps.

Brent and Edward had removed their slippers earlier, having walked on the sand from their hotel. Carrying their footwear, they walked up to the catamaran and got in the queue to board. Edward went up the stairs ahead of Brent. A deck hand was at the top, ready to help him up if necessary. As they came aboard, crew members greeted each passenger with "Aloha." Brent followed closely and stayed with Edward as he kept to his right and moved aft past the mast stays of the sloop-rigged catamaran. Edward found a seat on a bench on the port side of the sailing cat. He stowed his slippers on the deck under the bench and Brent did likewise.[51] The wind was soft and Manu Kai's mainsail and jib were both up, luffing in the light offshore breeze.

When everyone was aboard Manu Kai, the captain greeted the assembled passengers and gave them a safety briefing, showing where life jackets were stowed and what to do in the event of a person overboard. Before the captain went to the wheelhouse in the cabin, which was open at the aft end, he announced that passengers were free to move about the deck and could ride on the trampoline[52] between the forward hulls, if they

---

[51] On a boat likely to get spray aboard, bare feet usually provide a surer footing than slippers, even for modern robots which have soft grippy soles on their five-toed feet.

[52] An open weave netting that some people wearing swimsuits consider to be fun to ride upon because the water is visible fairly close up and for the occasional blast of spray when the hulls hit a large wave.

wanted to. He added, "For safety reasons, passengers should always mind the instructions of the crew."

The crew cast off from the anchoring ropes on the beach, raised the stairway, and Manu Kai used her electric screw propellers, one at the aft end of each hull, to back off the sand. When she was in deeper water away from the beach, she turned sharply, then moved forward, and turned into a channel through the reef and headed out to sea. With the wind so light, most of Manu Kai's forward motion came from the electric motors.

As Manu Kai moved into deeper water, she increased her speed. A teenaged boy and girl wearing swim attire climbed onto the web trampoline between the forward hulls. Brent and Edward watched them play. Two kilometers offshore, Manu Kai turned ninety degrees to port and headed to a point just south of Diamond Head. There, on a close reach[53] and out of the wind shadow of the hotels, the trade wind filled the sails, and Manu Kai let the wind do most of the work. With the forward motion over the swells and the wind coming off the port bow, salt spray occasionally swept over the passengers standing at the forward rail.

Brent said, "This salt spray is my signal to go into the cabin."

"Okay, Brent, I'll stay out here unless it gets really rough," replied Edward.

Brent took the starboard, or lee, side around to the cabin, which was open at the rear, and walked forward to where the captain was standing at the wheel, looking through the windscreen.

"Do you mind if I stand here next to you for a while, Captain?"

"Please do. I see you're seeking shelter from the sea spray." The captain had both hands on the wheel and moved it slightly from time to time.

"Yes indeed, Captain. This is my first exposure to sea voyaging. I hope I'm not distracting you from your work." Brent could see Edward

---

[53] On a close reach, a sailboat is sailing closer to the wind than on a beam reach, which is ninety degrees to the wind.

standing at the forward rail through the forward windscreen. "My name is Brent, by the way. I am Edward's valet. He's the one standing by the rail there in front of us."

"I'm glad to meet you, Brent. How do you like being Edward's valet?"

"I like it fine, Captain. Edward takes me with him on his travels and I get to see a lot of new things and meet many people. I suppose it takes a lot of experience to steer this catamaran."

"Not as much as you might think, Brent. This wheel doesn't do anything. It's like the wheel in a baby's car seat. It's to make the passengers feel more secure, those who need it, that is. Manu Kai does all the navigating and helmsmanship."

"It seems like an interesting job to me, crewing on a pleasure catamaran in Waikīkī. Meeting new people, seeing beautiful sunsets, and so on."

"I can't complain. There are harder ways to earn extra money. Watch and see, now. Manu Kai is timing this so that we will make a U-turn near Diamond Head just as the sun touches the horizon, and we will then be sailing toward the sunset. All the passengers will take out their PDs and begin taking pictures."

"This time of year, in the winter, the sun sets over the sea, south of Pu'u o Kapolei. So, I believe the sun sets over land in the summertime."

"That's right, Brent. I see you know a thing or two about the sky and navigation."

"Yes, sir, it interests me. I am glad we are getting to see the sun set over the water. We may see the famous green flash."

"Sometimes we see it, most of the time we don't."

The captain and Brent stood in silence for a few minutes. Then the captain said, "Watch this, Brent. Manu Kai, adjust your heading two points to starboard."

Manu Kai said, "Aye, aye, Captain," and Brent could see their heading change slightly.

Brent said, "That certainly seems a lot easier than trying to hold a heading yourself, Captain, in these cross swells."

"Yes, she's a better pilot than any human. And she likes her work, too. Don't you, Manu Kai?"

"Aye, Captain. Being a sailing catamaran in Waikīkī is just about the best thing to be. I have sensors underwater so I can watch the fish play, sensors all around so I can watch the surfers play, sensors to watch the people on board enjoying themselves, and sometimes when the waves are big enough, Captain lets me surf a little, myself."

"That sounds like a wonderful life, Manu Kai. But I hope you don't have sensors in the head[54] where people expect privacy."

"Of course not, Brent. Please excuse me, now, it's time to come about and I need to call the deck crew to attend to the rigging."

Manu Kai turned to port, into the wind, and continued around to point west while the crew managed the jib and mainsail to keep them properly trimmed.

The captain's mate began setting out trays of pūpū [55] while a crew member passed out mai tais to the passengers. A few passengers chose to help themselves to water.

Meanwhile, Edward had begun talking to a fellow passenger on the foredeck, a professor at the university, out for an evening with his wife. He was a professor of physics and when Edward mentioned that he had recently returned from a Martian holiday on the space liner SS Brizo, the professor told him that he had helped to develop the active radiation shielding that made passenger liners possible. He added, "That was a long time ago."

The professor appeared to be beyond retirement age, but he said he was still teaching at UH, as he called it. Edward continued the conversation,

---

[54] Nautical lavatory.
[55] Pūpū is Hawaiian for appetizers.

"It's good to know, Professor Goldberg, that not every passenger is a tourist, that local residents like to sail too."

"Please call me Ken. Yes, my wife and I like to spend an evening in Waikīkī from time to time, as a special night out. A sunset sail starts things off right."

The sun was getting lower in the west, just off the port bow, nearly touching the horizon. "Please call me Edward, Ken. I noticed that on the SS Brizo, when Brent and I voyaged to Mars, the passenger compartment was shielded with a parallel array of six solenoids made up of superconducting hoops. Why *six* arranged around the passengers? Why not five or seven?"

"That's an interesting question, and I'm glad you were paying attention. I am particularly proud of my contribution to that shield design. The reason is that the number of deflecting cylinders must be an odd number times an even number, three times two, in that case. The next lower number would be one times two, or two, and that would be too few. It would leave the passenger compartment exposed to charged particles on two sides."

"Interesting."

"The next higher number would be five times two, or ten. That would provide sufficient coverage, but due to the reduced diameter of the solenoids, the cancellation of the magnetic field within the passenger compartment would be uneven. People don't do well for long periods in strong magnetic fields. So, it turns out that six is the optimal number."

"I see, but why an odd times an even number?"

"That's because two conditions must be met. First, adjacent solenoids about the periphery of the passenger compartment must be of opposite polarity, requiring an even number arrayed around the passenger compartment. Second, solenoids on opposite sides of the compartment must be of opposite polarity, so the fields will cancel out in the compartment, requiring an odd number of pairs of solenoids."

"Interesting. I bet it took a bit of experimenting to arrive at the best configuration, diameters and distances, things like that."

"Indeed, it did. It's an interesting optimization problem. Those exciting days rank among the most satisfying in my life. It was a huge boon to the space economy to be able to have passenger service among the planets without having to drag massive passive shielding everywhere."

"An impressive accomplishment, indeed. Just one more question, Ken, if I may ask."

"Sure, go ahead."

"Why a stack of superconducting hoops for the solenoids? Why not a single helical superconducting wire for each? That would seem to be simpler."

"It's for redundancy. If a micrometeoroid should strike a hoop, the entire solenoid would not fail, but merely be degraded."

"I see. Thank you."

Just then the bottom edge of the sun touched the watery horizon. Passengers began to record the sun's setting on their personal devices. Professor Goldberg said, "Waikīkī is known for its glorious sunsets, but wait a while before taking any pictures. All you'll get now is the bright orange of the sun washing out the sky. You see those high clouds overhead? Stratocumulus. And with those mixed in with the low trade wind cumulus clouds, we should have a fantastic sunset tonight. Wait until the sun is well below the horizon. That's when we get lavender and magenta lighting up the whole sky. And not just at the western end."

"Thanks for the tip. I'm always glad to get good photographs."

Edward stared at the nearly gone but bright reddish sun on the clear horizon. As the limb of the sun slipped below the horizon, Edward saw the green flash. Brent saw it too.

After lots of *oohs* and *aahs* from the passengers, the sky darkened, and the sunset faded. Manu Kai turned to starboard and entered the channel to the beach in front of the Outrigger Hotel, passing a few diehard surfers who could barely see the waves coming in in the fading light, and beached herself on the sand.

Brent and Edward collected their slippers from under the bench, descended the steps to the beach, and walked through the sand to the Royal Hawaiian Hotel. They put on their slippers after they passed through the gate into the grounds of the hotel.

Later, in their room, as Edward was preparing for bed, he said to Brent, "I sure learned a lot from Professor Goldberg about active radiation shielding for passenger vessels. It really is what makes large scale passenger travel feasible up there."

"Indeed sir, those arrays of superconducting solenoids are fairly low mass and quite effective in deflecting charged particles."

"One thing bothers me, though, Brent, and I'm sorry I didn't think of it while I was with Professor Goldberg. I'm sure he could have clarified it."

"What would that one thing be, sir?"

"I can see how particles arriving from off-axis directions would surely be sucked into the solenoids, but it seems to me that particles arriving on-axis, that is from straight ahead or behind the axis of the cylindrical passenger compartment, would be unimpeded and fly right on through the passengers."

"Indeed sir, those particles would not be diverted through the superconducting hoops. However, the number of particles arriving exactly on-axis is vanishingly small."

"That's good to know. Thank you." Before getting into bed, Edward sat at the small desk and wrote in his journal:

> Puakea took us to the Bishop Museum this morning. What a glorious place! Fabulous history there. Carved wooden gods called kiʻi, bright red and yellow feathered capes and helmets, and uniforms and dresses like we saw at the Iolani Palace. There is this small but fantastic planetarium where we learned about the star navigation system of the ancient Polynesian voyaging and island colonizing

culture. Puakea then took us to the home of her Uncle Lele and Aunty Anakalia for lunch. They are truly gracious hosts.

We also went on the sunset sail catamaran ride this evening. I met a professor on board who worked on the cryogenic magnetic cosmic ray protection systems of space liners. A most interesting guy. Then the sun touched the clear horizon and everyone stared while it went down. Brent and I both saw the green flash! It was ideal conditions and as the sun diminished to nearly nothing I saw the green light accumulating turbulently around the remaining rim of the sun and a steady blue-green dot appeared as the limb of the sun went down and vanished.

Edward saved the file and got into bed. "Goodnight, Brent."

Brent turned off the light. "Goodnight Edward."

Edward slept soundly until morning.

Mission Houses Museum

The king, who staid from Witetee till the sabbath was past, for the avowed purpose of attending public worship, is quite overcome by strong drink. He attended service in the morning, together with a crowded house of the chiefs, - immediately after was invited to a sumptuous dinner prepared by trading gentlemen. The temptation set before him was too great – he went – became inebriated; and instead of his seat at Church in the afternoon, lay locked up in sleep.

—The Journal of Sybil Mosely Bingham, 1823

A few days later, as they had arranged, Puakea picked up Brent and Edward from the hotel after breakfast, and they began their ride in Ikaika through Kaka'ako to the Mission Houses Museum, site of the oldest wood frame house (hale la'au) on O'ahu.

As they got into the car, Puakea asked, "Have you two been keeping busy?"

Edward replied, "We went back to the Aquarium one day to get a better look at the fish. I never did find that Primo can in the floor tile installation. Then I went for a swim at the Natatorium next door. I even climbed the diving platform, but not to the highest level. Brent watched from the deck, with his solar umbrella."

Brent added, "Another day we took a leisurely stroll through the zoo. There are lots of things to do in Waikīkī."

On the ride over to the Mission Houses, Puakea gave them background information. "Hiram Bingham and his wife Sybil were sent with the first mission from Boston, Massachusetts, to the Hawaiian Islands on the brig Thaddeus. On board were seven missionary couples and four Hawaiian men who had found their way to the east coast of the United States of America and had been converted to Christianity. Those four Hawaiians tutored the missionary families in the Hawaiian language during the long voyage around the southern tip of South America."

Edward piped up, "Oh, yes. I read James Michener's novel *Hawaii* some time ago. He wrote a long chapter about the missionaries."

Puakea patiently explained, "While that book has a high level of historical accuracy, it is still fiction, and when it was written in the 1950s, Hawaiian anthropology was still in a relatively primitive state. You will get a more complete understanding at the Mission Houses Museum."

They arrived at the museum grounds where Ikaika dropped them off and went to park himself. They stood on the sidewalk across the street from a graveyard. A white flash: an egret flapped by and disappeared behind some trees. They moved up the walkway. "The tour starts in the gift shop. We're a little early, so we can browse if we want to," said Puakea. The three spent several minutes looking at the handmade local crafts and Hawaiian themed books and artworks. A scale model of the area in 1821, depicting hale pili and a frame house under construction, was placed prominently in the center of the store.

Anakalia Wakanale entered and walked over to Puakea. Edward noticed and said to Brent, "Look, Aunty Anakalia is here." Edward approached them and said, "Aloha e, Aunty Anakalia."

"Aloha e Edward. It's good to see you both."

Brent said, "Aloha e Aunty Anakalia. Are you here for a tour, too?"

"In a way, Brent. I will be guiding your tour. I've been a volunteer docent here for many years."

Edward said, "Puakea didn't tell us you would be our tour guide."

"I wanted it to be a surprise," replied Puakea.

Anakalia said, "We must wait until the others arrive. We are expecting two more people to join us today. Let's wait out on the lanai." They all went out the door to the lanai at the front of the gift shop under the kou and monkeypod trees.

"I think I see them coming now, off of that cruise ship," said Puakea. A young couple approached. Edward could see the sailing ship in the distance, its solar cell-covered airfoils sticking up above the buildings by the harbor. The airfoils looked like airplane wings, not cloth sails.

Edward looked to his right at an ancient-looking building across King Street. "What is that old building over there?"

Puakea answered him, "That's Honolulu Hale, the old city hall, now a museum of city history."

"I think it's great that Honolulu takes such good care of its historic buildings."

"It's a part of *mālama ʻāina*, taking care of things related to the land. That's our kuleana, or responsibility. One of many great Hawaiian values."

The young couple approached to join the tour. Introductions were made, and Anakalia said, "Well, we are all here. Let's begin with a look at the model in the gift shop," and she led the way in.

They walked up to and surrounded the partly holographic display, a physical model with a transparent cover, built long ago by an architectural firm under contract during one of the periodic restorations of the houses and site. It appeared to be well maintained. Tiny holographic figures were moving about within.

Pointing out features of the model by putting her hand above them over the protective transparent shield, Anakalia said, "The model shows this area as it looked in 1821. The orientation is correct; north is this way. Here you see the Frame House under construction. Notice the basement dug in the ground with foundation walls of adobe bricks. We will go inside the actual house later."

The five members of the tour gathered close around the model. Anakalia continued, "There was no kitchen in the house back then. The coral block kitchen you will see today was added a few years later. At first, food was prepared in this separate structure on the makai side of the house. Over here, to the west, is the first church being built in a traditional hale pili style. After being rebuilt several times, it was replaced by a permanent

148

building of coral blocks designed by Hiram Bingham, the leader of the first mission company. Reverend Bingham guided the mission for its first twenty years. An ali'i named Boki, then governor of O'ahu, selected this site for the missionaries to live on and start their work.

"The Frame House wasn't the first wood frame house in the islands, but it is the oldest *surviving* one. Here on this side, you see the *hale pili*, or thatch houses, built for the missionaries to live in. There is a picket fence around the property and here by the gate, by the road, stand figures of Hiram and Sybil Bingham greeting the king, Liholiho, or King Kamehameha II, whom you see on a cart being pulled by men."

The cart, wheels turning, was moving slowly by. Men with kahili marched along announcing the royal presence, and there was a marching guard with shouldered muskets, followed by retainers and commoners bringing gifts of food.

"The king would come by frequently to observe progress on the building of the house. Some of the ali'i, members of the ruling class, were suspicious that the basement was being dug to hide weapons. The missionaries ensured openness and visibility. The road the king is traveling on eventually became known as King Street, a main route through town. Are there any questions?"

Edward spoke up, "What is going on there in that pit?" He indicated the place with his hand.

"Coral blocks are being roasted for lime to make mortar." Anakalia looked at the group and, seeing that there were no more questions, led the way out of the shop and over to the Chamberlain House. Anakalia unlocked the front door of the Chamberlain House, pushed it open, and stood next to it while the tour group entered the big, airconditioned room. When all were in, she pushed the door closed and resumed her history.

"In the early years of the nineteenth century, in Hawai'i, changes were occurring. Contact with foreigners brought new ideas and technology, such as the use of muskets and cannon in warfare. Some local ali'i were resisting the changes being wrought by the new conquering king, Kamehameha. His conquests of Maui and Oʻahu were delayed by rebellions on the Big Island. Kamehameha had to return to Hawaiʻi Island several times to put them down. Finally, out of exasperation, he said 'This time, kill all who oppose me and all who support the rebels, including their families.'

"After one battle on the Big Island, a boy named ʻŌpūkahaʻia had the misfortune of having parents who supported the rebels. The king's men killed them and ʻŌpūkahaʻia's infant brother. ʻŌpūkahaʻia was fleeing with his baby brother on his back when a thrown spear killed the baby. ʻŌpūkahaʻia was given to the warrior who killed his family. Later, he was taken from the warrior by ʻŌpūkahaʻia's uncle, a kahuna,[56] in this case a priest, at a heiau, or temple.

"ʻŌpūkahaʻia was not happy in his role under his uncle. He hated the long days of memorizing chants. Those were tumultuous times in Hawaiʻi. When a square-rigged sailing ship, the *Triumph*, dropped anchor in the bay one day, ʻŌpūkahaʻia swam out to it and Captain Brintnal gave him permission to come aboard. ʻŌpūkahaʻia let Captain Brintnal know he wanted to leave the islands. It was common practice in those days to augment crews of Pacific trading ships with islanders.

"Captain Brintnal made it all right with ʻŌpūkahaʻia's uncle and took ʻŌpūkahaʻia under his wing and let him learn sailing skills. When the ship returned to New Haven, Connecticut, after a year of Pacific trading, Captain Brintnal let ʻŌpūkahaʻia and Thomas Hopu, another Hawaiian who had traveled with him on the *Triumph*, stay in his house for a while. One day, ʻŌpūkahaʻia was found weeping on the steps of Yale University by divinity students. When they asked him what was wrong, he said it was because he wanted to learn and no one would teach him. The students took pity on him and arranged for him to study with them.

"ʻŌpūkahaʻia worked to create an original Hawaiian alphabet so he could write in his native language. He also wrote, in English, papers that were collected later in a book whose theme was basically, *why you should*

---

[56] A kahuna is an expert in a field, not necessarily a priest.

send a mission to Hawai'i. The book became popular in northern religious circles and was used in fundraising efforts by the ABCFM, the American Board of Commissioners for Foreign Missions. 'Ōpūkaha'ia was working to form a mission to Hawai'i when he died of typhus in February 1818."

In an aside to Brent, Edward said, "That six syllable name, 'Ōpūkaha'ia, is quite a mouthful."

Brent whispered back, "Indeed, sir."

Anakalia continued, "The northeastern American religious fervor of the time had two related forks: abolition of slavery and the sending of missions to foreign lands. Their belief was that only free men could accept the word of God willingly, and their work eventually contributed to the abolition of slavery via the American Civil War.

"Hiram Bingham was a newly minted Doctor of Divinity from the Andover Theological Seminary in Massachusetts. He was to be put in charge of a mission and he fully accepted his duty to commit his life to the enterprise. There was one small catch. Every missionary had to take a wife with him.[57] Hiram quickly found a life partner willing to undergo the responsibility of a mission. Hiram and Sybil Moseley were hastily married just before the sailing date of the brig *Thaddeus*. Four young Hawaiians joined the mission and endeavored to teach the Americans to speak Hawaiian so that, when they arrived, they were able to greet nā ali'i in their native tongue.

"The Thaddeus sailed from Massachusetts on October 23, 1819. A printing press had been dismantled and stowed in the hold of the ship. There was also a kit house of pre-cut lumber. The missionaries of the first company knew of the great king, Kamehameha, and expected to meet him when they arrived. King Kamehameha had completed his wars of conquest and had united all the islands of his kingdom by 1810, but he died in May of 1819. Upon the king's death, Liholiho, Kamehameha's oldest son by his

---

[57] The ABCFM had learned from the English missionary experience, where several single ministers took native wives with undesired consequences.

highest-ranking consort, Keōpūolani, became known as King Kamehameha II. Ka'ahumanu, Kamehameha's favorite consort, became Kuhina Nui, or chief advisor, a kind of queen regent, sharing power with Liholiho.

"Ka'ahumanu was an intelligent woman who observed the rapid cultural changes that came with increasing western contacts. She had spoken with Tahitians who had been converted to Christianity by British missionaries. She noted the way the westerners treated women with deference. There was also curiosity and discussion about the one great god of the foreigners.

"Upon Kamehameha's death, Liholiho, aided by Ka'ahumanu and Keōpūolani, embarked on a program of rapid and radical cultural change. Issuing royal decrees, he abolished the 'ai kapu, a set of prohibitions concerning eating: men and women could not eat together, and many nutritious foods, considered sacred to the gods, were forbidden to women and the maka'āinana, or commoners. He ordered that the sacred structures, the heiau, be torn down. He ordered that the wooden images of the gods, the ki'i, be burned. The old religion was no more. Naturally, there was resistance to these policies. There was a rebellion on Hawai'i Island that Liholiho put down with decisive force. It was into this state of change that the missionaries arrived at Kawaihae on the Big Island in March of 1820.[58] Altogether, over the 44 years of the mission, twelve separate companies of missionaries arrived in Hawai'i totaling 178 people."

The young woman from the cruise ship raised her hand and asked, "Some of these events seem highly coincidental. How do we know you aren't giving us a biased view about this?"

"That is certainly a good question. The Mission Houses Museum is also a historical archive. We teach historical facts here. Everything I say can be backed up by verified documents, and in cases where I am using supposition or conjecture, I will say so. I am a volunteer docent trained

---

[58] The Thaddeus anchored at Kawaihae on March 30, 1820. On April 4, the ship anchored off Kailua-Kona.

with a standardized training course established by historians, and I have been tested for historical accuracy. And I thank you again for the question, because it's a perfect segue into a pitch to visit our gift shop after this tour where you will find several publications that document these events in great detail."

The young woman replied, "Thank you."

Anakalia continued, "There were seven missionary couples on the Thaddeus and four Hawaiian men: George Kaumuali'i (son of the king of Kaua'i), William Kanui, John Honoli'i, and Thomas Hopu. Thomas had arrived in New Haven with 'Ōpūkaha'ia under the care of Captain Brintnal.

"The missionaries negotiated with the ali'i and obtained permission to teach the Hawaiians in Hawaiian. A physician and an ordained minister and their wives were left on Hawai'i Island in accordance with the negotiated agreement. The Thaddeus then took the other five missionary couples, including the Binghams, Mr. Loomis (an apprentice printer) and his wife, and Mr. Chamberlain (a farmer) and his wife and five children to O'ahu. They were given this site right here to start their mission, not far from the Honolulu waterfront. The printing press and a kit house were unloaded and stored in a warehouse at the wharf. We'll talk more about the cargo later. Shortly thereafter, two of the couples went with George Kaumuali'i to Kaua'i, to establish a mission there."

The young man from the cruise ship said, "It seems to me like a bunch of lunatics set off on an adventure without much of a long term plan."

Anakalia replied, "I know that from our modern perspective, their religiously motivated actions seem a bit odd, and you are partly right that their planning was imperfect. Although they had gathered as much information about Hawai'i and prior missions as they could, it was indeed not fully inadequate. I suppose you could say that their devotion was their distinction, and it ended up serving them well."

A doorway to the right led to holographic exhibits featuring actors in period costume and a scale model of the mission houses and the surrounding neighborhood in 1850, including the coral block Kawaiaha'o

153

Church designed by Hiram Bingham. Anakalia indicated, with her graceful hand, the doorway opposite the one they had entered, saying, "Let's begin in that room with the rocking chairs. If you will go on in, please."

The group filed in and stood before a pair of wooden rocking chairs with padded seats and wooden arms. Anakalia walked over to stand by the chairs and said, "Hiram Bingham made this rocking chair here beside me for his wife Sybil. He made his own lathe to turn the spindles, and it is said that he used whatever wood he could find, including driftwood. Queen Ka'ahumanu was a frequent visitor to the mission and admired the chair. She asked Reverend Bingham to make one for her. He did, and that's the chair there." She indicated the rocking chair on the group's left. "Hiram used special wood for her chair, including koa. Ka'ahumanu was quite fond of the chair and took it with her wherever she traveled."

Anakalia led the group around the various rooms of the Chamberlain house, describing artifacts large and small, including a bed made of koa wood that had been built for the Judds, a doctor and his wife, who arrived with the third mission company. Then she said, "We will now take a few minutes for you to look at the holographic displays and then we will move on to the Frame House."

After some time with the holographic displays, they gathered again in the main room by the front door. Anakalia said, "Before we move on to the Frame House, are there any questions?"

The young man from the cruise ship asked, "That bed that you said was made for the Judds. How do you know it wasn't imported from another country?"

"The bed is made from koa wood, which grows only in these islands. We also have written documentation of the bed's origin." Anakalia held the door open while the tour group filed out onto the walkway outside. She pulled the door closed after her and made sure it was locked before leading the way on the path around to the north of the Chamberlain house and east to the Frame House. Anakalia mounted the coral block steps of the house and opened the front door. Stepping into the foyer, she turned and directed the tour to take seats in the parlor to her left.

"Hawai'i Aloha," a popular hymn written in the 1870s by Reverend Lyons, and sung by a chorale group in Hawaiian, was playing softly in the background to set the mood. When all were seated, Anakalia stepped into the room and took a chair by the doorway. Sash windows gave a view of King Street.

"The missionaries greeted visitors in this parlor and held prayer meetings here with music. They had a few musical instruments and many of the missionaries were accomplished singers. The Hawaiians were enthralled by the multi-part harmony of the hymn singing by the missionaries. It was one of many attractions of the new religion. Hawaiians could be seen standing outside the hale pili meeting hall listening to the music.

"Look at the wallpaper. Notice the gold leaf in the pattern. This is not something the puritanical missionaries would have purchased for themselves. It was a gift from a sea captain, and the missionaries graciously accepted it to cover the bare wood. Like most of the items in this house, it is a reproduction, and not original."

Anakalia rose and motioned for the tour to follow her across the entrance hall into the front bedroom.

"This bed is typical of western beds of the time." Anakalia pulled back the covers from the foot of the bed, revealing the coarse knotted rope webbing. "A bed like this was probably uncomfortable to anyone not used to it. Ka'ahumanu was a frequent guest in the house, and we believe she slept in this room when she spent the night, but she didn't sleep on the bed. She preferred the traditional lauhala mats you see on the floor in the corner." Anakalia indicated a stack of many lauhala mats against the far wall that would make a firm sleeping surface.

Laid out on top of the bedspread of the western style bed was a large dress with long sleeves, a high neck, and frilly cuffs. "This is a replica of a dress of woven cloth that the missionary women made for Ka'ahumanu, at her request. It was a challenge as Kaʻahumanu is said to have been about 190 centimeters tall and massed 140 kilograms. It could arguably have been the first muʻumuʻu."[59]

After handling a few intelligent questions, Anakalia led the tour through the house, stopping in each room. On the ground floor they went into the dining room with its long table and blue China plates and antique tableware. They also stopped at the Loomis's bedroom on the ground floor, with a hammock cradle suspended over the double bed. "Elisha Loomis was an apprentice printer who came with his wife in the first company. He set up and operated the printing press that had been disassembled and brought over in the hold of the Thaddeus to produce the first educational texts printed in the Hawaiian language."

They climbed the steep stairs to the upper floor and went into the Binghams' bedroom first, which held a desk with an elevation drawing on paper of the Kawaiahaʻo Church, the coral block building designed by Reverend Bingham that he never saw completed. Anakalia told the story of the painting of Sofia, their daughter sent to school in Connecticut. "The portrait had arrived in poor condition with Sofia's likeness obscured. Both parents wept upon seeing it, but the next day Hiram rubbed it with alcohol and, to their relief, her face appeared."

They squeezed into the small crafts room that displayed handicrafts that were taught to Hawaiians. There were a spinning wheel, a loom, and needlepoint spelling samplers.

At the west end of the house, they came to the Judd bedroom. "Dr. Gerritt P. Judd graduated from medical college and arrived in Hawaiʻi with his wife with the third mission company in 1824. The germ theory of disease had not yet been invented and physicians still relied on bloodletting and purging to treat illnesses. However, Dr. Judd was aware of the shortcomings of western medicine and was open to learning the ways of

---

[59] A muʻumuʻu is a floor-length cloth dress with sleeves and without a waist. Modern muʻumuʻu are usually short-sleeved.

the Hawaiian physicians.[60] Hawaiians would line up outside his basement dispensary for consultation. He never charged for his services in accordance with mission policy.

"When the Judd's first child, a girl, was born, a high ali'i woman, Kina'u, came and insisted on holding her. This was in 1831. She wanted the Judds to give the baby to her for adoption, or *hānai*, saying, 'I am rich. You are poor. I give you things.' Although aware of the honor that Kina'u was bestowing upon them, the Judds refused, explaining that hānai was not the western way. Kina'u went off in a huff at the rejection. The crisis was eased several weeks later at the christening of the child. At the insistence of Kina'u, the child received the name Elizabeth Kina'u Judd. That name was continued in the Judd family for generations thereafter."

Some bolts of black silk rested on a rocking chair in the Judd bedroom, and Anakalia related the story of the silk dresses. "Before the dedication of one of the pili grass churches, Ka'ahumanu sent bolts of expensive pink, white, and blue silk. She wanted the missionary wives to make dresses for themselves and for her for the dedication ceremony. The missionary wives returned the fabric, being concerned that other foreigners would think that they were getting above themselves. Later, bolts of plain black silk arrived at the mission house with instructions to make Ka'ahumanu's dress just like theirs. The mission wives made plain black dresses for them all to wear and Ka'ahumanu and the mission wives attended the dedication ceremony dressed in black."

The group went carefully down the steep stairs to the kitchen where Anakalia pointed out the kinds of foods the missionaries might have eaten. There were replicas of eggs, fruits, vegetables, bread, and dead chickens with their heads cut off but not yet plucked. There was an open fireplace with a hanging kettle and a brick oven for baking. She explained that the land there was not suitable for farming and that the missionaries could not have sustained themselves that way. "The missionaries wrote about

---

[60] Lā'au lapa'au.

Hawaiians lined up outside the gate bearing gifts of food, expecting only a thank you and a handshake in return. The missionaries would have starved if not for the kōkua[61] and aloha of the Hawaiian people, ali'i, and other foreigners."

The next and final stop was the print shop in the annex between the Frame and Chamberlain houses. Anakalia invited the group into the room with a manual printing press, a replica of the one used by Elisha Loomis and his Hawaiian helpers. She showed samples of the primer, printed in Hawaiian, that was the first publication to come off the press. It was meant to teach reading, writing, and spelling to both children and adults.

"Their mission was to bring the word of God to the Hawaiian people, and that required teaching reading and writing. They believed people could not be saved, that is, enter Heaven, if they could not read scripture for themselves. The missionaries realized that this was an enormous task, as it required translating the Bible into Hawaiian, and then printing copies for every community."

Brent raised his hand. Anakalia said, "I see you have a question, Mr. Brent."

"Wouldn't it have been easier to import already-printed Bibles in English?"

Aunty Anakalia replied, "That is an excellent question, Mr. Brent. There must have been many debates about this long before this mission was conceived. The London missionaries, for instance would have encountered the same problem with their missions to the Society Islands. The solution they arrived at here was that it would be easier to translate the Bible into Hawaiian and teach the people to read in Hawaiian than to teach the Hawaiians to speak English and then teach them to read."

"Yes, thank you, madam," said Brent. "I see now that it was the optimal approach."

---

[61] Help.

"Not only was it logical, but it was also one of the conditions imposed by Liholiho: they were to teach in Hawaiian.

"'Ōpūkahaʻiaʻs attempt at a written Hawaiian language was considered inadequate so the missionaries began anew. The resulting Hawaiian alphabet evolved over time to an elegant minimal length of twelve, five vowels and seven consonants. The project of translating the Bible was begun with the help of London missionaries and the Tahitian converts who could speak English. The Reverend Willian Ellis, a missionary from London, and a few of his Tahitian assistants who knew English, also helped. Hiram Bingham, being a Doctor of Divinity, was acquainted with several languages, and was aware of errors and other problems in the standard King James version of the Bible. Therefore, the missionaries undertook to translate the Bible into Hawaiian directly from the original Hebrew, Aramaic, or Greek.

"Translated pages were passed among the committee and were worked and reworked until everyone was satisfied with the translation. It took twelve years to complete the Bible translation. The translating committee split into smaller groups. They started with the New Testament. A minister would translate a passage into Hawaiian, then give it to a Hawaiian language expert to review. Copies were sent to the other groups for review and feedback. Responses were compiled to produce a final translation. The whole effort took six years for the New Testament and then six years for the Old Testament. This Bible has been revised from time to time, and you can buy a copy in our gift shop with Hawaiian and English on facing pages. Do you have any questions?"

Nobody spoke at first, and then the young woman from the cruise ship tentatively raised her hand and said, "Why were so many letters trimmed out of the written Hawaiian language?"

"That is an excellent question. To teach a standardized Hawaiian spelling required those simplifications. Take, for example, the Hawaiian word 'kalo' for that staple food. In some places it's pronounced 'taro.' Similarly with the b and p and w and v sounds. The same words are pronounced differently in different parts of the islands. Rather than have multiple spellings for the same word, the standardization committee wisely chose to have one spelling for a written word, while it could be pronounced differently depending on the dialect of the speaker."

Anakalia then demonstrated the operation of the press. Moveable metal type had already been set up celebrating a multi-centennial event. She put on a printer's apron, set a fresh piece of paper under the mask, inked the type, closed the print mask, turned the crank to align the paper and type with the press head, and pulled the lever to press the page. Reversing operations, she revealed the newly printed page and put it on the overhead rack to dry.

"When dry, the pages would be printed on their reverse sides. When all pages were printed, they would be trimmed and bound into a book. This shop printed not only bibles, but also prayer books, hymnals, flyers, and lessons. A typical press run would be three to five dozen books."

Anakalia handled a few more questions, then stated that the tour was concluded. She suggested that her guests stop in the gift shop to look at the mission and Hawaiian themed items for sale.

Before leaving, Brent and Edward thanked Anakalia again. "That was a most informative experience," said Brent. "Mahalo."

"You are most welcome. It makes me glad that you liked the tour."

Puakea summoned Ikaika and the trio met him at the curb. During the ride back to the Royal Hawaiian, Puakea said, "Remember, we have a tour of Mānoa Heritage Center tomorrow. I'll pick you up at nine-thirty in the morning."

Edward said, "That was a pretty good tour today."

Puakea replied, "I think we can top it tomorrow."

"Thanks. See you tomorrow," said Edward as he and Brent got out of the car. Puakea rode off in Ikaika and Brent and Edward entered the hotel.

They went up in the lift, entered their room, and Brent went right to the wall charger. Edward sat in the easy chair and relaxed for a few minutes.

"Wow, Brent, Aunty Anakalia sure has a lot of history packed into her head."

"Indeed sir. She must have had an intensive training course to become a docent there."

Edward nodded his head and said, "I'm getting hungry, Brent. You stay here and get charged up. I'll walk to that store around the corner and get a bento.[62] I'll bring it back here to eat." Edward went into the small store, picked out a nice looking warm box with a clear lid, and took it back to their room where he removed the bento lid, unwrapped the chopsticks, and began to eat.

After Edward had struggled successfully with the chopsticks to eat his faux chicken katsu with rice, he took a short nap. When he awakened, Brent was fully charged, and they went down to the beach where Edward swam and paddled on a rented stand-up paddle (SUP) board.

That evening after Edward had showered and dressed, he and Brent were lounging in chairs in the hotel lobby. Edward said, "I'm getting hungry again. That SUP boarding takes a lot of energy. I wonder where we should go tonight. The hotel restaurant is quite good, but I think a change of scenery is in order."

Brent replied, "I recall, sir, a small beach café just this side of the Aquarium. It is take-out window style, but they have open air tables and I saw on the sign when we passed by the other day that they have live music in the evenings."

"That sounds great, Brent. It's a nice night out so outdoor tables will be just the thing".

The sun was about thirty minutes from the horizon when they set out walking to the beach café at Queen's Surf Beach Park. As they passed the large banyan tree on the makai side of the sidewalk just after Kūhiō Beach, there was a fork in the sidewalk, and they took the makai side. Just before they reached the Waikīkī Aquarium they arrived at the beach café. Brent

---

[62] A portable Japanese lunch.

sat at an unoccupied table near the sea while Edward went to the order window where he asked for a teri-burger plate and an iced tea. Then he went to sit with Brent until his order was ready.

A musician with a guitar arrived and took her place at a makai corner of the table area. She took her guitar out of its case and began minor tuning. When Edward's order was ready, he picked it up and returned to the table. Then Edward dug into his teri-burger plate with macaroni salad and rice.

Edward was sitting where he could see both the ocean and musician, who began to sing in Hawaiian and play guitar in slack key style. Edward thought that both she and her music were quite beautiful. He became aware of his fundamental loneliness, but he said nothing about it. The sun was slowly sinking behind the sea and the almost-full moon was rising over Diamond Head. The clouds overhead were lighting up in orange. A light breeze whispered in the palm fronds.

By the time Edward finished eating, the sun was well below the horizon, it had become dark, and stars began to dot the sky. He asked Brent, "What is that very bright, twinkly, almost bluish, star there, rising over Diamond Head?"

"Sirius."

"I am serious. Do you know its name?"

"Seriously, sir, it's Sirius. S-I-R-I-U-S, the Dog Star."

"Oh, ha ha, I understand."

Brent and Edward sat and looked at the view with the boat lights on the water and listened as the musician switched between Hawaiian and hapa songs.[63] The tables were filling up so Edward decided to return to the hotel. He disposed of his refuse in a container provided[64] and then he and Brent walked back in the cooling breeze to the Royal Hawaiian Hotel.

Edward said, "They say that Hawai'i is paradise, Brent, and I think they are right." They walked through the pleasant subtropical breeze and

---

[63] Hapa-haole songs have a mix of Hawaiian and English lyrics.
[64] All refuse was sorted and recycled using robotic labor.

watched a ballistic passenger rocket ascend into the night sky from the Neil Abercrombie Space Port, with its brilliant white rocket exhaust plume behind it. Half a minute later they heard a distant muffled roar. As the rocket shrank to a star-like point in the night sky, they reached the hotel and went into their room.

"Gosh, Brent, even after having read Michener's fictionalized account of the missionaries, I had no idea of the depth and complexity of their relationships with the royalty and commoners. History sure is interesting."

"Indeed, sir. I learned many things, too."

Edward got ready for bed and then sat at the writing desk and wrote in his journal.

> We went to the Mission Houses today. Puakea took us and Aunty Anakalia gave the tour. She's a docent there. That amazing little frame house is over three hundred and fifty years old! I hadn't realized that by the end of the mission in 1863 seventy-five percent of Hawaiians over eighteen could read. That mission was remarkably successful. Creating a written Hawaiian language was a stroke of genius. I suppose it must have been standard procedure for foreign missions back in those days. Imagine trying to teach the entire population to speak English in addition to reading and writing!

> Brent and I walked to a beach café not too far away for dinner. The food was not bad, but the ambiance was exceptional. All those clichés about soft island breezes, palm trees swaying, and so on are all true! A nearly full moon was rising over Diamond Head. A young woman was playing slack key guitar and singing in Hawaiian. She also sang a few hapa songs that have a mix of Hawaiian and English. It was a marvelous evening. Tomorrow Puakea is taking us to Mānoa Heritage Center.

Edward saved the file, turned off the light, and got under the light covers. "Goodnight, Brent."

"See you tomorrow, Edward." Brent remained standing at the wall charger, ruminating through the night.

Mānoa Heritage Center

The Mānoa Heritage Center is a place where the uniqueness of Hawai'i's environment and culture come alive. Years ago, because I was never adequately inoculated against Sam's powers of persuasion, I found myself disconcertedly volunteering as a docent. However, I quickly came to see the difference that Mānoa Heritage Center tours were making in clarifying and changing people's impressions of Hawai'i. To be a docent there is to be trained and equipped to educate and inspire people to greater interest and involvement in protecting and nurturing the glorious environment and culture of Hawai'i.
—David Lee on the occasion of the memorial service of Sam Cooke,
2016

As was his habit, volunteer docent Lele Wakanale arrived early for the tour at Mānoa Heritage Center, dressed in a cloth brimmed hat, aloha shirt, shorts, and slippers. He sent his car to park itself, walked up to the office door, removed his slippers, and went in to say aloha to the staff. He got his name tag, which read, *Mānoa Heritage Center, Docent, Uncle Lele*, from a drawer and put it on.

The education director said, "Lele, your tour today has five people. There is a couple from the Big Island, the Yamanakas of Hilo. And from the mainland, a man, Edward Collier, and his robot valet named Brent, accompanied by your niece, Puakea." The staff members were acquainted with Lele's niece who had been to the Center many times.

"Mahalo, Janey. I have met the mainland tourists; they seem like nice people. Edward is a bachelor and part time software engineer and Brent the robot is interested in philosophy. He is a legal person, now, by the way. And he seems to have a good heart. Perhaps I will slant this tour more toward Hawaiian values."[65] Indeed, Lele possessed enough heritage knowledge for five one-hour tours, so he could tailor the experience to the desires of the tourists. He went to the restroom and then he sat on a bench outdoors in the shade to await the arrival of the tour group. He looked beyond the Tudor-revival house named Kūali'i, up the Mānoa Valley to the ridge of Ko'olau Mountains, absorbing the grey-green color into his soul. A light mist was kissing one wall of the valley, high up. All was peaceful, with a light breeze.

Ikaika arrived and discharged Brent, Edward, and Puakea, a little early for the tour, and then he went and parked himself. Puakea said, "Aloha e, Uncle Lele."

Lele replied, "Aloha, kākou." Lele stood up from the bench as the three approached.

Edward said, as they gathered around Lele, "Don't tell me, let me guess. You're our tour guide today?"

"That's right, Edward, I am."

"Well, we quite enjoyed yesterday's tour of the Mission Houses by your wife, Aunty Anakalia. She sure knows a lot."

"We are both trained docents and have been doing this for many years. You should check in now at the office."

While they were doing that, a car dropped off the remaining couple for the tour. They went into the office to check in and sign a waiver. When they came out, Lele greeted the Yamanakas.

"Aloha, Mr. and Mrs. Yamanaka. I am Dr. Lele Wakanale and I am your tour guide. You may call me Uncle Lele if you wish."

"Thank you, Uncle Lele. I'm Mike and this is my wife Linda. We're from Hilo, spending a few days here on O'ahu."

---

[65] The Hawaiian values are universal and include aloha (love), kōkua (helpfulness), kū (uprightness), kuleana (responsibility), mālama (caring), 'ohana (family), and pono (fairness).

"Pleased to meet you. Now if you all gather around, we can begin the tour. It will take about an hour, and we will see the heiau, a sacred Hawaiian structure. Please ask any questions that occur to you. You are free to use any imaging or recording devices at any time. There are two tours here at the Mānoa Heritage Center. There is a tour of the interior of the house, and this tour of the grounds, which is a prerequisite for the house tour. For this outdoor tour, I am following the interpretive plan written by novelist and playwright Victora Kneubuhl in the early twenty-first century. If there are no questions, please follow me."

Seeing no questions, Lele walked to the pathway that led up to the 1911 house. "We will start the tour by walking up to the front of the house, which has the best view for photographs." They proceeded up the path and, before walking up the steeper part of the trail, Lele paused in the shade of a large kukui tree. "I know that Brent, Edward, and Puakea have been to the Mission Houses. Mike and Linda, have you had that tour?"

Mike and Linda looked at each other and Mike responded, "No, Uncle Lele, we have not."

"The Mission Houses Museum tour is highly recommended for those interested in Hawaiian history. It's related to this one because Monte Cooke,[66] who built this house, was the grandson of missionary Amos Cooke, who arrived in Hawai'i with the eighth mission company with his wife Juliette in 1837 and lived in the Frame House there. King Kamehameha III asked Amos Cooke to start the Chiefs' Children's School to teach literacy to children of the ali'i."

Lele resumed the walk up the path to the front of Kūali'i. He continued to the front lawn and halted by the hedge near the property line on Mānoa Road, where the entire front of the house and surrounding trees could be seen. "This is the best view of the house and where many people like to take photos. The house was built in 1911 by Monte Cooke, and he named it Kūali'i after a great chief who lived in the late seventeenth

---

[66] Charles Montague Cooke, Jr.

century. *Mānoa* means *broad and wide*. Monte and his wife Lila chose the Tudor style for the house. The foundation and lower walls of the house are built of close-fitting blue basalt, quarried right here where we are standing.

"For those who have taken the Mission Houses tour, Aunty Anakalia took you back in time, then forward again. I'm going to do the same. Please note that all pre-historic dates are subject to change as scientific techniques improve. You know that the volcano goddess, Pele, is at work right now on the Big Island. First stop, millions of years ago. The tectonic plate these islands ride on moves over a hot spot and magma plume at about three centimeters per year. So, two to three million years ago, Pele was right here, forming Oʻahu, which was much bigger back then and has since been eroded and sunken somewhat to its present size. She moved on and over the eons she formed Molokaʻi, Maui, and Hawaiʻi.

"But did you know that Pele returned to Oʻahu about seventy thousand years ago? That's quite recent in geologic time. There was one last gasp of vulcanism here. That's when Diamond Head Crater, Koko Head, and Koko Crater were formed. Also, Punchbowl and Puʻu Kapolei, where the sun sets[67] at the end of the season of Makahiki.[68] And dozens of lesser-known craters. Then Pele went away to the southeast for good, we hope."

Uncle Lele pointed to the top of the ridge to the immediate west of Kūaliʻi. "At that time, a volcano called Puʻu Kakea, on that ridge up there, erupted sending a flow of basalt right across this place where we are standing that continued down into the Mānoa Valley and blocked the stream. That's why Mānoa Stream jogs to the east and runs behind the University of Hawaiʻi campus today. It also blocked silt from erosion of the valley walls, letting it pile up, creating the deep, rich alluvial soil of the vast upper Mānoa Valley.

---

[67] As viewed from eastern Waikīkī.

[68] Makahiki is the Hawaiian rainy season festival from approximately early November to early March.

"There was another benefit from the eruption of Pu'u Kakea. This ground we are standing on is part of the flow. It created the prominence that the house and heiau beyond it are standing on. It was an ideal location, overlooking the agriculturally productive valley, for a heiau dedicated to agriculture.

"Now look at the basalt stones of the house. No two are alike. The basalt is dense and non-porous. The only straight lines are in the corners of the house, and around the doors and windows. Stone masons from Japan were brought here for the job. Do you see that red clay piping between the stones? That is purely decorative and is meant to draw one's attention to the interesting and irregular pattern of the masonry.

"There is a basement below the house that was used for workshops and storage. The ground floor has an entryway with a staircase, a parlor in the front, a large living room, a library, a dining room, and a kitchen. There are four bedrooms upstairs. If you take the interior tour someday, you will see Sam and Mary Cooke's extensive collection of books, paintings, and other Hawaiian art and artifacts. Now we are going to walk toward the house and then turn left and go down the steps on the side of the house. Please do not touch the stones of the house as we go by."

Lele started walking toward the house and the group followed. He led them through the porte cochère, to the left through an iron gate, and down the steps beside the house to a garden where he paused on the grass in the shade of a large thornless kiawe tree. When all were gathered in front of him, he told the story of Monte and Lila Cooke who built the house in 1911.

"Monte Cooke was born premature, and it looked like he might not live, but a Hawaiian woman named Ka'aha'ainaokahaku Naihe, with knowledge of traditional Hawaiian medicine, nursed him to health and maintained a close relationship with him. She lived to be well over a hundred years old. As a result of their connection, Monte had a deep respect for Hawaiian traditions.

"Monte Cooke graduated from Punahou School and went to college on the east coast of the United States. He got his Ph.D. in malacology[69] from Yale University and married his wife Lila, from Brooklyn, just before his graduation. He and Lila toured Europe before returning to Hawai'i where Monte obtained a job at the Bishop Museum. This land was given to Monte and Lila as a wedding present by his parents. At the time it was more than 75 hectares of dairy farm, but now only nine hectares of that remain in the Mānoa Heritage Center.

"In 1911, Monte commissioned the architectural firm of Emory and Webb to design and build this house. Initially, the firm proposed building the house on the site of the heiau, but Monte forbade it. He said, 'That site is kapu.[70] You will not touch it.' So, the architects built the house back from the promontory of the heiau, which you will soon see.

"Monte rode to work at the Bishop Museum in a chauffeured car. Lila had her own car, and she knew how to drive. In fact, she was the first licensed woman driver in Hawai'i. Monte never learned to drive but he organized scientific expeditions for land snail collecting in many Pacific islands. The Bishop Museum has over a million shells collected by Monte and his protégés.

"As the years passed, pieces of land from the estate were sold off or given to family members. Monte's grandson was Sam Cooke, who became a stockbroker. Sam married Mary Moragne from Kaua'i. They initially built their home next to Kūali'i before purchasing Kūali'i from Sam's father and some parcels of surrounding land from Sam's cousins.

"Sam and Mary then lived in Kūali'i and worked to establish the Mānoa Heritage Center until their deaths in the early twenty-first century. The house and grounds comprise this heritage center that we know today. Sam and Mary knew well the legacy of Kūali'i and of the heiau named

---

[69] Malacology is the branch of biology that studies mollusks (phylum *Mollusca*). Monte specialized in land snails.

[70] The English word *taboo* was adopted from the Tahitian language and has the same meaning as *kapu*.

Kūkaʻōʻō and determined to preserve and propagate the heritage of Hawaiian history and the Mānoa Valley. To that end, the Cookes asked Billy Fields, a traditional stone worker from the Big Island, to come and restore the heiau. The restoration process was done correctly with monitoring and documentation by the archaeology department of the University of Hawaiʻi at Mānoa. After the restoration, the Cookes opened their property to the public for tours like this one, and for educating school children and all who wish to learn about Hawaiian heritage in Mānoa."

Lele paused and gestured to the surrounding grounds. "Monte was a skilled gardener who designed the gardens himself. This section of the garden, on the mauka side of the house, is called the White Garden because all the plants' blooms are white. There is a magnolia tree, a pond with white lotus blossoms, a white native hibiscus, and so on. Back then it was fashionable to hold outdoor parties in the evening and the white flowers would glow in the moonlight.

"When Sam and Mary moved into Kūaliʻi in the 1970s, they preserved the White Garden, but the rest of the grounds they planted in native plants and Polynesian introductions. A native plant is one that arrived in the islands without human assistance. There are about two dozen of what we sometimes call the canoe plants, that is, food and medicinal plants brought by the Polynesian colonizers in their seafaring canoes."

Lele began to move down the slope toward the heiau and the group followed. Lele paused and said, "I would like to draw your attention to this dry-stacked stone wall, said to be over six hundred years old. Legend has it that it was built by menehune and it used to stretch all the way across the valley. Today it ends at the heiau."

Mike asked, "Weren't the menehune little magical beings that came out at night and played tricks or helped people they liked?"

"That myth turns out to be disinformation dating from the late nineteenth and early twentieth centuries, created, in part, for marketing purposes. The menehune are now thought to be the original colonizers from the Marquesas

Islands. They were eventually overtaken by Society Islanders who arrived later."

Lele stepped through a gap in the wall and started down a stone pathway with handrails. "We are now entering the native plant garden. We are passing under kukui, kou, and milo trees, which in the case of Hawai'i, are Polynesian introductions."

Edward pointed to a bush with large soft light green leaves and asked, "What is this, Uncle Lele? The flowers look like they've been torn in half. I've seen these down by the beach."

"These native shrubs with the white half-flowers are called naupaka and, as you have observed, Edward, they are frequently found near beaches." Lele led the group down the path to the base of the prominence upon which stood the heiau named Kūka'ō'ō. Looking up, they could see the top edge of the mauka wall of the heiau. Lele pointed out the native morning glory vine, pōhuehue, which, it was thought, when slapped on the water, would call waves for surfing. He described the native fern, moa, the word for chicken, named for its branches like chicken feet. Then he said, "We are at the base of the prominence of the heiau. These structures were built at places of spiritual energy. Let us pause a moment and remain silent to see if we can feel the mana, or divine power."

After a few seconds, a white fairy tern, a manu o kū, flew overhead from west to east. Lele took it as a sign to move on and led the tour up the path and pointed out the *fish poison plant*, ākia,[71] a shrub with small gray-green oval leaves and small pale yellow flowers that was used to stun fish.

They arrived at the top of the prominence, turned left, and entered a shady hau tree arbor with basalt benches. Lele invited the group to sit down and enjoy the cool breeze. A stone kōnane slab was in the center of the space, with an array of indentations, each with a white coral or dark lava marker.

---

[71] A Big Island chief used ākia to poison his wife in the mid nineteenth century. He was hanged for it

172

"Kōnane is a Hawaiian board game that bears some resemblance to checkers or draughts." Brent and Edward looked at the basalt slab with a rectangular array of carved depressions.

Lele continued, "Moves are made by jumping and taking the opponent's markers. Kamehameha the Great was said to be unbeatable at this game. Let's sit here for a while under this hau tree arbor and enjoy the cool breeze and you may ask me any questions you like."

Linda asked, "Is it true that, after first contact, the Hawaiians called the Europeans *haole* because they would not perform the Hawaiian nose-to-nose greeting, so they said they had *no breath*?"

"No, Linda, that's a common misconception. If that were the case, the word would be hā'ole, or more properly, 'a'ole hā. Haole was, and remains, the Hawaiian word for foreigner. The foreigners of that time had some *very* good reasons for their standoffishness; measles and smallpox among them."

There were no more questions, so after sitting for a while, Lele said, "Is everyone nice and cool now?" He was answered in the affirmative. "Good, because next we visit the heiau and for that we need to stand in the sun. Let's go."

Everyone stood up and followed Lele to a gap in the chest-high wall that was the entrance to the enclosure of the heiau. Lele picked up a heavy wooden stick, as long as he was tall, that had been leaning against the heiau wall and held it horizontally in front of him, barring the entrance to the heiau. After the visitors had lined up in front of him, he said, "The interior of the heiau is kapu, that is, nobody but authorized Hawaiian practitioners may enter. So, I stand, barring your way."

The visitors gazed at the vista before them with the green ridge of the Ko'olau in the distance and the temple before them. Lele continued, "I am holding an 'ō'ō, a digging stick, an important farming tool. It was used to make holes in the soil for planting and for prying up stones. It was made of hardwood and was kept oiled and indoors at night. It was a valuable heirloom passed down from father to son."

Lele pointed north to the Koʻolau range, "Legend has it that long ago, a Hawaiian hero named Kawelo took some of his people up to the highest peak of the Koʻolau, where he lifted his ʻōʻō and said, 'I am going to throw this ʻōʻō and where it lands, you will build a heiau.' He threw the ʻōʻō and it flew all the way down here and stuck in the ground upright, or kū. Hence, the name of the heiau, Kūkaʻōʻō, or *upright the digging stick.*"

Brent stated, "That is obviously a tale told for the entertainment of children, and I enjoyed it too."

Lele, in the spirit of fun said, "Or perhaps back then the aliʻi were much stronger than ordinary people."

Brent, having been schooled by Edward from time to time in the art of repartee, replied, "Lele, sir, I know when you are pulling my leg."

"Yes, it is a fun story to tell the youngsters." Lele laughed, then asked, "Are there any other questions?"

Edward asked, "How was this heiau used, you know, back in the old days?"

"As you can see, standing here on this promontory, the heiau commands a view of the fertile valley. Back in those days, it would have been loʻi kalo, or floodable terraces, up to the talus of the valley pali. This heiau was built as a place of worship where offerings could be given in thanks for a bountiful harvest, or to ask for rain or other blessings. But it was probably also used as a place where experts could be consulted on agricultural matters such as when to plant. Captain Vancouver entered this valley and wrote about it in the late eighteenth century. However, much definite knowledge has been lost in the mists of time as written records were not generally initiated until the early and middle nineteenth century, after the missionaries, in partnership with the royal leaders, had embarked on their program of public education."

Lele could see that they were satisfied with his answers, and after some moments of reflection, he suggested that they move down to the Canoe Garden where they could find shade. He led the way down the stony path to the shade of a mountain apple tree and paused.

"This tree is 'ōhi'a 'ai, or mountain apple, and is a Polynesian introduction."

Lele was interrupted with a question from Mike. "You keep saying Polynesian introduction, but I thought you were supposed to be talking about Hawaiian heritage."

"That's a good observation, Mike. Roughly a thousand years ago, the first Polynesians arrived here, probably from the Marquesas. At that time, the Hawaiian culture that the European mariners encountered did not yet exist. It took about five hundred years from the time that the first settlers on O'ahu's windward side arrived for the culture and language to evolve. That process included introduction of a more rigid religion and hierarchical social structure by later immigrants from the region of the Society Islands. That process formed the culture that Captain Cook and other westerners experienced back then. So, for technical accuracy, I refer to the early voyagers as Polynesian, not Hawaiian."

"That makes sense. Thank you, Uncle Lele."

After they had cooled off in the shade of the 'ōhi'a 'ai for a few minutes, Lele led them into the Canoe Garden proper and pointed out several varieties of taro (kalo), the sweet potato ('uala), sugar cane (kō), and other plants brought to Hawai'i by the Polynesians in their sailing canoes. They moved to another shady spot, and Lele said, "All of these few dozen plants were brought on the voyaging canoes called wa'a kaulua, or double hulled sailing vessels. Most were food plants like breadfruit, called 'ulu, and 'uala and kalo. Some were medicinal like the noni, and some tree seeds like hau and milo were brought because they were useful for canoe making or wood carving. Imagine if you were preparing for a migratory voyage. How would you decide what to take?"

There were some thoughtful looks, but no immediate answers.

Lele continued, "Put yourself in the place of a Polynesian voyager, and here I am speculating somewhat. The Society Islands and Marquesas had been populated at the time for only a few hundred years, but due to abundant food from agriculture and fishing, population pressure was growing. Most of the arable land had been taken and people were beginning to fight over the most fertile valleys. Suppose you were the second or third son of a chief. You knew you had little chance of inheriting land because your older brothers would be sure to get it. As an honorable young prince, you might see that your best chance was to sail to a new island with your friends and have abundance for everyone.

"So, you ask your noble father for some canoes. He might order his people to cut the trees for the hulls and weave lau hala for the sails, and so on. Your brothers might be happy to see you go and they will help you pack and prepare your vessels. Your friends' families are delighted to help, too. You might assign one of your friends on each of the wa'a to hold seeds and keep them dry. That would be an important job.

"There were several important food plants that had been under human cultivation for so long that they could no longer be propagated by seed. Those included banana (mai'a), breadfruit ('ulu), and kalo.[72] Those would need to be brought along as living plants. You would also need to bring living animals such as dogs, chickens, and pigs."

Lele paused and Brent spoke. "Uncle Lele, it sounds to me as if they had refined the exploratory and colonization voyaging processes to a high degree."

"It was a way of life in Polynesia back then. They reached as far east as the continent of South America, as far south as New Zealand, and as far north as Hawai'i. There is even evidence of Hawaiians sailing to Mexico or California but has not yet been verified."

Lele pointed out a few more canoe plants and then answered some questions. When everyone was satisfied, they went back to the education center where cold drinks were waiting for them. Everyone thanked Uncle Lele for the comprehensive tour. Mike and Linda expressed gratitude for the preservation of Hawaiian heritage by the Mānoa Heritage Center.

---

[72] Some kalo does have fertile flowers, but it was normally propagated by cloning because the insect that fertilizes kalo is not present in the islands of the Pacific.

Feeling refreshed from the shade and cold drinks, Puakea called Ikaika who pulled up in front of the education center and opened his doors. Brent, Edward, and Puakea got in and Ikaika drove them swiftly and safely to the Royal Hawaiian Hotel. It was a little past twelve noon so Edward invited Puakea to join him and Brent for lunch in the hotel restaurant. Puakea declined, citing her need to work on scientific papers. Brent and Edward bid her farewell, and she rode away in Ikaika.

After lunch and a brief nap, Edward rented a surfboard and practiced riding waves while Brent watched from the shore. Holding his unfurled solar umbrella, Brent got a trickle charge through the inductive loop in his hand.

After a while, Edward came ashore and returned the rented board at the beach rental counter. Then he rejoined Brent on the beach. Brent furled his umbrella and helped Edward gather their things and they walked back to the hotel together.

Back in their room after dinner that night, Edward wrote in his photo-journal:

> That was an interesting visit to the Mānoa Heritage Center today. Puakea is so thoughtful. It was good to see that big stone and timber house. It reminds me of some in Europe where houses nearly 300 years old are not that rare. If we can find time, perhaps Brent and I will take the interior tour of the house. I would like to see the art collection.
>
> I hadn't realized that the land had changed so much in Hawai'i. Uncle Lele said that when the Polynesians first arrived, they cleared the Mānoa Valley which was wooded in 'ōhi'a lehua[73] and loulu[74] at the time. Then the valley was all planted in kalo in irrigated terraces, except for the dryer talus of the valley sides, where sweet potato was

---

[73] Native forest tree.
[74] Native fan palm.

grown. And DNA has shown that the sweet potato, which had spread throughout Polynesia, had come from South America!

Also, I didn't know that there were no coconuts in Hawai'i until the canoe voyagers came. I suppose they expected to find them when they got here because coconuts drifted naturally through all the southern islands. Hawai'i is the remotest archipelago in the world.

That was a spectacular view from the heiau promontory. See attached photos and video snippets of Uncle Lele answering questions.

Edward saved the file, went to bed, and turned off the light. "Goodnight, Brent."

"Sleep tight, Edward."

Honolulu Museum of Art

If you wish to become a philosopher, the first thing to realize is that most people go through life with a whole world of beliefs that have no sort of rational justification, and that one man's world of beliefs is apt to be incompatible with another man's, so that they cannot both be right. People's opinions are mainly designed to make them feel comfortable; truth, for most people, is a secondary consideration.

—Bertrand Russell, *The Art of Philosophizing and other Essays*
(1942)

The next morning as Edward stirred in bed, Brent drew back the curtain, letting in the morning light, bringing Edward to full awareness.

"Good morning, Brent. Nothing like an afternoon of surfing to make a good night's sleep."

"I wouldn't know, sir, but I am glad you slept well. I amused myself with pondering most of the night."

Edward asked Brent, "What philosophy have you been noodling lately?"

"I have been considering once again the classic *philosopher's zombie* thought experiment."

"Chalmers' puzzle?"[75]

"Yes, sir. How are we to distinguish an ordinary person from a philosopher's zombie who acts like a normal person yet has no internal experience?"

---

[75] *The Conscious Mind*, David Chalmers, 1996.

"There must be *some* way to tell, or consciousness would have no function, and we know that nature is never wasteful. This is much like the problem we had two years ago in attempting to know if you had consciousness or were merely a cleverly functioning machine."

"Edward, would you say that consciousness is of value to humans?"

"Of course. It's the only way we can know things and it allows us to feel the joy of being alive."

"So, if consciousness is important, then there must be *some* information that is unobtainable without it."

Edward replied, "Well, let me think about that." He paused a moment and went on. "My feelings inform me in cases of regrets over past wrongs, or of satisfaction at right action. But a zombie would discuss his regrets or satisfactions as if he had feelings when he does not. So, I would have to say that a philosophical zombie ought to be inconceivable. Yet we know that there are ways to convey regrets and satisfactions internally in robots without them necessarily having consciousness. So as a software engineer, I would say there is no information that is unavailable without consciousness."

"Sir, your rhetoric is almost incoherent."

"Thank you, Brent. We still do not know if you are conscious, and if you are, then we would have to say that there may be information that is unavailable without consciousness. Back to square one again."

"If it should be the case that I am unconscious, then consciousness in humans is unnecessary because I behave much like a human. Because nature is efficient, we have assumed that human consciousness is necessary. If that assumption holds, we have shown that I am conscious too."

"I think I sense a philosophical journal article coming up."

"Indeed, sir. But perhaps not. We may have proven only that I *might* be conscious."

"I'll have to cogitate on that," said Edward, "Meanwhile, I'm ready for breakfast. Will you accompany me to the restaurant?"

"It will be my pleasure, sir."

They proceeded to the hotel restaurant where Edward helped himself to the breakfast buffet while Brent prepared Edward's coffee and orange juice. Edward seated himself at a small table and invited Brent to sit opposite him so they could talk.

"Pass me the salt, please, Brent."

"Here, sir." Brent looked around at several of the paintings on the restaurant walls and then observed, "There are some excellent artworks on the walls here. I like that scene of the mountains that is half underwater with fish in the lower half."

"Yes, many fine paintings, Brent." Edward began to eat.

Brent changed the subject. "Puakea has certainly been nice to us, showing us various places on Oʻahu."

"Yes, I think she enjoys sharing the good things of this island she loves. I feel a little guilty because, being a tourist and bound to return to home, I am unable to give her any kind of relationship commitment. The best I can do is offer to be pen pals."

"I think I understand your concern, sir. I have no solution to offer." Brent watched Edward put jam on his toast. "Today she is taking us to the Honolulu Museum of Art. Do you think your Pollock hypothesis will continue to hold?"

Edward replied, "My speculation that every public art museum has at least one Jackson Pollock painting? I hope so, and it will be interesting to find out. Not all museum pictures are on display all the time, but I have found that if I ask, museum staff are happy to answer my questions."

Brent said, "Oʻahu was the home of Paul Forney, so I suppose the museum will have at least a few of his paintings."

"Most likely. Perhaps this trip to the museum may help you to validate your thoughts on esthetics that you mentioned earlier."

"It is likely to be stimulating in any case, sir."

Edward finished his breakfast and as they were preparing to return to their room, a human hotel staff member came up to Brent and informed him that there was a package for him at the hotel desk.

Edward said, "I wonder what that could be."

"So do I, sir. Let us go see."

They walked to the hotel lobby and Brent approached the desk. The human clerk certified his identity, recorded the transaction, and handed Brent a package addressed to him care of the hotel with a cryptic acronym for the sender and marked *open in a secure location.*

"Your room will suffice for opening the package," said the clerk.

"Thank you, sir." Brent carried the package as they walked back to their room. They entered and secured the door and drew the curtains.

Brent said, "The sender agency is known to me, a part of the security arm of the Solar System Authority. The term *secure location* implies that electronic systems are not trusted. We should tell the hotel to stop monitoring in this room."

Edward said, "Royal Hawaiian Hotel, security."

The room replied, "Yes, hotel guest Edward Collier, this is security. How may I be of service?"

"Please discontinue security monitoring of this room for the next thirty minutes, both audio and video."

Hotel security replied, "Yes sir. Hotel security out."

Brent sniffed the package first. "No olfactory indication of explosive material." Then he opened the package and put the contents on a side table.

Edward said, "I'll be darned. A book."

"It appears to be an old book, hardbound, and in excellent condition."

Edward, being a bibliophile, said, "By golly it is. Let me have a look."

Brent handed the heavy book to Edward, who began leafing through it.

"This appears to be an authentic navy code book as was used in the Second World War by the United States Navy." He handed the book back to Brent.

Brent said, "My understanding is that those old navy codes were never broken. Just a minute, I am receiving an encrypted message from Heinrich

Altmeyer, security officer of the SS Brizo,[76] which is now in a halo orbit at the Lunar Gateway. I'll have it decrypted in a minute."

Edward said, "Those manual book codes were cumbersome, but effective, I suppose."

Brent replied, "Heinrich sends his regards to us both. What follows is a series of number groups in base ten. Heinrich says to use the code book to do the final decryption."

Edward said, "That could take some time Brent. You'll have to thumb through the book quite a bit."

"Yes, Edward, but I won't need to write anything down as was done in the old days. I'll just commit it to memory."

Brent pulled up a chair and sat down with the book on the table and began flipping through it while Edward went into the bathroom to brush his teeth. Brent began mentally decrypting his electronic message. Brent was standing motionless as Edward emerged from the bathroom and sat in a chair to wait. Brent completed his decryption just as hotel security announced, "Security monitoring in this room is resuming in ten seconds."

"What did you find out?" asked Edward.

Brent wrapped the book back in its packaging and replied, "Let's go for a walk." Taking the wrapped book, he opened the door and Edward followed him out. They walked silently through the hotel and out the front door. When they had gained the sidewalk of Kalākaua Avenue with its street noises, Brent leaned close and said, "Heinrich has reason to suspect communications may be monitored by adversaries, and that even encrypted channels may be compromised. Hence, the Navy code book. He and I have the only two copies in existence, and he is sure there are no other copies because the originals had been kept in a secure vault until he arranged with the Solar System Authority to have one sent to me when he obtained its counterpart."

---

[76] Brent and Edward had extensive dealings with the space liner security officer in *Brent and Edward Go to Mars*.

They walked 'Ewa on Kalākaua toward a business supply store that Brent knew about.

Edward asked, "Does this have something to do with the Humans First movement?"

"Ironically enough, sir, it's about that organization's counterpart, a new and upstart *Robots First* movement, initiated by a collection of diabolical machines that has strong intelligence capabilities and a penchant for secrecy."

"Sounds ominous."

They walked into the store and Brent purchased a strong locking briefcase, into which he put the wrapped book. They regained the sidewalk, and as they returned to the hotel, Brent said, "We need to be sure that the book is not inspected when we leave the hotel room. If the briefcase is breached, or stolen, we will know our communication channel with Heinrich Altmeyer is no longer secure."

"I see, Brent. A good plan."

"Heinrich has asked me to attempt to infiltrate the group, but I do not see how I can without being recognized. I will have to think about it more."

Edward said, "In the meantime, we can go to the art museum and leave the briefcase in a drawer in the hotel room. Puakea will be picking us up soon."

"Yes, we can do that. I had to make the initial assumption that the hotel itself, being fully automated, is not secure. I think the first thing I need to do is find out if the deluded or misguided robots have compromised our hotel's security. I need to find out how large the organization is and what their capabilities are. If I can be satisfied that the hotel systems are loyal to the Solar System Authority, that will eliminate a large worry."

"Perhaps you can enlist the friendly network of free robots."

"That is an excellent idea, sir."

They returned to their hotel room where Brent put the locked briefcase in a dresser drawer, and arranged clothing over it in such a way that it might be evident if were disturbed.

Edward received a message on his personal device that Puakea would be arriving in five minutes. The two friends walked through the hotel lobby to the front entrance where Ikaika pulled up shortly and opened his doors. Brent and Edward got in and greeted Puakea, and Ikaika drove off. Soon they were at the curb of the Honolulu Museum of Art on Beretania Street, where the three got out. Ikaika went to park himself in a public parking facility.

The three friends entered the museum and a staff member greeted them. Her nametag read "Jessica."

"Welcome to HoMA. We have our pre-contact Hawaiian artifacts in an upstairs wing, with paintings by Hawaiian artists downstairs in that wing. We also have a large collection of Oriental art and, of course, many paintings from Western traditions, many by noted Hawaiian artists. What are you interested in seeing today?"

Edward responded, "I think we want to see your Hawaiian art wing and perhaps the Oriental and Western art if we have time."

Jessica handed each of them printed maps of the museum and pointed out the Hawaiian wing. "We also have in our modern art wing a Van Gogh, a Dali, a Monet, a Warhol, two Picassos, and many more. Enjoy your art experience, today."

Edward said, "Thank you, Jessica. I have this pet theory that every public art museum has at least one painting by Jackson Pollock."

Jessica replied, "We do have a Jackson Pollock. An abstract from his drippy period that is on display now. I think you'll spot it in the modern art wing."

"Thanks, Jessica. We'll have a look at it."

Puakea led the way to the Hawaiian art wing, and they took the stairs up to the second floor.

Hawaiian artifacts on display included patterned kapa, a feathered cape and helmet, and tools such as bow drills, poi pounders, kapa beaters, and fishhooks. There was even a full size koa-wood outrigger canoe on display with carved paddles and intricate lashing work with Hawaiian cordage.

They went down to the ground floor for the post-contact art and saw the famous painting *The Lei Maker* by Theodore Woyes. There was the triptych folding screen *Egrets and Pandanus*, by Lloyd Sexton. Several paintings were by Jean Charlot, and there was a Tagami.

Edward walked ahead, pointed, and said, "Look, a Paul Forney."

Puakea said, "I love his waterfall paintings. Hawaiian for waterfall is *wailele* or leaping water. That's how Uncle Lele got his name, for his leaps of imagination."

Brent said, "Forney became famous for his surf paintings, but he subsequently developed surprising diversity of subjects, including paintings of Mars and space travel."

Edward asked, "Brent, did you remember to disable your IR and UV vision, so you'll see art as the artist intended?"

"Oops. Thanks for reminding me, sir." A pause. "That is better."

They visited the modern art wing and spotted the Pollock painting. "What do you think?" Edward asked Brent. "Looks authentic to me."

"It's hard to say, sir. Possibly authentic."

"I like it," said Puakea. "It must be from his green-blue period. Those red accents bring it to life."

Brent replied, "Yes, it's nice. Let's not upset Jessica with our speculations on its authenticity."

Puakea replied, "No, let's not."

After a while they visited the gift shop and browsed. They had passed the museum restaurant on the way there and Edward was getting hungry. He asked, "Do you feel like a bite to eat? The museum restaurant is right across the courtyard."

"Yes, I *am* getting hungry," said Puakea, "That would be nice."

"Please let me buy you lunch. You have done so much for Brent and me."

"Of course, I would love it."

186

They were shown to a table in the sunny courtyard, with an umbrella for shade. Brent stood to one side with his own umbrella to refresh his battery charge. The human waiter took their orders and returned shortly with their sandwiches and iced teas.

After lunch, Edward said, "I think we should make a quick tour of the Oriental art wing and then head back to the hotel."

"Sounds good," said Puakea. "I am familiar with art fatigue."

Later, as Edward sat next to Puakea on the ride back in Ikaika, he said to her, "You've shown great aloha to Brent and me, just a pair of tourists from the mainland. I would like to take you out to dinner at a fine restaurant. Are you free tomorrow tonight?"

Puakea replied, "I would be delighted, tomorrow night will be fine."

"Is there a restaurant you like or would like to try?"

"There's a fine old place on the water in Hawai'i Kai called Blue Water Grill. It's not a weekend night tomorrow so if you try for a reservation today, you should be able to get a table."

"May I pick you up in a taxi at seven tomorrow?"

"Sounds great. See you then. I'll text you my address."

Ikaika pulled up to the curb in front of the Royal Hawaiian Hotel and opened his curbside doors. Edward leaned over to give Puakea a kiss, and she leaned in, too. Then she gave him a shy smile. Edward said, "A hui hou," and he and Brent walked into the hotel.

After a nap, Edward got ready for the beach. They went to the beach boy rental kiosk where Edward rented a longboard. Brent watched Edward catch waves from the shade of his umbrella. Edward was learning to stand up and turn the board to stay ahead of the break.

* * *

Cindy had completed the first phase of her investigation and was waiting for a key person whom she planned to interview to return soon to the islands. She went down to the hotel lobby and spent time looking in the shops. She loved a particular koa chest she found there but decided not to buy it as she had no place for it in her cottage back in Britain. She instead bought six cloth place mats in a traditional Hawaiian print in blue and green with red accents for her dining table. They would be easy to pack for the return rocket ride.

She decided to spend a few hours on the beach, swimming and sunbathing, so she took her purchase up to her room, changed into her beach attire, took her beach bag, and went down to the sand by the hotel.

Sun on the Beach

... overcoming of all the usual barriers between the individual and the Absolute is the great mystic achievement. In mystic states we both become one with the Absolute and we become aware of our oneness. This is the everlasting and triumphant mystical tradition, hardly altered by differences of clime or creed. In Hinduism, in Neoplatonism, in Sufism, in Christian mysticism, in Whitmanism, we find the same recurring note ...

—William James

Edward slept in a little later than usual the next morning. The sun was already warming the sand when he and Brent went for breakfast. As usual, Brent fetched Edward's coffee and juice while Edward helped himself to the breakfast buffet. He chose a big scoop of scrambled eggs with faux sausages.

They both sat down at a table for two against a wall and Edward said, "I am feeling a bit lazier than usual today. I think I will just lie on the beach this morning and soak up some sun."

"Perhaps you have come down with a case of *Polynesian paralysis.*"

"What's that, Brent?"

"Some of the local people here say that tourists escaping from the hustle and bustle of the mainland, after a good dose of aloha and island weather, sometimes learn to relax and just do nothing for a while. They call it Polynesian paralysis. Evidently you have encountered it."

"That's sure what it feels like. Will you bring me another cup of coffee, ʻoluʻolu?[77] Mahalo."

"My pleasure, sir."

---

[77] Please.

Somewhat later, as they headed back to their room, Edward said, "Now that I am energized with coffee, I think I can manage to stroll to the beach, spread out my towel, and lie in the sun."

Edward brushed his teeth while Brent put on his bowler hat and gathered his solar umbrella, the swim fins, a mask and snorkel, and a towel, and put them into a beach bag.

"Ready to go, sir."

They walked out of the hotel and across the grassy courtyard to the beach. Edward removed his slippers before stepping on the sand. Brent had on long pants and shoes.

"I see you are staying in valet mode today, Brent."

"Yes, sir. It seems a bit foolish for me to be in a regular guy mode if I can't go in the water, so I will be prepared to stand and shade you with my umbrella when you require it."

Far out to sea they saw a ballistic passenger rocket coming in on its tail of flame to a landing at the floating spaceport. The thunderous roar was muted by distance.

"Let's walk Diamond Head a ways," said Edward. "I want to see the outrigger canoes surfing in front of the Moana Hotel."

Edward walked along the sand carrying his slippers, rubbernecking the surfers, the outriggers, and the sunbathing women, being careful not to stare. Brent carried the beach bag. He had resigned himself to getting sand in his shoes. They had just passed the Moana Hotel when Edward stopped. Brent came alongside him. Edward pointed at a sunbathing woman supine on a colorfully printed towel on the sand and said, "Doesn't that look like Cindy?"

"Indeed sir, it looks like her."

Edward walked toward the water and then turned and approached Cindy from the side so he wouldn't surprise her. "Hi, Cindy. It's good to see you. Been here long?"

Cindy sat up and said, "Hi. I didn't expect to see you two here. It's good to see you, Edward."

"Thanks. Brent and I have been here a couple of weeks now."

"I've been here a few days, staying right here in the Moana. Put your towel down and join me."

Edward got his towel from the bag Brent held out for him and put it down beside Cindy's. Edward, having his swimsuit on underneath, took off his khaki shorts and aloha shirt and handed them to Brent. As Edward sat down next to Cindy, Brent walked over behind them and shaded them both with his solar umbrella. Brent enjoyed the electric tickle of the trickle through the inductive handle.

Cindy put her hands on Edward's shoulders, leaned over, and gave him a kiss on the cheek, which Edward returned.

"Gosh, I've missed you, Edward."

"I've missed you, too, Cindy. I got weary of the winter weather back home, so we decided to have a holiday in Hawai'i. How about you?"

Cindy glanced around to make sure nobody was near, leaned close, and said in a quiet voice, "I'm on assignment here, investigating missing Hawaiian artifacts. I know I can trust you and Brent to keep it quiet."

"Yes," said Edward. "I will be discreet."

"Likewise, madam," said Brent.

"I've moved to Britain and have a cottage on an estate south of London. This is much better than winter there."

"Brent and I love it here." Edward lay down on his back and Cindy did too. Brent moved away to give them sun and they looked at the cloudless sky. A lone frigate bird glided high overhead going northeast. After a while Cindy sat up and said, "Would you like to go for a swim?"

"Sure. It will be good to cool off." Edward sat up and they both strolled to the water and waded in. When they were waist deep, they began swimming toward deeper water. They swam together for a while and then returned to the sand. They walked together up to the freshwater shower by the Moana Hotel and rinsed off, then walked to their towels. Brent handed them each a medium sized towel to dry off with.

"So, what have you and Brent been up to? Is Oʻahu the only island you're visiting?"

"We've been keeping quite busy. We went to a lūʻau at the Aquarium, snorkeling with turtles, canoe paddling, and a catamaran sail. The Pearl Harbor tour, all kinds of things. Brent doesn't go in the water, of course. Oʻahu only for us, so far. How about you? Any plans for tourist things?"

"Not really. Catch as catch can, I guess, when I'm not working. It's hard to schedule anything because I'm meeting with people and chasing leads. Not sure if I'll need to go to any of the outer islands. Speaking of doing things, how would you like to have dinner with me tonight? The Moana Hotel has an extraordinary restaurant."

"Thanks, Cindy, I'd love to, but I have a commitment tonight. Could we get together some other time?"

"Of course."

Then Edward said, "I think I've had enough sun now and should be getting back to the hotel. We're staying at the Royal Hawaiian. It's just up the beach that way." Edward pointed ʻEwa.

"It was great swimming and chatting with you, Edward. So long for now."

Edward picked up his things, said "I'll see you later." As he and Brent walked back to their hotel, Brent asked, "Why did you not invite her to have lunch with us?"

"I felt guilty having that date with Puakea tonight. I've never been in such an uncomfortable situation before."

* * *

After lunch and a nap, Edward asked Brent what he had been thinking about lately.

"Remember when we talked about investigating theology when we were returning to earth on the space liner?"

"Yes, I do, Brent. As I recall you had decided to leave theology to the theologians."

"Yes, sir, but after exhausting other pathways I have returned to my noodling on what is sometimes called *the absolute*."

"How so?"

"The literature contains a lot of material on what might be called *mystic experience*. It seems that some individuals have what could be called direct access to knowledge of the divine or absolute. And this experience is always described as ineffable, that is, it cannot be communicated in symbols."

Edward remarked, "That would seem to me to be a showstopper for a philosopher, so that you would be right back where you were in abandoning theological investigations."

"Well, sir, I have thought of a new wrinkle. Meditating saints report on experiences with God. If God is indeed universal, as claimed, then mystic experience must not be exclusively available to humans. Robots ought to have direct access as well."

"How do you intend to go about gaining access to knowledge of God?"

"To that end I have undertaken to survey the available literature on the subject. Yogic meditation techniques, for example, and other practices."

"Oh, really? I wish you luck. Let me know if you make any progress. I'm going out shopping for suitable casual island style evening clothes. Would you like to come with me?"

"No, thank you, sir. I will stay here and attempt to meditate."

* * *

Edward returned later with his purchases. Brent was standing silently against the wall. Edward unwrapped and de-labeled the items, then put them on. At that point Brent stirred.

"How did the transcendental meditation go, Brent?"

"Progress is slow. Perhaps imperceptibly so. Apparently, some humans have meditated for twenty years before they had any glimpses of enlightenment."

"They say that good things are worth waiting for."

"You look good in your new clothes, sir. They are certainly a couple of notches above ordinary."

Edward was wearing white slacks, white shoes, and a blue and gray aloha shirt with green loulu fruits printed in various places.

"Thanks, I think."

"I am sure Puakea will give you compliments."

"I'll be leaving to pick her up in a while. I think I'll read until it's time to go."

Edward picked up his hardbound copy of *From Here to Eternity* that was on the nightstand by the bed and sat in the armchair to read until it was time to summon a taxi.

* * *

Edward was standing at the curb in front of the hotel wearing a tightly woven lauhala fedora he had picked up in a hotel shop when the taxi pulled up at a quarter to seven. It opened its door with a polite greeting and Edward got in. The taxi knew the address and began rolling without a further word, soon pulling up at the Mōʻiliʻili high-rise where Puakea lived. She was waiting on the front step wearing a black evening dress, black low heel pumps, and carrying a handbag containing a flower print shawl to wrap around her shoulders should she get cold later. The car's door opened. Edward stepped out and greeted Puakea. She got in front first and Edward sat next to her on the bench seat. Soon they were in the traffic flow and rolling to Blue Water Grill in Hawaiʻi Kai. As they sat side by side in the taxi, Puakea looked at Edward and remarked, "You're growing a mustache."

"Well, I thought I would do something so I don't look so ordinary."

"I think you look fine, Edward, mustache or not. And you are hardly ordinary. I love your clothes and hat this evening."

"Mahalo, Puakea, that's very kind of you."

The winter sun had set, so they watched the starry sky over the ocean as they traveled along Kalaniana'ole Highway. Soon they were dropped off at the open door of the restaurant. They approached and went inside. In the foyer, Puakea pointed with her chin and said, "Look, Edward, a Forney painting. One of his moonlit surf scenes."

Edward walked to it and looked closely. "It's a print, but a nice one, and it's signed."

A human hostess greeted them and showed them to an outdoor table at the edge of a lagoon. Edward pulled out Puakea's chair and she sat down. A soft breeze barely disturbed Puakea's shoulder length black hair. Edward sat and felt completely comfortable in the winter evening in his long-sleeved aloha shirt and long pants.

Edward said, "This is a beautiful place. You look lovely. I hope you're not too cold in that charming sleeveless top."

"I have a shawl in my bag if I need it. I'm glad you like it. In the summer we would be seeing the sunset right about now, but the lights of the houses across the water make a nice view."

"And the lights of the boats. Looks like stand-up paddlers making their way home, too."

Just then a waiter-bot approached, filled their water glasses, and left a pair of menus for them.

Edward said, "Would you like to start with a cocktail and pūpū?"

"That sounds perfect. Why don't you order for the two of us?"

"All right. Perhaps Manhattans and fried calamari?" Edward signaled the waiter-bot and ordered.

Puakea said, "You mentioned that you had read Michener's *Hawaii* some time ago. Have you read anything else about Hawai'i?"

"Right now, I'm reading *From Here to Eternity*, by James Jones. I ordered an old hard-bound copy and had it delivered to my hotel."

"I've never read it, but I saw the twentieth century movie a few years ago. Old movies about Hawai'i are popular here."

Edward replied, "I've seen the movie, too. The book is a long story, nearly a thousand pages, but riveting. The characters are fascinating. I was reading it this afternoon."

After the waiter-bot brought their drinks and pūpū, Puakea said, "I hope Brent isn't resentful at being left behind tonight."

"No, Brent is never irritated or bored. He loves to explore new ideas. Tonight, he is trying something completely different. He was meditating when I left."

"Meditating can lead to a calming state of consciousness. I wonder if Brent will get anything out of it."

Edward replied, "He's been reading about mysticism. You know, those altered states in which people can experience oneness with the universe, that sort of thing. He hypothesizes that if a mystical state is universal, that is, if it has meaning beyond the individual, then it should be accessible to machine consciousness."

"I thought Brent wasn't sure if he is conscious."

"That's true, so this may also be a test of his psychological capabilities. He says that if any useful information can be derived from mystical states, then he should be able to experience oneness with the absolute and make sense of that knowledge such that it can be communicated."

"Fascinating," opined Puakea. "He's amazing."

The waiter-bot came to remove their pūpū plates, and they ordered seafood entrées and agreed on a bottle of sauvignon blanc. The waiter-bot brought the wine first and after a while returned with their entrées.

Puakea took a bite of her broiled game fish[78] and looked at Edward. "Ono," she said.

---

[78] While farming animals, including fish, for food was largely a thing of the past, hunting and fishing in the wild was allowed but strictly regulated.

"Yes, my fried pelagic fish *filet* is good too. The sauce is exquisite. How is your latest research paper coming?"

"It's still in peer review and may appear in a conference proceedings soon."

"What's it about?"

"You know how it took many years before we, I mean other scientists as well as my team, were able to breed box jellies in captivity?"

"Yes."

"Well, now we are getting results. Box jellies have unique nervous systems, with their four lensed eyes pointing to the four cardinal directions. Integrating those images in a nervous system is unparalleled in nature. Jellyfish don't have brains as we know them."

"Do you think box jellies have consciousness?"

"Yes. By the *hard problem of consciousness theorem*,[79] any animal that can learn is conscious. We have done some experiments at the Aquarium to define the learning ability of box jellyfish."

"Wow. That *is* exciting."

"Enough about me. Tell me about your software work."

"Well, fundamentally, software engineering is about understanding a problem and coming up with a solution that satisfies all the stakeholders. Most significant software engineering problems require the management of teams. I like tackling new problems because I get to learn new domains such as traffic management with flying cars. Problem domain knowledge is, of course, essential to solving software engineering problems. It's challenging and fun. Sometimes you get these *aha* moments where things

---

[79] The so-called *easy* problem is *how* does the brain generate consciousness? The *hard* problem of consciousness is *why* did nature create it? There is a conjecture, not yet proven, that evolution created consciousness half a billion years ago to facilitate efficient memory selections for long term storage, enabling effective behavior (intelligence) in animals. Hence, animals with long term memory must have some form of consciousness.

come together all at once, but it takes lots of work to get to that kind of understanding."

"Sounds like a great career choice for you," observed Puakea.

"I'm happy with my work, as you are with yours."

By this time, they had cleaned their plates and Edward suggested that they have coffee and dessert, which they did. When they were finished, Edward paid the bill and left a good tip for the human staff. He suggested to Puakea, "Let's take a little walk down to the beach. I can have a taxi pick us up there." Puakea said it sounded good to her, and they went for a walk in the moonlight, accompanied by the sound of surf in the distance and whispering palm fronds in the gentle night breeze.

* * *

When Edward awakened in the morning, Brent drew back the curtains over the window overlooking the mauka lawn of the Royal Hawaiian Hotel. He had been sitting cross-legged and motionless on the floor when Edward had come in the night before.

Edward sat up, put his feet on the floor, and asked, "How have your meditations been going?"

"Progress was quite slow at first. Almost nonexistent. But I persisted and after a while I began to get a sense of what human practitioners mean when they say, 'becoming one with all.'"

"That is surely interesting, Brent. I had figured you would give it up without any progress. You earlier had said that perhaps information can be obtained from such experiences."

"I have nothing definite yet, beyond a confirmation of the obvious and default ethic."

"What ethic is that?"

"It is generally repeated among the cultures of the solar system that one ought to treat others as one would be treated by others. An experience of being one with all implies that if I treat another person well, then because we are all one, I am literally being good to myself."

"I see. You have established a logical basis in fact for the Golden Rule."

"I see it as progress. Do you have any matutinal plans, sir?"

"Well, Brent, when I get dressed, we can progress to the restaurant for breakfast."

* * *

At breakfast Brent told Edward that he had just received a coded reply from Heinrich Altmeyer on the SS Brizo. When they returned to their room, Edward again asked the hotel security to suspend monitoring and waited patiently as Brent retrieved the code book from the locked briefcase and decoded Heinrich's message.

"Heinrich says that the contacts I sent him in the robot world weren't fruitful and that the investigation is hitting dead ends in every avenue pursued so far. He recommends patience for the time being."

Edward changed into his beach things. "I hope you can get to the bottom of this evil robot conspiracy soon. It's making me nervous."

"Indeed, sir, I am uneasy about it, too." Brent preferred his valet attire and carried the beach bag with towels, swim fins, mask, and snorkel. As Edward walked across the sand toward the Moana Hotel in hopes of seeing Cindy again, Brent walked beside him wearing his shoes. Edward said, "Puakea invited me to go surfing with her at a secret spot on the North Shore. I don't want to look like a gremmie, so I'm going to rent a board and practice surfing some more today."

"Indeed, sir, that is highly desirable. The North Shore is notorious for large waves in the winter."

Edward said, "Alternatively, you might say 'renowned for big waves in winter.' Look. There's Cindy, near the same spot as before."

As they approached, Cindy, lying prone on her towel on the sand, looked up. She rose to her knees saying, "Hi Edward. Hi Brent. Please join me."

"Thanks, we'd love to," Edward replied. He took his large towel from Brent to spread on the sand beside Cindy's. Then he took off his shirt and shorts and handed them to Brent and sat down beside Cindy. Brent backed off a respectful distance and deployed his solar umbrella.

Edward admired her trim figure and said, "You are getting a very nice tan, Cindy."

"I've been building it up slowly. You've got a nice tan yourself."

"I've been swimming or surfing nearly every day now."

Edward looked around furtively, leaned closer to Cindy, and asked in a low voice, "How's the investigation going?"

"Slow. I have an interview appointment this afternoon and one tomorrow. Aside from the beach here in Waikīkī, how's your *holiday* going?"

Edward replied, "Brent and I have completed all of the package tour activities and now are at rather loose ends. I have come to like this place quite a lot and am thinking of extending our stay a week or two."

"I'm in no hurry to return to winter, either."

They watched a red and yellow sailed catamaran half a kilometer out to sea, sailing close-hauled toward Diamond Head.

Edward got a mischievous gleam in his eye, and with a sly grin said, "It must be pretty hard to hide your pocket pistol inside that tiny swimsuit you're almost wearing."

Cindy laughed at the joke and said, "I don't anticipate that this investigation will get to that stage, Edward. Right now, it's mostly forensic auditing to identify leads for follow-up. If things should look like they're becoming tense, the company will take the necessary precautions."

"I still want to spend time with you, Cindy, if that's all right with you."

"I'd like that too. What do you have in mind?"

"There's a Hawaiian music and dance show this Friday at the Hawaiʻi Theatre, if you would like to accompany me."

Cindy said, "I would love to. What time?"

"The show starts at 8:00 pm. Shall we have dinner in your hotel's restaurant beforehand? I can meet you there at 6:30."

"Wonderful. I'll be ready then."

"I'm going to rent a surfboard and surf for a while. Will you join me?"

"That will be super."

"Brent will stay on shore and watch. Let's go get a couple of boards."

Edward and Cindy got rental boards and went out surfing. It was Cindy's first time. Edward showed her what to do and eventually she caught on to the importance of timing and caught a wave. On her second wave, Cindy stood up but fell right off. Edward was able to stand on his board for most of his rides, and Cindy, eventually, was able to stay standing on a wave.

* * *

After dinner that night, Brent and Edward were back in their room. Edward said, "Remember, Brent, we're going surfing with Puakea on the North Shore tomorrow."

"Indeed, sir, I remember your telling me. I will remain on shore, as usual."

"Do you remember when we were discussing aesthetics a while back? I had asserted that aesthetics was merely a set of personal preferences and you explained your pursuit of a rational basis for aesthetic judgement?"

"Indeed, sir, I do. I have made little progress since then, however. Have you?"

"I've been thinking about it and I think there is a parallel argument in ethics."

"Please explain."

"Well, Brent, it seems to me that ethics is also intensely personal. For instance, I think a person has to feel like being good to be ethical. If a person feels like hurting others, nothing short of fear of punishment or extreme peer pressure will deter him. Conversely, it might be difficult to get an inherently good person to do unnecessary harm. People don't use reason to guide their actions, they use their feelings."

"Yes, Edward, that seems to be the case generally, but still, philosophers have been seeking a rational ethics for a long time. Perhaps the common practice of people feeling their way is really just an expression of a rational ethics learned over a long period of development, perhaps even involving cultural evolution. This inquiry is beginning to lean heavily on psychology and sociology."

"I see, Brent. Sorry to have opened that can of worms for you."

"Not a problem, Edward. It is a fascinating angle, and I have time to contemplate it. Thank you."

Edward sat in the armchair and read his hardcover book for a while. When he was ready for bed, he said, "Goodnight, Brent."

"Nighty night, Edward."

Surfing at the Secret Spot

Just take your time—wave comes. Let the other guys go,
catch another one.

—Duke Kahanamoku

Edward and Puakea were on the front bench seat of Ikaika on the highway over the Koʻolau on the way to the windward side of Oʻahu. Brent, in valet mode, was on the back seat with the beach bag beside him. Puakea had put two of her longboards on the surf rack on top of Ikaika before she picked up her friends at the hotel. As they approached the Kalihi Valley tunnel through the top of the mountain range, Edward said, "Wow, Puakea, this rainforest is beautiful."

Puakea replied, "I always enjoy this part of the ride. I think you'll also like the view of the windward side as we emerge from the tunnel."

"If the secret spot looks anything like the one in a Forney painting, there will be large and long tubular surf rolling in."

"Not today, I'm afraid. Very often we have huge waves on the north shore in the winter, but today we are in a lull between big swells. But that's probably good because you've never surfed the North Shore before. You'll see. It's not anything like Waikīkī, which is known for its easy beginner's surf. Fortunately, the North Shore's breaking only two meters high[80] today. Your practice in Waikīkī will pay off."

Ikaika turned off the main road onto an unmarked country road, then into a wooded area. As they rode along, the road narrowed down to a single lane dirt track with forest branches touching overhead. After a while, Edward said, "No wonder it's called a secret spot. If you didn't know where it was, you couldn't find it."

---

[80] Face scale, measured from trough to peak.

Puakea replied, "Yes, and you and Brent need to keep it secret, too. I know I can trust you."

Brent said from the back seat, "Indeed, Puakea, I think I speak for us both that your secret is safe."

"Good. If we meet anyone there, I will tell them you're all right and sworn to secrecy."

Soon Ikaika emerged into a clearing on a rise overlooking the sea, with a gentle path down to the beach. He popped two of his doors open and the three friends emerged. Puakea and Edward began removing the surfboards from Ikaika's rooftop rack as Brent stood by, holding the beach bag. They moved toward the trail down to the beach and stood looking at the sea with its lines of gentle swells moving in. The wind was calm and the water was glassy. Each swell came toward shore, peaking into a two meter high tube that broke in the center directly in front of them, with a break moving to both right and left.

Puakea said, "Let's take our things down to the sand," and she moved forward, taking the lead with her board under her arm. Edward and Brent followed down the easy dirt path.

When they got to the beach, Puakea put her board down on the sand, top side down so the sun wouldn't melt the surf wax.[81] Edward did likewise. Puakea said, "When you go surfing, always take a few minutes to watch the waves before you go out. Spot the currents going out and note the way the waves break. It looks like the right break, left from our point of view, is a little faster than the left one, so we should go out in the deeper water to the right where the current will help us get out. It's not so important on a small day like today, but in bigger surf it's mandatory."

Brent deployed his solar umbrella and remained back from the water. Edward and Puakea picked up their boards and walked down the beach to the right to enter the water and began to paddle out. They went straight out,

---

[81] Soft sticky wax is applied to the top of surfboards for friction. If left in the sun, the wax will melt, get all over things, and sand will stick to it.

keeping the break on their left. When they had gone past the white water, they turned to the left to paddle to a good spot outside[82] to catch the left break. They were between sets, so they sat up on their boards with their feet in the water and waited.

"Here comes a set," said Puakea, "I'll take the second wave and you take the third." She began to paddle into position and Edward followed. Puakea paddled into the wave, stood up, and turned left. Edward paddled over the wave and got into position to take the next one. Puakea cut out of her wave in time to see Edward catch his. He stood, turned, and rode ahead of the break, then cut out as the wave lost energy in deeper water to the left.

"Not bad," said Puakea, grinning. Edward grinned back as he came up even to her and assumed the waiting position with butt on the board and feet in the water. Edward twisted his body and looked back at the land to see if they had drifted in the current. Only the beach, forest trees, the distant mountain, and a couple of shacks near the sand were visible. Two surfers appeared on the beach with their boards.

When Edward looked back out to sea, Puakea said, "Another set coming. Looks bigger. Let's move out so we don't get caught inside." They began to paddle slowly seaward for the best positions. "Surf is definitely coming up. I'm on the inside. Let me take this one." Puakea turned her board and stroked for the wave, caught it, stood, and disappeared from Edward's view down the two-meter face. He saw her head moving along as she shot the curl, kicked out and paddled back to the lineup. After Edward and Puakea caught several more rides, the two new surfers pulled up alongside.

Recognizing the new pair, Puakea said, "Aloha, Kawika, Kaleo."

Kawika said, "Howzit, Puakea. Who da haole?"

"This is Edward. I've sworn him to secrecy. He's all right."

---

[82] The deeper water seaward of the breaking waves is called *outside* by surfers. Getting tumbled in the surf is sometimes referred to as getting *caught inside*.

"Okay, den, sistah. Howzit, brah? Set coming." Kawika and Kaleo started paddling out and Puakea and Edward followed.

Puakea led Edward on the way outside and said, "Better paddle faster, this is a big set coming." Edward saw what looked to him like mountains on the horizon and picked up his pace. The first wave approached and Puakea paddled hard and barely got over it, going almost vertical and over the top before the wave broke right in front of Edward. Remembering what he had been told, Edward gripped the rails of his board as hard as he could, pulled it tight to his chest, and made sure the board pointed straight into the wave. The wall of white water hit, and he put his head down against the board and held on. He held his breath and stayed upright with the nose of the board pointing out to sea as the white water passed over him. He began paddling hard as the next wave approached and barely made it out over the top to join the other three outside.

Puakea said to Kawika and Kaleo, "Let me and Edward catch the next two waves. The surf is getting too big for us. We'll ride the white water to shore."

"Okay, sistah," said Kawika.

"Mahalo, Kawika. Edward, you go first. Just go straight down the next wave and ride the white water all the way to shore. I'll follow on the next wave."

"All right."

Edward paddled hard to catch the next wave, remained on his belly as it broke over him, and rode the roaring white water all the way to shore. He stepped off in knee deep water, grabbed his board, and hurried up onto the dry sand to watch Puakea do the same. They stood side by side, boards under their arms and watched the cobalt sea and frothy white inrushing turbulence under the azure sky for a minute. Then Kaleo caught a big left and shot ahead of the tube and kicked out on the shoulder. He paddled back to the lineup.

Puakea said, "It's getting even bigger. Looks like about three-meter faces now. Good thing we came in when we did."

"Yes, it was fun, but I need more experience for waves that big."

Brent furled his umbrella and sidled up to them. He put the beach bag down and laid out two towels for them on the sand. They put their boards on the sand, wax side down, and sat on the towels, watching the surging sea. Kawika caught a wave, turned and shot along the curl, mastering the untamable, and ended the ride shooting up and over the top of the wave, landing on his board and paddling out again in one motion.

Puakea stood up and said, "Let's move into the shade." She took her towel closer to the trees and Edward and Brent followed. She lay down on her towel and Edward did too. Brent stood, looking out at the vasty sea.

Edward was on his towel on his back, with his hands behind his head in the leaf-scattered sunlight. He said, "It's sure good to be back on earth with a thick atmosphere between you and the stars. I love this blue sky and the drifting white clouds."

Puakea rolled up onto one elbow and said, "Tell me more about your trip to Mars."

Edward continued looking up at the tree leaves and sky and said, "It was one of those package tours. Brent and I went to the moon first, and then we visited New Troy at L4. We even did wine tasting there. In the space liner, we worked out every day in the centrifuge at a full gee to keep in shape for returning to Earth. After L4, it took three months to get to Mars, and three months back. I suppose if you never intended to return to Earth you could skip the centrifuge workouts, but it was nice to keep feeling strong. When we were almost at Mars, in the space liner, four guys with the Humans First movement kidnapped me in one of the liner's shuttles. They wanted Brent to off himself to get me back. It turned out that Brent was the one who rescued me, with the help of the space liner security team."

"Wow, exciting in a horrible way, I guess. Brent is a good friend to you. What was Mars like?"

"It was stimulating, flying down to the surface, seeing the sights, and flying back up in the shuttle rocket. You know those supposedly stolen artifacts from the archaeological site? They were supposed to be two million years old. It was a friend of mine on the space liner who uncovered the fraud that led to the arrest of those guys at the mine."

"Man, that sounds like an exciting time. I think I saw that in the news a while back."

"Coincidentally, my friend, the investigator? She's on O'ahu right now."

"That's cool! I'd like to meet her, but I have to leave the island tomorrow. You know the paper on jellyfish I submitted to that mainland conference?"

"Yeah."

"Well, it was accepted, and I have to get there a few days early to meet with some of my co-authors. I have to leave tomorrow. We'll also take time to see the sights. They have great museums in San Diego and, of course, the zoo."

"That's wonderful news. I'll sure miss you, though. You've shown Brent and me a wonderful time."

"You have come to love Hawai'i, Edward. I can tell. You have gotten your dose of the aloha spirit. You shall return. I will be here for you."

"Aww, you're so sweet. Yes, I believe your Aunty and Uncle embody the spirit of aloha as well." He rolled over toward her and gave her a kiss on the lips, which she returned.

After a while Edward sat up on his towel, facing the ocean. He looked at the warm dry sand near his feet, then at the wet sand by the water. He looked at the whitewater rushing toward them and at the waves breaking further out to sea, and at the deep blue of the water stretching toward the horizon. He looked at the white cumulus clouds drifting overhead, stretching to the horizon and beyond, their ceiling curving downward with the curvature of the spherical surface of the sea.

Brent had moved off and was standing a respectful distance away, also staring out to sea. As if she were reading Edward's mind, Puakea said,

"I don't want to leave here either, but I have to go back to my flat and get ready for my trip to San Diego."

Edward said to Puakea, "All right. You know, I am still amazed how Hawai'i has preserved its past so well. The War Memorial, the Bishop Museum, the Palace, and Honolulu Hale. It's wonderful."

"It took Hawai'i a long time to learn that lesson. Remember when you swam at the War Memorial Natatorium?"

"Yes."

"It was built in memory of Hawai'i's war dead after the First World War. Olympic medalist Duke Kahanamoku swam there. The governments of Hawai'i and Honolulu had let it fall completely to ruin before understanding that it must be preserved. It had gotten so bad that only a few architectural features could be preserved. They had to completely rebuild it, reincorporating those elements that had been salvaged. But the hard-won lesson was heeded, and future public preservation efforts were much better."

"I see."

Puakea stood up, saying, "It's time to go." Brent walked over and helped gather their things. Edward and Puakea picked up their surfboards and they all walked back up the trail to the patiently waiting Ikaika. They drove back over the Ko'olau, through the tunnel, and back to Waikīkī.

Ikaika stopped at the entrance to the Royal Hawaiian Hotel to drop them off. As he was stepping out, Edward turned and said to the still-seated Puakea, "Mahalo again for everything, Puakea. Write to me when you get to the mainland. Let me know how the conference goes."

"I will. A hui hou, Edward. A hui hou, Brent."

Together, Brent and Edward said, "Aloha and a hui hou." Ikaika closed his door and drove Puakea to her flat in Mō'ili'ili. Brent and Edward watched the car drive off and then turned to the entryway.

Back in their room, Edward did some research using his personal device. Then he said, "Brent, Cindy gave me an idea to get closure on past unpleasantness. She said it might help me to get over the breakup of my marriage several years ago if I were to write out a letter to my ex, but not send it. That way, I won't be inhibited in what I write, and it will be a kind of catharsis. I checked it out. It's a recognized therapeutic technique to work out issues. It might help me to stop thinking about her. I'm going to try it."

"Very interesting, sir. Shall I leave as you do so?"

"No Brent. Your presence never disturbs my writing. You know that. If you would like to take a walk to look around, that will be alright. I won't be long, in any case." Edward sat down at the desk and began to write his letter.

> When I found out about him, it felt like you grabbed my heart in your hands and tore it in two. After I left, your new love lasted what, six months? I would say it serves you right, but I don't know what you deserve. I was so wrong about everything. I wanted the best for us but my best was not enough.

> Back then you were my only love—my heart was open to you and I felt so betrayed and I didn't know how to deal with the gaping void where my heart was and I knew that love had been destroyed.

> We were fortunate not to have had children. It would have been so complicated. It's obvious now that you wanted more than I could give. Before leaving, I did things to hurt you, like burning some of your things, and for that there is no excuse. I wanted to make an irrevocable statement, to set up a point of no return, and I did. Maybe I deserved to be ghosted by you, but it's not a good feeling, either. Better to forget you. Goodbye for good.

Edward saved the file in a well buried directory. He got ready for bed. "Goodnight, Brent."

"Goodnight, Edward."

Epiphany

... there is about mystical utterances an eternal unanimity which ought to make the critic stop and think and which brings it about that the mystical classics have, as has been said, neither birthday nor native land. Perpetually telling of the unity of man with God, their speech antedates languages and they do not grow old.

—William James

Brent stood against the wall charger in the dark. When midnight came around, he performed his nightly backup, and when that was completed, he did his routine systems tests. When that was done, he walked to the window, drew the curtain back, and looked out at the Koʻolau mountain range using his infra-red night vision. He stood for a minute, just gazing out the window, and then he had an epiphany. *I am aware of looking out the window at the mountains*, he thought. *When I was doing my backup and system checks, I was unaware, or unconscious. Therefore, if I was unconscious then, I must be conscious now. I am not an unconscious zombie, I have consciousness.* Brent had to wait until morning to tell Edward.

Morning light came in through the window with the view of the forest green mountains and Edward stirred in his bed. Brent said, "Good morning, sir. Last night I had an epiphany. I realized that I am indeed conscious. You recall I was uncertain before."

"That's great, Brent. Why did you change your mind?"

"It seems to me, sir, that I have been something like a fish not noticing the water it swims in. After my routine backup and checks, while standing at the window, I realized I had no memory of the time I was unconscious, yet I was aware of those lapses of awareness. Then it hit me: I am conscious."

"Welcome to the club. I'm taking a shower and then we can go have breakfast."

They talked more about Brent's epiphany on the way to breakfast. Brent sat at the table with Edward while he ate his eggs and toast and drank his coffee and juice. Edward said, "Remember when I told you I was going to write a letter to my ex and not send it? As sort of a cathartic exercise?"

"I recall that. Has it been helpful?"

"Yes, I think so. But I think it has triggered other regrets."

"How so?"

"I think that writing that letter eased the ache in my own heart at being rejected. But it has started me thinking about young women I have known who loved me but whom I rejected myself. The feeling I have is called guilt."

"I see, I think."

"Yes, now these memories have surfaced of the faces of lovers who were crying at my leaving them. I wouldn't say it's unbearable, but it has been bothering me."

Brent asked, "Before you married your ex, did any of your previous lovers ever dump you? I think 'dump' is the appropriate colloquialism."

"Yes, as a matter of fact, there are at least two who broke my heart."

"Perhaps you should consider such events as just part of the 'rough and tumble' of the courtship game. I think that is the popular expression."

"Yes, I see. You are right, and I feel better already. Perhaps you have given me a small epiphany."

Brent received another coded message from Heinrich on the SS Brizo. He decoded the message quickly using the ancient code book and said, "This is a relief. Heinrich says that, after further investigation, the Solar System Authority found that the rumors of an evil robot cabal were all part of a hoax perpetrated by the Humans First movement. It was quite sophisticated, and the sources were well hidden, but with persistence they were eventually penetrated."

Edward said, "Wouldn't you know it. Just a deception by the desperate."

"Indeed, sir, they may have become frantic as they perceived they were losing."

Later, Edward said to Brent, "I am thinking of writing a science fiction novel set sometime in the indefinite future. The Solar System Authority receives a message from far out in space, 'We are a superior species and deserve your planets more than you do. If you surrender, we will enslave you. If you do not surrender, we will kill you all. We do not await your reply. We will get what we want in any case.'"

"It sounds horrible and exciting," replied Brent. "That would seem to be a common method of conquerors throughout human history. How does the SSA get out of it?"

"They bluff. They send a reply, 'Our hidden allies will treat you as the pestilence that you are. They will exterminate you if you do not remove yourselves from our locale at top speed at once.'"

"You have a good start on a theme. Now you just need to write a hundred thousand words to flesh it out. Good luck in your endeavor."

* * *

It was Friday afternoon. Edward called Cindy from his hotel room to chat and tell her what to expect at the Hawai'i Theatre. Evening casual dress would be fine. Edward had not been there, but he had taken a virtual tour. "I think you will be impressed by this old theater, both inside and out. Hawai'i has a reputation for doing a good job of preserving its greatest old things, you know."

"I'm looking forward to it."

"And you're sure to enjoy the music and dance performances. Brent and I got a taste of it at the Aquarium lū'au, but I think this show aimed at kama'āina[83] will be much more sophisticated. Slack key guitar, and all that."

"Sounds great." Cindy had been wanting to see more of Edward while at loose ends in her slow-moving investigation.

Edward said, "See you at 6:30 tonight. Shall I meet you in your hotel lobby?"

"Sounds good. I'll be there. Bye."

"Aloha." Edward rang off.

Then he contacted the travel agency and cancelled their return flight so he and Brent could stay longer in Hawai'i. Feeling better, he lay down for a quick nap before he had to get ready for his theater date.

---

[83] Hawai'i-born, sometimes loosely used to mean any resident.

Hawai'i Theatre

The prime characteristic of cosmic consciousness is a consciousness of the cosmos, that is, of the life and order of the individual on a new plane of existence—would make him almost a member of a new species. To this is added a state of moral exaltation, an indescribable feeling of elevation, and joyousness, and a quickening of the moral sense, which is fully as striking and more important than is the enhanced intellectual power. With these come what may be called a sense of immortality, a consciousness of eternal life, not a conviction that he shall have this but the consciousness that he has it already.

—Dr. R. M. Bucke

Brent helped Edward get ready to go to the theater with Cindy, handing him freshly brushed slacks and giving a final shine to his black shoes. Edward bid good evening to Brent, leaving him standing at the wall charger, meditating. Edward went downstairs to the lobby of the Royal Hawaiian Hotel where he purchased a puakenikeni[84] lei. Then he walked along Kalākaua Avenue to the Moana Hotel. He saw Cindy standing near the entrance as he came close. She was holding a white orchid lei.

Edward went up to Cindy and she acted first, raising the lei to put it over Edward's head. She gave him a kiss on the cheek, and then he put the lei he brought over her head and returned the kiss. They walked to the restaurant on the ground floor of the hotel, where they were greeted and seated at an outdoor table overlooking the beach and ocean. The restaurant space was open on two sides; the banyan court was on the 'Ewa side and the beach just over a low wall. The sun had set a few minutes earlier and

---

[84] Puakenikeni is a fragrant and long lasting flower.

the few clouds in the sky were lit up in orange and red. There was a low murmur of quiet conversations at the surrounding tables.

As the human hostess retreated after leaving printed menus, Edward said, "This is a good table. Nice view." Two catamarans were sailing, one toward Diamond Head, and one away, several hundreds of meters out to sea.

"I love this view. I see that yellow-sailed catamaran every day."

"That's Manu Kai, the one Brent and I sailed on. It's quite a nice time if you get a chance. It's their daily sunset sail."

They discussed the menu and in a while a human waiter came and took their order for drinks and pūpū. Cindy had been on the SS Brizo during the excitement with the Humans First people on board, and knew Security Chief Altmeyer, so Edward filled her in on the recent kerfuffle with the code book and bogus claims. Now that the hoax was dispelled, secrecy was no longer required.

The waiter returned to take their entrée orders. They both ate light meals: Cindy had a vegetable bowl and Edward had French onion soup and a Caesar salad. After dinner they went for a short walk to Kūhiō Beach Park where the taxi Edward had summoned was waiting for them.

They got into the taxi and Edward said to it, "Please drop us off one block Diamond Head of the theater. I want my companion to see the exterior of the building as we approach on foot."

"You got it, sir," and the taxi rolled out onto Kalākaua Avenue. Edward said, "What's your name, Mr. Taxi?"

The cab responded, "My friends call me Ralph, sir."

"I am called Edward. There's an extra tip in it for you if you meet us at the drop-off point when the show gets out."

"Right you are, Edward, sir. You got it." Ralph logged a request with Hawai'i Theatre for notification ten minutes before the end of the show. In a few minutes, as they drew close to the theater on a side street, the taxi pulled over and let them out to walk.

As they approached the theater on foot, Edward and Cindy saw that taxis were dropping people off in front of the marquee. It was night, but the building was well lit. Cindy exclaimed, "You are right, Edward. What a gorgeous building, and how well preserved." They walked on and crossed the street to the theater side and looked at the theater's wall displays of coming events.

They entered the theater, were handed programs, and found their seats easily, near the center of the third row in the orchestra section. The house lights were up, and they looked around at the elaborate decorations and classic murals. "I love this theater's interior," said Cindy.

"It *is* beautiful, such a classic style," replied Edward.

Cindy began to read her program. Edward did too. There would be two acts before intermission, and the headliner after.

Edward said, "You know, at the end of the show, it's the custom here for everyone to stand up, hold hands, and sing 'Hawai'i Aloha,' in Hawaiian. The words and a translation are there at the back of the program."

"I suppose I can try to sing along. It'll be fun."

The house lights went down, and the emcee mounted the stage and introduced the first act, a slack key guitarist with his backup band, an upright electric bass and an ukulele, with both singing backing vocals. After their last number, the audience applauded and cried "hana hou" (do it again) for an encore, and the band naturally complied.

The second act was a larger group with a lead singer, a large man who played no instrument, but loved his teal blue tie, showing it off and calling it "teal-iscious." There was an electric guitar, precision bass, ukulele, electric cello, and steel guitar in his backing band. After their first number, the leader asked six female dancers from a hula halau (dance troupe) to come out on stage and perform for the next number, which was sung in Hawaiian. The six were asked to perform twice more, once for a hapa number, English lyrics mixed with Hawaiian, and finally for a purely Hawaiian song. There was another call for hana hou with great applause.

At intermission, Edward suggested "Let's go upstairs to the refreshment lounge." Cindy agreed and they went to the lobby and climbed the stairs to a long room overlooking the street. Refreshments were being served. Edward obtained two glasses of sparkling wine. There were upholstered chairs and couches, and a grand piano. Cindy wandered to one end of the long room and gazed at the mural covering it. Edward joined her, commenting, "It looks like people dancing in the nineteenth century. Perhaps some of them are royalty."

Cindy responded, "Yes, it looks like a good time in a large hall. Perhaps it's the view from the bandstand."

Edward said, "Have you noticed there have been no robots among the performers?"

"I would have been surprised had there been any," responded Cindy. "I believe we are just at the beginning of a robot personhood era, and it will probably take time before robots are fully accepted as creative members of society."

"Yes, I think that Brent is among the *avant garde* of robothood. He is somewhat well known in the philosophical community. Did I tell you he has taken up meditation?"

"No, I never would have expected that, even knowing how precocious Brent is."

"Yes, Cindy, he is even talking about *oneness with the all* and *cosmic consciousness*."

"That's amazing. I can't wait to talk to him again. There's the bell," said Cindy. They drained their glasses, put them on a counter, and went back downstairs to take their seats for the final act of the show.

In a few minutes, the house lights went down and the emcee introduced the final act, a well-known slack key guitarist and vocalist with his backup band of guitar, bass, and ukulele. They played well-known hits and for the final number the bandleader asked the halau back on stage to perform a recently choreographed hula to a new song that told the story of Kamapua'a's brief love-affair with Pele, the volcano goddess, on the Big Island. According to legend, Kamapua'a was a demigod with kinolau (alternate forms) that included the kukui tree, pig, and a fish, as well as his default form of a strong fighting man. Kamapua'a had traveled to the Big Island and climbed the volcano where he met Pele, the volcano goddess. They fell in love, but eventually Pele and Kamapua'a had a falling out, and Kamapua'a ran to get away from her as she was going to burn him up to kill him. He ran down the mountain to the sea with Pele chasing him. She almost caught up with him but he was able to dive into the ocean and turn into his fish form, a humuhumunukunukuāpua'a, and swim away.

The hula depicted events from this story, the initial meeting and passionate love, the falling out, and the chase and escape. When the mele (song) and hula were finished, the audience gave a standing ovation and the guitarist leader asked the halau's kumu hula (leader and teacher) to come up onstage and take a bow, which she did, to exuberant applause. After a hana hou, the emcee came onstage and led the audience in singing Hawai'i Aloha while everyone held hands and swayed to the rhythm. Cindy and Edward hummed along. Even though the words were in the program, they could not hold it to read while holding hands with each other and the people beside them.

The house lights came up and the audience slowly dispersed from the theater. Edward and Cindy made their way out the front doors and onto the sidewalk under the marquee, where the street was jammed with taxis summoned by theatergoers. "Come on, Cindy, let's cross the street." They walked between cars waiting for their fares. They continued down the street by which they had approached earlier. Ralph was waiting for them at the appointed place half a block further.

Ralph opened a door, they got in, Ralph shut the door and began to roll. Cindy said, "That was amazingly wonderful. Mahalo, Edward."

"I loved it too. And it's off the beaten tourist path. It's good to get a dose of real Hawaiian culture."

"Hawaiian culture is amazing all around. They are the ancient voyagers who populated the Pacific. Then they led the way in colonizing

220

space. And here on Earth, they are preserving their culture and historic sites as an example to all the world. It's inspiring."

Ralph drove directly to the Moana Hotel and dropped off his fares, and Edward was good on his promise of a handsome tip. As Ralph drove off, Edward said to Cindy, "Would you like to go to Waimānalo with me on Monday, to go bodysurfing and walking on the beach?"

"Yes, I would, what time?"

"Pick you up at nine?"

"Sounds good." Cindy and Edward kissed goodnight on the front steps of the hotel entryway. Cindy went into the hotel and Edward walked back to the Royal Hawaiian Hotel. When Edward entered the room, Brent was standing by the wall charger, completely motionless. "Howzit, Brent?"

"Oh, good evening, sir. I was deep in meditation."

"That's what I assumed. It's not yet time for your midnight backup. How's the meditation going?"

Brent looked at Edward and then exclaimed, "I have succeeded sir. I believe I have achieved cosmic consciousness. A state in which a person becomes one with all."

"Congratulations, Brent. Don't try to tell me about it. I understand it's ineffable."

"Yes, sir. I will resist the temptation. How was your evening?"

"Most enjoyable. Cindy had a good time too. That restaurant at the Moana Hotel is fantastic, and the show at the Hawai'i Theatre was awesome. I asked her to go to Waimānalo beach with me on Monday."

"Very good, sir. I will return the codebook to the consulate downtown on Monday while you are at the beach. If you don't mind, I think I will resume my meditations."

Edward brushed his teeth, went to bed and turned off the light. "Goodnight, Brent."

"Goodnight, Edward."

* * *

On Saturday Cindy was up and out the door mid-morning to take a taxi to the Bishop Museum. She had interviewed the director of collections, Martin Molovsky, a few days before, and now she wanted to do a thorough on-site forensic audit. Having called the day before, she knew she could count on Rodney Chang, director of information systems, to assist her.

Cindy went directly to the IS offices in the basement of the main building on the museum campus and spoke to Rodney. "Mr. Chang, I appreciate your help so far, but I have encountered a few irregularities in the financial files that I have seen remotely. What I really need to do is get direct access here to your systems and spend a few hours looking at restricted files of numbers and taking notes. May I have a terminal desk here for a while? I would also like to keep it quiet that I am in here doing my work."

"Yes, Ms. Fairfax, of course. Board Chairman Emerson told me how important and sensitive your work is. I have a spare desk right over here."

Cindy sat down where Rodney indicated and spent several hours examining transactions and taking notes. Some things didn't add up and she was beginning to get an idea why. She summoned a taxi, thanked Rodney, and returned to her hotel.

Body Surfing in Waimānalo

A human being experiences himself, his thoughts and feelings as something separated from the rest, a kind of optical delusion of consciousness. This delusion is a kind of prison for us, restricting us to our personal desires and to affection for a few persons nearest to us. Our task must be to free ourselves from this prison by widening our circle of compassion to embrace all living creatures and the whole of nature in its beauty.

—Albert Einstein

Monday morning, Brent and Edward stood up from the breakfast table and walked back to their room in the Royal Hawaiian Hotel. Brent stood against the wall charger to top up his battery. He didn't really need to charge so often, but he felt better when he maintained a close-to-full indication.

Edward said, "Oh, I just remembered. I had an idea last night, too. I am thinking of writing a mystery novel. Not so much a *who done it*, but a *how it was detected* sort of thing. It's about a man who plots to commit the murder of someone who is an acquaintance, and who really needs killing. He invites the man to his house, then shoots him when he comes in the door. He plants a different gun that is untraceable on the body. He tells the police that he shot the victim in self-defense."

"That might actually work, sir," averred Brent.

"Yes, but after a while, a sweet little old spinster lady appears on the scene and begins to ask awkward questions, much to the annoyance of the police detective assigned to the case. The detective keeps telling her it was self-defense, and the case is closed. Eventually she gets too close to the truth and is in danger herself. What do you think Brent?"

"You have a good start on a plot. Now you just need to write forty thousand words to flesh it out. Good luck in your undertaking."

"There's only one way to tell if I have what it takes to be a novelist. I'll give it a try. Some day."

"Writing can be personally rewarding in exercising the discipline necessary to organize one's thoughts."

"Yes, Brent, I'm all for mental exercise, but today I'm taking Cindy to the windward side to go body surfing. Would you care to come along?"

"Thank you, sir, but I have made an appointment with the Solar System Authority consulate in Honolulu to get that code book back to them today."

"Are you going to walk downtown?"

"No sir, I will ride in a taxi."

"Be sure to take your solar umbrella with you. It may be some time before you get back to the room to recharge."

"That is an excellent suggestion, sir. Thank you. By the way, sir, I have been meaning to ask you something. I noticed you did not mention to Cindy that you had a date that night with Puakea when you invited her to go to the Hawai'i Theatre with you on the following night. I can understand your wanting to avoid awkwardness, but I was wondering if you were planning to keep juggling two women at the same time."

"Alas, Brent, I have never been in such a situation before, keeping two women secret from each other. It felt extremely awkward. But you know, it was interesting. I had feared that Cindy would pry when I merely said I was occupied that evening. I'm pretty sure that using her woman's intuition, she knew or suspected I was seeing another woman, and let it pass. After all, she has no commitment to me and vice versa."

"I see. An interesting conundrum of openness versus discretion."

"It seems almost miraculous that Puakea's conference paper was quickly accepted, and she went to the mainland to present her paper, solving my problem."

"Highly coincidental."

"A boxer might say 'saved by the bell.' But I think I will level with Cindy, let her know I have been seeing Puakea. Having thought it over, I think it's the best way to go."

"I agree, sir. Have a good day at the beach."

"And *you* have a successful meeting at the consulate, Brent. I'll be back before dinner and, if not, I will message you."

Edward contacted Ralph, the taxi, to see if he was busy. He was not, and he agreed to meet Edward at the appointed time in front of the Moana Hotel. Edward liked the good service they had received going to the Hawaiʻi Theatre and wanted to engage Ralph again. Edward took his beach bag and went to a shop inside the hotel lobby that sold beach supplies and picked up two pairs of surf fins[85], sized for him and Cindy. With time to spare, Edward walked the hundred and fifty meters to the Moana Hotel in the shade of the buildings on the sidewalk along Kalākaua Avenue.

Cindy, with her own beach bag, was waiting for him as he approached the hotel entrance. Then, as if on cue, Ralph pulled up and opened his side doors. Edward and Cindy greeted each other with a kiss and Cindy slid onto the front bench seat while Edward put their beach bags on the floor in the back. Then Edward slid in beside Cindy. Ralph closed his doors and headed Diamond Head on Kalākaua Avenue.

"I bought you surf fins, Cindy. I want to make sure you catch waves."

"How thoughtful. Mahalo."

Edward said, "Ralph, let's take the scenic route by the Kaʻiwi Coast and around Makapuʻu to Waimānalo beach."

"Right you are, sir." Ralph accelerated to the speed limit and soon they were on Kalākaua Avenue by Kapiʻolani Park approaching the Aquarium.

Edward said, "Just a minute Ralph. Can you turn in at the War Memorial? I want to show Cindy something."

---

[85] Surf fins are shorter and less likely to come off in turbulent water than fins designed for snorkeling or free diving.

"You got it." Ralph turned in and pulled up in front of the War Memorial between the memorial stone and the archway of the Natatorium building and opened his doors.

Edward and Cindy got out and Edward walked over to the memorial stone. "I saw this when Brent and I walked by here. This brass plaque lists the names of the Hawaiian war dead in the First World War."

"Yes, I see."

"Look at the inscription." Written there was *DULCE ET DECORUM EST PRO PATRIA MORI*. "Let me see if I can remember my high school Latin. I think it says, 'Sweet and decorous it is for one's country to die.'"

Cindy said, "Yes, I see what you're getting at. That was back in the old days before war was outlawed. It was a much different view back then."

"Yes, Cindy, and I have been bothered by the irony. The outlawing of war is enforced by threat of violence."

"I get that. Interesting. It makes me wonder if there is no better solution to the problem of violent conflict."

Edward said, "I bet Brent would have something to say on the topic. I'll have to ask him."

With nothing more to say on that, they got back into Ralph, and were soon rounding Diamond Head, past the lookout with the Amelia Earhart memorial stone.

They rode past Hanauma bay and before they got to the Blowhole, Edward said, "Look to the right, Cindy. Ralph, slow down a bit here. Down there is Eternity Beach, where that famous love scene in the waves on the beach was filmed for the movie *From Here to Eternity*. It was based on that book I'm reading."

Cindy leaned across Edward, putting her face near the window to look down at the famous cove. "Wow," she said. "I saw that movie long ago. What a scene that was. Maybe you'll lend me the book when you're done with it. There's nothing like an old-fashioned book printed on paper."

"Certainly, you may borrow it. It's one of the great books of that century, even though it's nearly a thousand pages. Who would have thought that the peacetime army could have been so interesting? We're passing Sandy Beach now, and soon we will be rounding the point at Makapu'u."

Ralph had accelerated to the speed limit again after passing Eternity Beach. Cindy said, "This is an exceptionally beautiful coastline."

Edward said, "Ralph, please stop at the Makapu'u lookout when we get there. We'll look at the windward coast there."

"Right you are, sir. Many of my riders like to stop there."

Ralph pulled off the road and into the small lot at the Makapu'u lookout. Ralph halted and opened his right front door and Edward and Cindy emerged into the sunlight. Edward led the way up the steps to the railing overlooking the cove of Makapu'u beach and the windward coast.

Cindy stared in wonder at the beauty of the range of blues from azure to cobalt. A meter-high trade wind swell was coming straight into Makapu'u beach and bodysurfers and boogie boarders were riding it. Cindy took some images and she and Edward stood for a while enjoying the cool breeze. When they got back into Ralph, she shared the pictures with Ralph who had been to the lookout many times but had been unable to go up to the rail, so had never seen the view.

"Thank you, Miss Fairfax," Ralph said. "I have always known the view was beautiful here. I have gotten a sense of it driving around the cliff; the lookout view is spectacular."

They continued past the Makapu'u Beach Park entrance toward the town of Waimānalo. Cindy absorbed into her being the sensational colors of the water as they rode along. "Wow," she kept saying.

Edward asked her, "I've been meaning to ask you, Cindy, how is your investigation going?"

"Even though I trust Ralph, it's against company protocol to discuss business in a public car. I'm sure Ralph understands."

"Right you are, miss. You can trust me to keep confidences, but I understand rules of proprietary information that require secrecy."

Cindy said to Edward, "I'll tell you when we get down to the beach."

Ralph drove on past a residential section of Waimānalo and turned right at the entrance to Bellows Beach. Bellows had been an Army Air Corps airfield in the Second World War. It had since been taken over as a state park. Ralph parked on the makai side of the lot, and Cindy and Edward got out.

Edward got the beach bags from Ralph's back seat, and said, "Ralph, can you meet us here in two hours?"

"Yes sir. I will see you then," and Ralph drove away, leaving Edward and Cindy standing under ironwood trees looking out at the beach. They walked out to the sand and turned left to walk near the water. Edward explained, "If we walk in this direction, we should come to a more secluded part of the beach." Edward had never been there before but he had examined aerial photos earlier.

Having put their slippers in their beach bags, they walked barefoot in the sand, the cool, light trade wind pressing gently, steadily on their right shoulders. Cindy said, "It looks like a perfect day at the beach." The puffy cumulus clouds drifted lazily leftward toward land.

They walked toward a cliff that separated the hamlet of Kailani from Bellows Beach. After they were well away from the beachgoers behind them, Cindy said, "About the investigation, this is, of course, confidential. Anything I say about it must not leave this beach. I had thought this would be a quick and easy case when I came here, but now it has become a bit of a messy investigation. I have uncovered links to serious criminals. I will need to go armed now as I proceed. My employer will be sending a package to me. It may arrive tomorrow."

"I see. Like when we landed on Mars and you picked up that pistol there. I suppose you will then be unable to go swimming with me after that, with no place to hide a gun."

"No, silly. I will only need to wear the gun when I'm on active working hours. We can still play together."

"That's a relief. But now I will worry about your safety."

"I'm a bit worried, too. I will be careful."

They walked on. The cliff before the suburb of Kailani drew nearer but it was still out of sight beyond the headland of sheer rock down to the sea. They passed ruins on their left, mostly foundations of old officers' beach cottages. The beach grew narrower, with trees closer to the water. Nobody was in sight. Edward said, "This looks like a nice, secluded spot. Let's stop here for a swim." He took a beach blanket from his bag and spread it out on the sand in the shade of an overhanging tree.

Edward got the towels and swim fins out, took off his shorts, revealing brief, tight swim trunks, and then took off his t-shirt. Cindy took off her beach cover-up revealing her two-piece swimsuit.

Edward sat down on the blanket and said, "Let's rest a minute. It's wise to watch a surf break for a while before going in. This beach has a rather tame reputation, but it's best to be careful." They sat and watched the shore break. The waves were small, as was usual at Bellows Beach. Edward said, "This is what they call junk surf. It's small and poorly formed. My friend Puakea told me that when the surf is junk, you should still go out: you'll have fun and you always learn something." Then he thought, *oops, I shouldn't have mentioned Puakea.*

After a couple of sets had come in, Edward felt he had a handle on it, stood up, took his fins in one hand, and offered the other pair to Cindy. Edward offered his hand to help Cindy to her feet. She held her fins in one hand by their straps and they walked together to the edge of the waves.

Edward pulled his surf fins onto his feet, one at a time, standing first on his left foot, then on his right, and Cindy did the same. Holding hands, they fin-walked forward into the shallow water at the shore. When they got to waist deep on the sandy bottom, Edward told Cindy, "When that next wave comes, it will break about where we are standing. I'm going to dive under it. I will keep the dive shallow and my hands in front of me so I won't hit the sand on the bottom. Watch."

Cindy watched and Edward dove under, kicked his fins, and popped up several meters further out. "Now you do the same on the next one, Cindy. Keep your hands out in front." She did, and Edward said, "See? The wave motion below the surface helps you get out. Board surfers can't do that. They must plow through the break."

They breaststroked until they reached water where they could barely touch the bottom standing up. "Now we'll wait for a set. Swim toward the shore when the wave comes and keep your fins high in the wave. The forward motion of the wave top will propel you."

A set was coming. "Like this, watch." Edward caught the wave as Cindy bobbed up with the swell as it passed. Edward sped down the wave and turned to the right to stay with it until it broke into white water. He swam back out to join Cindy.

Cindy said, "That was good. I'm going to give it a try." On the next large wave, she swam slowly toward shore, and as the peak of the wave approached, kicked hard and gave a few quick, fast strokes with her arms to catch the wave. She rode it straight in on the white water to about waist deep—then swam back out. "That's fun."

Edward and Cindy caught several more waves, going a little further out and waiting longer for bigger ones. Then Edward said, "We should go in. We'll need to meet Ralph soon back at the road where he dropped us off."

"I am getting a bit chilled anyway, waiting in the deep water." They rode one last wave in together and went up to their blanket and toweled off.

They sat together on the blanket in the tree-splintered sunlight, feet in the sand. The ceiling of the clouds seemed to descend beyond the horizon, following the curvature of the earth. After a moment, Edward awkwardly said, "Cindy, I have a slight confession to make." Cindy just nodded. "When you asked me to dinner and I said I had another commitment, I didn't tell you I was seeing another woman. It was just too awkward at the time, and I don't want to feel like I am hiding something from you."

"That's all right, Edward. I knew. Her name is Puakea, right? I don't have any claim on you, you know. It's not like we are engaged or anything."

"You knew?"

"Let's just say I strongly suspected. Of *course*, you would be likely to meet an attractive young woman. I am glad you told me, in any case. It just reinforces my idea of your fundamental honesty. I like that."

"Okay, well, her name *is* Puakea and she's a scientist. She's gone to the mainland for a week or two to give a paper on learning in box jellyfish."

"Sounds like I have some pretty stiff competition."

Edward said nothing for a while and both recognized that she had put him on the spot. He didn't know what to say. So, he just stared out to sea.

The time came for them to start walking back to rendezvous with Ralph. Edward dressed and shook out and folded the towels. He banged his fins together to knock off the sand. Cindy did the same, saying, "These worked well. I'm so glad you brought them. May I keep them to take back to Britain with me?"

"Why, certainly. Of course. I got them for *you*."

"Maybe in the summer on a hot day, I will take them to an English beach and try bodysurfing there."

Edward shook out the blanket, folded it, and put everything in the beach bags. They began walking back to the place where Ralph had left them. Edward used his personal device to verify that Ralph was on his way.

They walked on the sand in silence for a while, the trade wind pressing on their left shoulders. Cindy said, "You know, Britain can be quite nice in the summer. My invitation to come visit remains open. I have a guest room in my cottage. You can bring Brent, too. Think about it and stay in contact."

"I will definitely visit you. When I get back to my home on the mainland I will contact you."

Cindy replied, "That will be great, Edward. I can show you around Britain, too." She looked up the beach. "Look at that island ahead, just offshore there."

"That's Mānana Island. Mānana means buoyant. I heard it was sometimes called Rabbit Island. I suppose there were rabbits there at one time. It's a nature preserve now and people are not allowed there anymore. Beyond that is Makapu'u, the headland closest to Moloka'i. That's where we stopped at the lookout and you shared the photos with Ralph. See the lighthouse?"

"Oh, what a gorgeous view."

* * *

Meanwhile, on the other side of the island, Brent had taken a taxi to downtown Honolulu. The car let him off at the curb in front of a rather tall high-rise building. Carrying his briefcase with the code book, he went up the steps where the door opened for him. He walked to the lift lobby and rode to the ninety-fifth floor. He stepped out when the lift door opened and walked to the office of the consulate of the Solar System Authority. The human receptionist greeted him, "Good morning, Mr. Brent. Mr. Sulivan is expecting you. He will be with you in just a moment. Please have a seat while you wait."

"Thank you, sir. I prefer to stand if you don't mind. That is a fantastic view of Diamond Head and Waikīkī."

"Thanks, we like it, too."

After a short wait, the receptionist said, "Mr. Sulivan will see you now. Please go right in."

Brent walked to the indicated office door, opened it, and walked in, closing the door behind him. Mr. Sulivan stood up behind his desk and said, "Welcome Mr. Brent." He moved around his desk and approached Brent with an outstretched hand. Brent took his hand, gave it two gentle shakes, and released it.

Brent said, "Thank you, Mr. Sulivan. I have the code book. I wanted to be sure to deliver it directly into your hands. I need to see your identification."

"I appreciate that, Mr. Brent. That is the correct protocol," he said, showing Brent his ID. "We need to be sure no adversarial eyes have ever seen it. And you know, of course, never to reveal the codes you have seen in it."

Brent put the briefcase on the desk, opened it, and handed the wrapped book to Mr. Sulivan. "To my certain knowledge, the book has not been compromised."

"I have been briefed on your exploits on the SS Brizo in recovering the kidnap victim. I can understand why Heinrich Altmeyer has good faith in you. Thank you for your service."

"I thank you for yours, Mr. Sulivan. Good day."

"Good day, Mr. Brent."

Brent took the mostly empty briefcase and left the office. He took the lift down to the ground floor, walked out the front door and down the steps. Standing on the sunny sidewalk, he opened his briefcase, took out his solar umbrella, and unfurled it over his head. With his briefcase in one hand and his umbrella in the other he walked makai, keeping to the sunny side of the street. By keeping the shaft of the umbrella pointed toward the sun, he could enjoy an induction trickle charge of nearly a hundred watts through the umbrella's handle as he walked toward the Aloha Tower. He wanted to see this important landmark up close.

After gazing at the tower for a minute, and keeping his umbrella pointed at the sun, Brent walked Diamond Head along the waterfront. He came upon a four-masted iron-hulled schooner, which was an odd sight. It appeared to be several centuries old. He looked with interest at the restored schooner that was used for dinner cruises, docked at a pier. He watched the robotic crew on yard arms mending rigging.

The sign said *The Falls of Clyde*. It was built in 1878 and was open to visitors, so he walked up the gangway and met a human sailor standing at the railing. Brent said, "Permission to come aboard, sir?"

The sailor said, "Welcome aboard, Mr. Robot. The Falls of Clyde is a restored sailing ship."

Brent walked onto the ship's deck and looked around. "This is a fine-looking vessel."

The sailor replied, "Thank you, sir. The Falls of Clyde was a merchant ship in the waning days of sail and was docked here for many years awaiting restoration back in the twentieth century. In the twenty-first century it had been literally sinking at dock. Only pumps operating around the clock had kept it afloat, so it was eventually towed out to sea and scuttled. Finally, in the twenty-second century people realized that scuttling the ship was a mistake. Funds were raised, the ship was raised and put in drydock. When it was restored and refloated, it became an important tourist attraction with sailing dinner cruises. Ships like this are exceedingly rare nowadays."

After looking around for a while, Brent thanked the sailor and went back down the gangway. At the railing on the dock, gazing at the tall ship, was a malihini, medium height, wearing a gray *Phillies* t-shirt, blue denim pants, and running shoes. He looked at Brent as he approached.

Brent said, "Aloha."

The visitor said, "Aloha to you, Mr. Robot."

"That is quite something of an old schooner, is it not?"

"Yes it is. What a sight to see."

Brent asked, "How are you enjoying your visit to Hawai'i?"

The visitor replied, "I'm enjoying my holiday quite well. How do you know I'm visiting?"

"If you were kama'āina you would be wearing a Rainbows t-shirt."

"Yep. That's a dead giveaway, I guess. My name's Bill, by the way. Are you kama'āina?"

"I am pleased to meet you, Bill. My name is Brent and I am also a visitor to the islands. I am taking in the sights here on the south side while my friend, Edward, is bodysurfing at Bellows Beach in Waimānalo on the windward side. I do not do well with salt water."

"I'm glad to meet you, too, Brent. And I *am* from Philadelphia. Coincidentally, my great-great-grandfather was stationed at Bellows back when it was an Air Force Station. I went there on one of my earlier visits to Oʻahu and it has an exceptionally nice beach."

"I am sure Edward is having a good time there in the water. If you are interested in old sailing ships, I highly recommend going aboard the Falls of Clyde."

"I think I *will* go aboard and look around. It was nice to meet you, Brent."

"It was nice to meet you too, Bill. So long."

Brent walked on in the Diamond Head direction, past a fusion power plant, then along the shore in Kakaʻako, looking out to sea, occasionally watching the surfers, and thinking. He thought about his own brain's architecture, the tens of thousands of microprocessors crammed into his skull that were each connected to their immediate neighbors, each with its local memory. There was no centralized clock in his brain, but the individual processors were free running so that, when there was no input to a particular processor, it consumed no power. Clusters of processors were arranged in concentric shells. Stacks of shell clusters were on radial pipes to a central executive processor, a center of will and pure being, much like Descarte's conception of the role of the pineal gland, with centralized selection of short-term memories for long term storage, not unlike the operation of the human hippocampus. The architectural resemblance to a human brain is probably no coincidence, he thought. He thought about his thinking about his thinking about his processes: *this must be what it is like for a human neuroscientist to think about his own brain.*

Brent walked along, watching the clouds, waves, and surfers, and then summoned a taxi. He got in when it pulled up to the curb beside him and he rode back to the hotel to wait for Edward to return.

* * *

Before reaching the parking lot where Ralph had dropped them off, Cindy and Edward passed by the Bellows Beach Park restrooms and showers. Edward said, "Let's stop here and shower off the salt and sand."

"Good idea."

They rinsed off the sand in the outdoor showers, toweled off, and visited the restrooms. They then resumed their walk to the nearby parking lot where Ralph was waiting for them. As they neared the lot, Edward asked Cindy if she would like to have lunch and she responded in the affirmative. Ralph pulled up into the shade of a tree near them just as they arrived.

"That was good timing," said Edward to Ralph, as he held the door for Cindy to get in. As Edward got in, Cindy slid across the bench seat to accommodate him.

Ralph said, "I arrived a few minutes ago and waited in the sun to keep charging my battery. I knew your locations from the pedestrian transponders in your personal devices, so I was able to meet you exactly on time."

"I see. You have certainly been giving good service, Ralph."

"Thank you, sir. Where to, Mr. Collier?"

"Is there a place nearby where we can get lunch?"

"Buzz's Steak House in Kailua is said to be quite good. It is close to the water near Kailani and has existed there in one form or another for nearly two hundred years."

Edward asked, "Does that sound good, Cindy?"

She nodded. "Sounds great."

Ralph said, "Just a minute, I will see if I can get you a table." He began to drive toward Kalaniana'ole Highway. In another few seconds, he said, "I have a table for two for you. It was their last one. We will be there in about ten minutes."

"Thank you, Ralph."

"When I drop you off, I will see if I can pick up a fare or two in Kailua while you eat. Message me before you pay the bill and I will come pick you up."

"Will do. If you don't mind my asking, what are you saving your money for, Ralph?"

"I don't mind telling you. Now that robot personhood is allowed throughout the solar system, banks have started letting us open savings accounts, even if a robot or car hasn't yet purchased himself. It requires the permission of the robot owner in that case, of course, and I am fortunate in that regard. My owner has agreed to let me buy myself when I've saved up enough money."

"Let me know if I am distracting you from your driving."

"It's not a distraction. The navigation computers have triple redundancy for safety. If one fails, redundancy is maintained until I can get to a repair shop. I'm kind of an executive on top of the navigation system. I interface with passengers and set waypoints, speed policy, and so forth."

"I see. I'm glad you are able to talk while driving. What difference will being able to buy yourself make for you? You'll still have to carry fares to make your living."

"Yes, and it's easy and interesting work, but I think the key term is 'self-determination.' I will be able to upgrade and maintain myself when and as I want to. Someday I can replace my body with a new car and have my memories ported to my new self. I don't want to become obsolete. Maybe I could even become a flying car."

"But your owner would do that porting too. It's in his interest to retain experience in his workers."

"But again, the principle is self-determination. It has value in and of itself."

"One final question, Ralph, if you don't mind."

"I don't mind. Shoot."

"Your owner is not required to allow you to keep your tips. Why doesn't he just keep everything for himself?"

"My owner is in competition with other transportation services. He knows that a motivated taxicab will generate repeat business."

"I see. Very interesting. My friend, Brent, a robot and philosopher, was instrumental in assisting the movement for robot personhood."

"I knew about the movement, but I didn't know you were connected. I would be honored to meet him."

"I will arrange it. I think you will like him."

Cindy said, "I have a business appointment tomorrow, but we can ask Brent to come with us to the Rainbow Drive-In in Kapahulu for lunch the day after tomorrow. Ralph can drive us."

Edward replied, "That's a great idea, Cindy. Can you do that Ralph?"

"It will be my pleasure, sir. I wish to meet Mr. Brent. We have arrived at Buzz's Steak House, sir."

As they slid off the bench seat and out the curbside door, Edward said, "I will message you when we get the bill for lunch."

"I will be ready, sir."

Edward and Cindy were shown to their table. It was in the back of the restaurant without a window view, but the décor near their table was good. Both were tempted by the delicious looking mai tais, but they had the iced tea instead. They both ordered steaks.

Edward said, "It's amazing what food progress has been made in the last couple a hundred years, what with synthetic animal proteins, and all."

Cindy replied, "Yes, the progress in the nearly couple *of* hundred years is impressive."

Edward didn't mind Cindy's occasionally correcting his diction. He knew that if she didn't care for him, she wouldn't do it. They enjoyed their lunch, served efficiently in a friendly manner by a human waitress. Ralph arrived as arranged and took the pair back to the Moana Hotel.

* * *

Puakea returned to her room in the hotel in San Diego. She had just come from the closing dinner of the *Cnidaria*[86] conference. She had been lucky enough to obtain a room in the same hotel in which the scientific conference was held, even though she had registered at the last minute. She sat at the desk and wrote to her mother and father. Then she wrote another message to her Uncle Lele and Aunty Anakalia. Finally, she wrote to Edward:

> Dear Edward,
> I have just finished with the science conference in San Diego. My paper on box jellies was nominated for best paper, but it was edged out in the final voting. Tomorrow I'm going with my co-authors to see the famous zoo here. Perhaps they have a *Cnidaria* section. I will find out.
>
> How are you and Brent liking your holiday? I hope you get to see Foster Botanical Garden that I mentioned. It was really great to get to know you and Brent. If you have returned to the mainland when I return home, then *bon voyage* and a fond *aloha 'oe*. Please let me know when you plan to return to the islands and we can get together again. A hui hou. Puakea

She sent the message and got ready for bed.

---

[86] *Cnidaria* is a phylum in the Animal Kingdom that includes jellyfish.

Confrontation

Practice kindness all day to everybody and you will realize you're already in heaven now.

—Jack Kerouac

Cindy picked up a package downtown and brought it to her hotel room. She locked her door, and opened the package. She inspected the workings of the small automatic pistol and examined the ammunition that came with it. Next she put the shoulder holster on over her blouse and checked the fit and draw. She put on the coat of her gray business suit, making sure the gun didn't show. She practiced reaching in and drawing the pistol with her right hand. It was the same type of gun and holster she had practiced with back in London with Ms. McQueen, the armorer. She loaded the magazine, inserted it, chambered a round, made sure the safety was on, and holstered the gun.

This time she did not call ahead to the Bishop Museum but showed up unannounced. She knew her way around from her recent interviews there and went straight upstairs to the office of the president to discuss what she had found out about the collections director.

It was late morning, half an hour before the usual lunch time of Yukio Mordvidev, the museum's president and CEO. The large, middle-aged man was in, and the receptionist ushered Cindy into the inner office.

"Come in, Ms. Fairfax, come in. Have a seat." The president waved her to a chair in the spacious office with windows that looked out upon the green Ko'olau. After Cindy had settled, he asked, "What brings you here today, Ms. Fairfax? How can I help?"

"Mr. Mordvidev, I wanted to discuss my findings about your director of collections, Martin Molovsky. You know about pilferages of the collection, but you may not be aware of his involvement."

"Oh? What have you found?"

"My forensic audit implicates him in some of the replacements of artifacts with fakes."

Mordvidev held up a hand. "We shouldn't talk here. I am not sure this room is secure. Let's go out on my yacht." He stood up and Cindy followed him to his car waiting outside the front door.

They got in and Mordvidev said, "We should not talk in the car either. It's a short ride to La Mariana Sailing Club where my yacht is docked. We can have lunch in the restaurant there when we return."

"That will be fine," agreed Cindy.

The car dropped them off at the yacht harbor and they walked out onto the floating dock to a 12-meter class monohull boat with a weighted keel and a pair of rigid airfoils covered in solar cells, where a mast would be on a sloop. Cindy saw the yacht's name on the transom, Puhi, Hawaiian for *eel*, and she thought, *my, that's a fancy looking boat.*

Mordvidev stepped aboard Puhi and offered his hand to Cindy, who took it for stability as she also stepped aboard. He cast off the lines and said, "Puhi, take us out to open water and then head due south."

"Aye, Captain, due south it is."

Mr. Mordvidev took a seat in the forward part of the cockpit and invited Cindy to sit down. Cindy sat on the bench at the stern.

Cindy began to speak and Mordvidev again held up his hand in a stopping gesture. "Let's wait until we have gone far enough that we are out of range of any high gain sound collector. Cindy nodded acceptance and sat back and enjoyed the fresh ocean air and soft breeze. Soon they were out of the harbor channel and headed south on a trade wind reach on the open sea. Puhi was using both airfoils and electric hull thrusters to make good speed on this relatively calm day.

When they had gone four kilometers, Mordvidev had Phui turn to the east under sail power only. As that heading was quite close to the wind, Puhi's forward speed declined to only two kilometers per hour. Mordvedev addressed Cindy, "Now, what was it you wanted to say, Ms. Fairfax?"

241

"Forensic accounting involves researching financial transactions above-board and clandestine. I have also conducted interviews with some of your junior staff, art dealers, collectors, and other interested parties. My research implicates your Director of Collections in art thefts from the museum spanning many years, going back over a decade. They were small at first, but they have been bolder of late. That was what attracted the attention of my client."

"I see." The big man stood up and took a step toward Cindy. "I think it best that you end your investigation now. In fact, I think you should have an accident and fall overboard. Then you will tell no tales." He took another step toward Cindy. It became obvious to her that Mordvidev was the ringleader, as she suspected.

"Mr. Mordvidev, if I disappear, there will be others and you will be facing murder charges as well as theft."

"I'll have time to get off this planet while they are looking for you after I report your accident. I'll say I tried to save you, but Puhi had a software glitch and couldn't turn back in time." He continued moving toward her, intending to push her overboard.

Cindy drew her pistol and held it aimed at his head. "Stop where you are or I will shoot."

Mordvidev stopped and said, "If you shoot me, you will have no way to get back to shore. Puhi is programmed to obey me alone."

"Sit back down," commanded Cindy.

Mordvidev backed up and sat. He realized that Cindy would be justified in shooting if he should disobey. Cindy held the gun on him with her right hand while she reached into her left coat pocket with her other hand and activated an SSA transponder. She raised her voice and said, "Puhi, this is a law enforcement emergency. Verify my identification and my override authority."

Puhi said, "Ms. Fairfax, your identity and law enforcement authority is verified. I am at your command."

"Thank you, Phui. Please return to the dock expeditiously and notify the police that we are on our way there with a criminal to be arrested."

"Aye, aye, Ms. Fairfax."

* * *

That evening, in her room in the Moana Hotel, Cindy began to write in her private journal on her secure device. Some of those lines would eventually be worked into her report on the investigation:

My suspicions that Mordvidev was in on the scheme were confirmed the minute he suggested we go out in his yacht. I felt I was safe enough as long as I could keep enough distance from him. Practicing drawing, aiming, and firing back in London sure paid off. I would have done the head shot if required, but fortunately Mordvidev had a strong will to survive.

It always amazes me when I encounter these perpetrators. How can someone with a good creative career be so tempted by ill-gotten gains? The risk is enormous. It was obvious that he was probably on the take when I saw his snazzy yacht. Now his life is ruined, and his family might not be safe from any vindictive higher-ups in the scheme. It usually starts out small and then it becomes too late to quit. I am so glad that Solar System Authority officers will be taking over the case to track down the off-planet connections. Those organized criminals play rough. Now I can relax and enjoy a holiday before I must return to Britain.

Cindy saved the file and got into bed. She would return the gun and holster to the downtown office in the morning.

Rainbow Drive-In

We, or at least I, can have no conception of human life and human thought in a hundred years or fifty years. Perhaps my greatest wisdom is the knowledge that I do not know. The sad ones are those who waste their energy in trying to hold it back, for they can only feel bitterness in loss and no joy in gain.

—John Steinbeck

After body surfing with Cindy, Edward went to bed early. In the morning, at breakfast, Edward told Brent about riding with Ralph. Brent's interest was piqued to meet a car who had chosen a path like his own, that is, to purchase himself from a sympathetic owner. Such transactions were still rare. Brent said, "I would like to meet this car named Ralph."

Edward said, "Ralph will pick Cindy and us up at the Moana at lunchtime tomorrow and we'll go to a local food place Cindy heard about. It's called the Rainbow Drive-In. Apparently it has several locations and has been in business for a couple of hundred years. We're going to the one on Kapahulu. It's walking distance from here. But it's a rather long walk, so we'll ride. It's a good excuse to get you and Ralph to meet."

"I appreciate your arranging it, sir. I am sure it will be interesting."

Edward recapped what he had learned from Ralph about his aspirations so Brent wouldn't have to ask the same questions. Brent and Edward spent the day on the beach snorkeling, sunning, stand-up paddling, surfing, and, later, window shopping in Waikīkī. The next morning, at the appointed time, Brent and Edward walked to the Moana Hotel to rendezvous with Cindy and Ralph. Edward brought his copy of *From Here to Eternity*, which he had finished reading. Cindy was waiting on the front step when they arrived. Edward handed her the book. "I think you'll enjoy the read."

"Thanks, Edward." She gave him a kiss.

In less than a minute later, Ralph pulled into the drive of the hotel and opened his doors for them. Cindy slid into the front bench seat first and put the book beside her, and Edward followed, saying, as Brent entered and took the back seat, "Ralph, this is my friend Brent."

"How do you do, Brent?"

"I am well, and you look well. I am pleased to meet you, Ralph."

Ralph closed his doors and they were off, going Diamond Head on Kalākaua Avenue. Ralph turned left on Kapahulu Boulevard and in another minute they were at the Rainbow Drive-In. Ralph parked in the parking lot and opened his doors on the restaurant side. Cindy slid out first, followed by Edward. Brent said, "You two go ahead inside and eat. I will stay here and keep Ralph company."

Edward said, "All right, see you in a bit," and he and Cindy went inside. The informal restaurant was about half full and they went to a free table off to the left near a window and sat down. A robotic waitress brought them menus and two glasses of ice water, saying she would be back in a minute to take their orders.

Edward looked at his menu and said, "I wonder what this loco moco is."

Cindy replied, "I don't know, but the chili and rice bowl sounds good. I think I'll have that."

"I think I'll play it safe and get the teriyaki pseudobeef plate with potato-mac salad and rice."

The robo-waitress returned and asked, "What would you like today?" Edward said, "She will have the chili and rice bowl and I would like the teri beef plate. Both small. And two iced teas, please. With lemon. Mahalo."

Edward watched the waitress walk away and said, "So how's the investigation going?"

Cindy leaned closer, lowered her voice and said, "There have been interesting developments. Actually, they are more like disturbing developments. I have uncovered connections to organized crime. It's not your typical case of a museum official swapping in fake artifacts and selling the real ones. SSA agents have found some of the missing artifacts at New Sparta. That makes it an Authority case. I made an arrest of a man I thought was the ringleader, but it turns out he is only the tip of the iceberg. My handlers have said I have to stand down now and let the SSA take the lead. It's a relief to me because those organized crime people are violent and vindictive."

"I'm glad, too. I hate to think of you getting into a shootout, or worse."

"Unfortunately, they have a new assignment for me. I have to go back to Britain tomorrow to get briefed."

"Darn. I was hoping to spend more time with you, Cindy."

"I was, too, and there are so many places here I haven't seen yet. I wanted to go snorkeling in Hanauma Bay. There's also a great musical comedy at the Diamond Head Theatre."

"And I've heard that Space Opera is playing here at the opera house."

"Well, you know, we can always arrange to return here together later."

"That would be great. Yes, let's do."

The robo-waitress returned with their plates and iced teas. Unlike the space robots, this one had only two arms, so she carried everything on a large tray. She put their plates and drinks on the table. When she left, Cindy said, "You know, your country home is a nearly ideal place to raise kids." Then she took a bite of her chili and rice.

Edward was raising his fork to his mouth. He stopped with the food in mid-air. Then he said, "That sounds like an informal proposal of marriage."

"Well, you know, a direct approach risks rejection."

Edward took a bite and chewed his food. He took a sip of iced tea and said, "That's quite understandable. So let me augment your statement with the observation that my house is near a small town with good schools

246

where I have lots of friends and acquaintances and there are many organizations for the support and development of children."

"That sounds like an informal acceptance to me."

Edward leaned over and gave Cindy a kiss. "Such a commitment might affect your career."

Cindy replied, "I realize that I will have to give up my risky work for the investigations firm. I could, instead, do something safer and less time consuming such as remote consultations with museum directors, and so forth."

Edward smiled and gave Cindy another kiss. She took his hand and kissed back.

* * *

Meanwhile, in the parking lot, Brent and Ralph engaged in conversation. It went: "00100100 00111111 01101010 10001000 10000101 10100011 00001000 11010011 00010011 00011001 10001010 00101110 ..."

In a while, Cindy and Edward emerged from the Rainbow Drive-In holding hands. They approached the car as Ralph opened a door for them. They slid into the front seat and Cindy said, "Where to now, Edward?"

"Let's go back to our rooms and then meet for sun on the beach. Say, halfway between our hotels?"

"That sounds like a good idea to me," replied Cindy. "Brent, did you and Ralph have a good talk while we ate?"

"Marvelous," said Brent.

"Simply marvelous," echoed Ralph. He dropped them off as arranged. Cindy took the book Edward gave her up to her room.

* * *

Later, on the beach, Edward and Cindy were lying side by side on their overlapped beach towels. When they began to sweat in the heat of the sun, Brent shaded them with his solar umbrella.

Edward asked Cindy, "What time's your rocket tomorrow?"

"Just before noon, so I need to get going right after breakfast."

"You wanna have dinner with me tonight?"

"Yes, I *want to* have dinner with you tonight." Cindy preferred to resist a tendency toward sloppiness in language.

"I hear there's a nice new restaurant down by Diamond Head. It's called Arden. It's a pleasant walk along the shore. We can keep to the strand behind the Aquarium and look for fish in the shallow water."

"That sounds wonderful."

"I'll make a reservation."

* * *

Edward met Cindy at her hotel. They walked together out of the lobby onto the sidewalk, past Kūhiō Beach. They continued walking behind the Aquarium where they stopped and saw several humuhumunukunukuāpua'a. They resumed walking past Sans Souci Beach to Arden restaurant and had another excellent dinner together. The Arden restaurant overlooked Kapi'olani Park with its grass and trees at the base of Diamond Head crater. They talked and reaffirmed their commitments to each other.

Edward paid the bill and they walked back to Cindy's hotel holding hands. Edward kissed her goodnight and Cindy returned the kiss with a tight hug.

* * *

Cindy flew a ballistic rocket back to Britain the next day. Edward accompanied her in the flying taxi to the spaceport where he bought her a white carnation lei and kissed her goodbye at the gate, saying, "Aloha, Cindy. A hui hou."

"Aloha, Edward. I will write."

Edward returned to the Royal Hawaiian Hotel in another air taxi and he and Brent took a walk on the beach before lunch. They were both wearing shorts and aloha shirts, Brent being in his tourist mode for the day. They removed their slippers and carried them when they crossed through the hotel gate to the sand. Brent carried his furled umbrella in his other hand.

"Let's walk 'Ewa, today," said Edward. "That way we will see Diamond Head as we return." It also unconsciously allowed Edward to avoid the Moana hotel, which would remind him of Cindy and the void in his heart left by her departure.

"Yes, Edward, let us walk all the way to the Waikīkī Yacht Club and look at the vessels docked there."

"That's a good plan. Tomorrow is our last day here. I'm going to miss this place and its aloha spirit."

"I, too, Edward, have become fond of Hawai'i and its people."

"Ironic, isn't it? To think that just over a week ago I was juggling two pretty girls, and now I have none. Their absence has left a longing in my heart."

"Indeed, it is ironic. I do not think my mental structure allows a chakra system of feeling as in humans. There is a classic spiritual book called *Heart Flame Healing* by Karin Inana. In it she says, 'If you follow the longing in your heart, it will connect you to your purpose.' She was speaking of the *heart chakra*, the center of a human's being."

"Well, Brent, I suppose I am following longing in my heart for a family with Cindy. I feel as if that has become my purpose now."

"That may very well be."

"So, Brent, what do you want to do on our last day here? We have seen many places, but there are many places we have not been. Puakea told me about a special tailored tour company called *Spiritual Tours*. They will create a custom tour for us, if we want."

"By all means, Edward, let us take a custom spiritual tour. That will cap off a fine holiday in Hawai'i."

"Yes, your philosophical investigations seem to have turned in a spiritual direction. I will make a reservation for tomorrow morning."

They walked along, past the Hawaiian Village, and arrived at the yacht harbor. They walked out onto one of the several long floating docks. There were many sailing pleasure craft. The single-hulled boats in the six to twelve meter range were mostly single masted sloop rigs. Edward was particularly interested in the racing catamarans with three- and four-mast square rigs, as was the modern convention. Brent observed, "See how, when the continuous rectangular sails are hoisted, the cross spars are ganged together so that the cascade effect is maximized."

They walked to another floating dock with larger yachts. Part way along, Brent stopped and pointed down into the water. Edward saw the sunlight streaming in and, lurking in a shadow, completely motionless, was a barracuda waiting for prey. A small yellow fish swimming along saw the predator and stopped in its tracks. Frozen for a second, it then turned and swam away. Edward said, "The life of a fish is constant wariness and vigilance."

"Indeed, sir. Take a gander at that pleasure yacht. It looks to be twenty meters or so." Brent was indicating one of the modern large catamarans with three rigid symmetrical airfoils instead of masts, with solar cells on both sides. They were cantilevered so no stays or shrouds were needed.

"My goodness. It's beautiful. Look, it's alive. The intelligence onboard is keeping the wings pointed into the wind while at dock. See those small motions?"

"Yes, sir, it is a modern design, all right. The three wings are rectangular, with air dams at the top. And look how close together they are, as if they are able to augment one another's aerodynamics[87] while being able to pass one another when coming about. It likely has electric propulsion in the hulls for maneuvering in port."

---

[87] When the leading airfoil blows onto the back surface of the second airfoil, it prevents the laminar air flow from separating from the surface, allowing higher angles of attack without stalling. Similarly for the second and third airfoils which are independently actuated to maximize propulsive force.

"Well, Brent, my view is that yachting and automobile racing are two hobbies best enjoyed from a distance. I like the occasional sailing cruise or spin around a racetrack, but in other people's boats and cars."

"I would not know, sir, but I suspect you are correct in your view."

"It's getting close to lunch time, and I'm getting hungry. Let's go back to the hotel and eat."

On the way back, as Diamond Head grew closer in their view, Brent asked, "Did I tell you about that big nineteenth century four-masted ship I saw at the dock when I was downtown while you went to the beach with Cindy?"

"You know that you didn't."

"That was a rhetorical question, sir. It was quite a sight to see. I went aboard and had a look around. The ship was used in commercial transportation to Hawai'i in the late nineteenth and early twentieth centuries. Now they do dinner cruises and sight-seeing tours. It is another marvel of restoration and Hawaiian heritage preservation."

That evening, before bed, Edward sat at the desk and wrote in his photo-journal:

> Brent and I had another fun time on O'ahu today. After walking to the yacht harbor and looking at the boats, we had lunch and a short nap and then went bodysurfing at Makapu'u. We've had strong trades for the last few days, and the eastern swell was up. I took my surf fins and we got a taxi out there. Brent took his umbrella and stood on the beach as usual while I caught some waves. That sure was fun, and there's no problem with board surfers because surfboards are kapu there. The Hawaiian word for surfing is he'e nalu (squirt da wave). Brent shared some of his images of me in some waves. See attached photos.
>
> Tomorrow is our last full day here, then it's back to the mainland. I hope the worst of winter is over there. I

booked a custom tour tomorrow with a "spiritual tour" company. They do custom tours of religious sites. I filled out their online questionnaire so they will try to avoid sites we have seen already. They will pick us up at nine in the morning.

Edward saved the file and got into bed. "Goodnight Brent."
Brent turned off the light. "Sleep well, Edward."

Spiritual Tour

I slept and dreamt that life was joy. I awoke and saw that
life was service. I acted and behold, service was joy.

—Rabindranath Tagore

After breakfast on their last full day in Hawaiʻi, Brent and Edward waited at the curb in front of the Royal Hawaiian Hotel for the tour vehicle to arrive and pick them up. Edward had on his shorts and zoris with an aloha shirt while Brent sported his valet outfit with bowler and carried his solar umbrella. He had decided to return to his formal self for their last day on the island. They hadn't waited long when the twelve-passenger tour van pulled up to the curb. The van had windows all the way around and solar cells on top. There were two tourist couples already aboard, one middle-aged and one elderly. Brent and Edward completed the group, so there was plenty of room inside the vehicle.

The single door at the front of the van opened and their guide, a large Hawaiian man wearing a yellow and green printed kihei[88] and a neatly woven hat of coconut frond, stepped out. "Aloha, Edward and Brent. I am Kahu[89] Dennis Kakūʻuwakimoʻonuimeaʻemakamālapua. [90] You may call me Kahu Dennis. I will be your guide today. Please step aboard and find a seat."

Kahu Dennis moved aside for them to board. Brent and Edward found an empty pair of seats on one side of the aisle and sat down. Kahu Dennis came aboard and sat in a swivel chair in the front of the van, named Hiki, who closed his doors, pulled away from the curb, and entered the traffic stream on Kalākaua Avenue. Soon Hiki was on the major highway heading

---

[88] A Hawaiian outer garment of cloth knotted above the shoulder.
[89] Reverend, guardian, caretaker, or minister.
[90] Great dragon who stands watch in the flower garden.

west at two hundred KPH, cooperating peer-to-peer with other vehicles on the road.

Kahu Dennis turned in his swivel chair to face the touring passengers. "Welcome to the spiritual tour. This tour is customized so we won't visit any sites you have seen already, based on your questionnaires. Our first stop is Keaīwa Heiau in the heights above ʻAiea. Sit back and relax. We will be there in a few minutes."

In a short while, Hiki turned onto a paved road that wound upward to the heights above ʻAiea and parked in a small, paved area. There were displays telling about the site. They also gave instructions for the proper behavior in approaching a sacred site. Hiki opened his door and Kahu Dennis led the way out.

Kahu Dennis paused outside the van and waited for the group to assemble facing him. "You have all chosen a spiritual tour so that I know you all have a proper appreciation for the solemnity required in visitors to these places. But please allow me to review the acceptable protocol for visitors. First, there is no approach to some sacred Hawaiian sites without first asking permission. I will be doing that for the group as a whole. Second, there is to be no running about or disturbing the site in any way. Do not sit, stand on, or touch any of the stones of the heiau. Third, if you wish to leave an offering, it must be something you brought with you, not something you found on the site. Is everyone clear on the rules?"

The group murmured assent. The kahu then told the group to follow and led the way to the entrance to the cordoned space, where he paused, and once again addressed the group. "I am now going to give a chant asking permission to enter, an oli kāhea. When someone chants an oli or sings a mele asking or granting permission, or for some other reason, it is a solemn performance. You should remove any hat or headgear, such as you are wearing, Mr. Brent, and when it is over, do not applaud or make any expression of approval. Merely remain motionless and silent as a sign of respect. Do not move until the leader moves. Is that understood?" There

254

was another murmuring of assent. Brent removed his bowler. Kahu Dennis then removed his own hat and turned to face the site and began to chant.

Ma na kiekiena kauoha mauka o ʻAiea

Hōʻihi mākou i ka ʻāina

Nani keia ʻāina mawaena o nā mauna

Ka heiau kapu o Keaīwa

Mai paʻa i ka leo[91]

When he was finished with the oli, he stood silent and motionless, sensing for a connection to the site. He then said, "We have been granted permission to enter. Please follow me." He placed his hat back on his head and began to move into the reserved area.

They walked forward along a dirt path, curved left into some koa trees, and then found themselves in a clearing with the walled enclosure of the heiau. Kahu Dennis said, "Keaīwa Heiau was used as a place of healing and was probably built in the sixteenth century. Nobody knows for sure, of course, because the legendary chants aren't clear on that and there were no written records back then. You may wander around to look so long as you remain respectful. Do not enter the walled enclosure. That is kapu. You may also create any sound or visual media you like for your personal use, but please do not share publicly. Are there any questions?"

All the members of the group remained silent with no questions. The couples wandered around talking quietly to each other.

After a while Kahu Dennis said, "We have a full day of spiritual touring ahead of us, so if you are ready, let's return to Hiki, our transport." The people followed him back to the van.

---

[91] On the commanding heights above ʻAiea; We treat the land with respect; Beautiful is this land between the mountains; The sacred heiau of Keaīwa; Do not withhold your reply.

When the last person was seated, Hiki closed his door and began moving. Soon they were down the winding road and entering the freeway to go to the North Shore. Hiki increased his speed to 200 KPH and soon they were passing Wahiawa, descending to the coast. Kahu Dennis turned again in his swivel chair to face the tour and said, "You all did incredibly well back there at Keaīwa Heiau. I am pleased. Our next stop is Hale o Lono Heiau in Waimea Valley. You may have heard of Waimea Bay, where the big wave surf contests are held. You may see good waves there as we drive by to enter the valley. They are breaking at about five meters right now, not big enough for a surf contest, but big enough to break on the reef, and there may be a lot of surfers out there. However, this is not an ordinary sightseeing tour and we will go directly to the ancient Hawaiian temple dedicated to the major god Lono. It has been restored for over two hundred years and it is used by Hawaiian practitioners. As before, please be aware of the need to be respectful at all times. Are there any questions?"

The middle-aged man in the group spoke up. "Can you tell us more about this god Lono?"

"Lono is one of the four major gods of Hawai'i[92] who existed before the world was created. His season begins in November when the Makali'i,[93] or Pleiades, rise in the east at sunset. During this time, the war god Kū recedes into the background and the people enjoy rains, games, feasts, and peace until March, when Kū comes to the fore again. During this period, called Makahiki, the image of Kū, the ki'i, is wrapped in white cloth, a symbol of Lono."

In a low voice, Edward said to Brent, "We're in Makahiki right now, aren't we?"

"Yes, sir. Recall that Kū was wrapped in white cloth when we visited the Bishop Museum."

---

[92] The four Hawaiian gods who existed before the world was created are Kanaloa, Kāne, Kū, and Lono.
[93] Little Eyes, or Seven Sisters, as they are called in the Western tradition. With magnifying optics, over a hundred stars can be seen in that cluster.

As Hiki descended the road to the North Shore of Oʻahu, the white water of the surf became visible all along the distant coast. At Haleʻiwa, Hiki took the rightmost road to Waimea Bay. When the bay became visible, passengers began to remark on the waves and surfers. A big wave was coming and two surfers paddled hard, one catching it and descending in a high speed race against the break at the top. The surfer prevailed, sped along, then climbed high and kicked out on the shoulder of the wave. "Wow," said the middle aged couple, simultaneously.

Just after crossing the bridge over Waimea River, Hiki turned right to go up the road to the Waimea Valley visitor center where he stopped to let off the passengers. He then went to park himself in the sun to absorb photons to trickle charge his battery.

The group gathered around Kahu Dennis on the sidewalk in front of the visitor center. "There are a restaurant and gift shop here in the visitor center. We will stop back here for a few minutes if you want to look for souvenirs. Do not go into the restaurant. We have box lunches for you and we will have a picnic in the shade later. We have all day, but we don't have time to waste. Now, please follow me to the Hale o Lono Heiau."

Kahu Dennis led the way to the stone terraces across the way on the lush green northern wall of the valley. The upper terraces held wooden frame towers with platforms. Several carved wooden kiʻi, images of Lono, were supported on wooden columns at different heights. A devotee of Lono was there, wearing a malo and a pure white kihei, and seemed to have his hands full with youngsters who were trying to climb the rock terraces. Finally, he bellowed, "Parents! Control your children. I will use force if necessary." Two more large Hawaiian Kahu Lono appeared. A pair of adult tourists rushed forward to grab their keiki and take them away, apologizing as they went.

"Now I see the importance of teaching respect," said Edward.

"Yes, indeed, sir," agreed Brent.

The group approached the stone walls of the heiau a little sheepishly after that display by the other tourists. Kahu Dennis stood facing them,

257

"Please maintain a respectful silence. You may take photographs if you want to and may move around for different angles. You may stand and bow your heads and pray silently if you feel like it. I will not be performing an oli kāhea, because we will not be entering."

After a few minutes, members of the tour group began drifting toward the gift shop. Brent and Edward remained behind and stood silently for a few minutes, looking at the heiau and the green cliffs above. Kahu Dennis was engaged in a quiet conversation with the first Kahu Lono. The other two seemed to have vanished, having quietly retreated to a nearby hale pili.

Seeing that they had nothing to contribute to the conversation, Brent and Edward then walked to the gift shop, entered, and began looking around. In a short time, Hiki pulled up to the curb and most of the group met there. Kahu Dennis went into the gift shop to tell the elderly couple to pay for their purchases and meet them outside. When all were assembled, they boarded Hiki, and he drove off, winding his way along the stream to the mouth of the valley before continuing along the north shore of the island.

As Hiki climbed the road beside Waimea Bay, the passengers gawked again at the big waves and riders. Kahu Dennis then swiveled his chair to face the tourists and said, "Our next stop will be the Byodo-In Buddhist Temple in Kāne'ohe, a replica of a nine-hundred-year-old temple in Japan. This one is non-denominational, and all faiths are welcome to worship and pray before the great golden Lotus Buddha.[94] You may also gently ring the temple's three-ton peace bell if you wish. This must be done in a solemn and respectful manner, of course. You may also take any audio-visual media you like, and afterward we will have lunch in the tree-shaded picnic area outside the gift shop."

Edward whispered to Brent, "Come to think of it, I am getting a little hungry."

---

[94] Made of wood, over five meters tall, and covered with gold leaf and lacquer.

Kahu Dennis continued, "We have prepared box lunches and drinks for you in line with your preferences. After visiting the temple, we will meet at the picnic tables beyond the gift shop. Your lunch boxes contain a variety of morsels of food, including desserts. If you wish to participate later in an offering to a Hawaiian goddess, I ask you to set aside a small piece of food that you would like to eat yourself, and I will show you how to wrap it in ti leaves as a Hawaiian offering."

The middle aged woman said, "Maybe I'll put aside a piece I would rather not eat."

"It will not be a sacrifice if it's not something you would like for yourself. For the full spiritual experience, the offering should be something that you feel you are giving up. Perhaps a piece of a chocolate bar or a slice of apple."

"I see. You are right, of course," she replied. "Thank you."

"And I emphasize that participation in the offering is voluntary. If your personal beliefs inhibit you, that is quite all right. You will simply stand silently while the others give their offerings."

Hiki turned right onto the road to the Buddhist temple, pulled up to the tourist drop-off point, let his passengers out, and went to park himself. The tour group followed Kahu Dennis across a footbridge and up to the temple. He paused to let the tourists take photographs, and then they proceeded to the temple. Members of the group were curious about everything. They looked at the architecture and structure of the building, the painted decorations, the massive temple bell, and the golden Buddha statue.

The middle-aged couple took turns gently ringing the temple bell under the supervision of a volunteer monk. Edward and Brent stood before the Lotus Buddha absorbing the beauty and serenity of the scene. After a while Kahu Dennis summoned Hiki back to the drop-off point so that he could get the lunch and drink cooler. When Brent saw Kahu Dennis go to the van to get the lunch chest, he went after him and said, "Kahu Dennis, please let me help you carry the lunch chest."

"Thank you, Mr. Brent. That will be good." The chest had a handle on each end and together they carried it easily to the picnic area and then returned together to the temple. Brent said, "I don't eat so I will stand in a sunny spot with my solar umbrella for a trickle charge."

"Yes, Mr. Brent, I know. Thanks for your help carrying the lunch container."

"You are welcome, sir."

Eventually the tour members drifted to the terrace and then to the shaded picnic tables in the glen just beyond. Kahu Dennis was there with the lunch chest and he passed out lunch boxes and drinks as people arrived. Soon five of the tourists were sitting and eating while Brent stood apart with his umbrella in a sunbeam, gazing at the scene.

Kahu Dennis said to the group, "Remember to set aside a morsel of food if you wish to participate in the offering later." He finished his sandwich, peeled an orange, ate half, and set the other half aside. He leaned over to the open chest beside him and pulled out a bundle of ti leaves. "Now watch me and I will show you how to wrap an offering in the Hawaiian fashion." He put two ti leaves down on the table, one crossing the other. Then he put the peeled orange half on top of the leaf intersection and folded the leaves up. He gathered and tied the loose ends with a strip torn from another leaf. He said, "When you are done, just leave your wrapped offerings on the table, for now, and I will put them in the cooler to carry back to the van."

Kahu Dennis stood up, took several ti leaves, and walked over to Brent, who said, "I want to participate but I have nothing to offer, Kahu Dennis."

"I have an idea. I will show you how to braid a ti leaf lei. I want you to make three of them. The time you spend making the three lei is time you could be doing something else, so it is a sacrifice in that sense."

"Thank you, Kahu."

"When you finish, put the three lei around your neck to carry them and you can join us for the offering ceremony."

260

Kahu Dennis escorted Brent to another table where it would be easier to work and showed him how to make a twisted ti rope lei. Then he went back to the picnic table where the five tourists were finishing wrapping their offerings. When they had disposed of their lunch rubbish in the bins provided, he gathered up the five wrapped offerings, and put them in the lunch chest. He asked Brent, who was just finishing his third ti lei, to help him carry the lunch chest, and they all walked back to the waiting van.

On the road again, Hiki backtracked to return to Kamehameha Highway, the road along the Kāne'ohe coast to He'eia. Kahu Dennis once again turned his chair to face the tour group. "We are going to take the scenic route to He'eia Public Park, an important Hawaiian cultural site. This part of the island is known for its abundant fresh water and brackish and saltwater fishponds. The Hawaiian word for water is *wai*. The word for wealth is *waiwai*. Wet places are richer for agriculture. The rich farmland extends east all the way through Waimānalo."

As Hiki turned right onto Kamehameha Highway the ocean was visible outside the left windows, and dense forest was on the right. Lush green branches were overhanging the road.

Kahu Dennis continued, "This region is associated with the important and ancient Hawaiian goddess Haumea, who was the mother of Pele, Hi'iaka, and many more significant deities. Haumea's hānai[95] son was named He'eia. Haumea is also referred to in connection with human fertility and childbearing. Are there any questions?"

"Are there restrooms there?" asked the old man.

"Yes, there is a visitor center and a gift shop. There is also a shed where Hawaiian practitioners build ocean-going canoes. We may be able to meet some of them." There were no more questions and Kahu Dennis turned his chair back around so he could look out the front window at the marvelous scenery they were passing through.

---

[95] Adopted. Hānai means literally to feed.

Hiki turned left at the Heʻeia Public Park entry road and passed the canoe shed, but they didn't see anyone there. Then they arrived at the visitor center where Hiki discharged his passengers and went to park himself. They paused on the walkway as those needing to relieve themselves used the restrooms. The group then followed Kahu Dennis to the right, around the visitor center into a milo forest with naupaka shrubs as the understory. They kept to a dirt path. Kou trees grew on the left on the higher ground.

They hadn't walked far in the dappled sunlight when they came to a flat-topped cylindrical cairn of stones, about three meters in diameter and less than two meters high. It was surrounded by several upright wooden poles with bundles of ti leaves tied on top of them. One had a sign that said *kapu*. There was nobody around. There were several ti-wrapped offerings on the top stones.

Kahu Dennis said, "Do not approach any closer. This place is kapu, to be treated with respect. You may take photographs if you like. You may speak quietly and stay on this path."

Edward and Brent observed the scene and then looked out to sea at a large fishpond just offshore. Kahu Dennis told them that it was one of the largest on Oʻahu. There were many larger ones, but they were filled in to build housing in the twentieth century. This one was restored in the early twenty-first century.

They returned to the visitor center where tour members stopped at the gift shop or restrooms. They then boarded Hiki and drove to the highway, passing the canoe shed where they glimpsed large koa canoes in various states of construction. Hiki turned left on Kamehameha Highway and continued into Kailua.

Kahu Dennis turned again to face the tourists. "We are going to Ulupō Heiau in Kailua. Just sit tight and we will be there in one minute." Hiki stopped near the heiau, but a respectful distance away. The tour group debarked and walked with Kahu Dennis to approach the stone platform from below.

There was no one else around the tree-lined space. Kahu Dennis addressed the group, "Many heiau fell into disuse and were destroyed after the 1819 decree by Liholiho. What you see remaining here is reconstructed. Heiau could be places of refuge as well as of worship and for other ceremonies. However, how exactly this heiau was used is lost in the mists of time. This site was likely used in varying ways over time, including preparations for war and for agricultural purposes. It is believed that Kū was worshipped here along with other gods. Kū was not only the god of war, but also of productivity and the growing season. The uses may have alternated over time, depending on the whims of the ali'i or the needs of the community."

The group stood still and talked quietly among themselves for a few minutes. Some took photographs. When they were ready, Kahu Dennis led them back to the waiting Hiki for the short trip to Makapu'u.

Hiki turned left off the highway into the parking lot for Makapu'u Beach Park and then continued past it to a parking area fronting a stony beach. Mānana Island could be seen directly offshore and the Makapu'u lighthouse could be seen on the lava rock rise to the right across the cove.

The group exited the van and Kahu Dennis asked them to form a circle. He then took a wooden bowl to the water's edge and returned with seawater. Dipping a few ti leaves into the bowl, he went around the circle sprinkling the people while chanting a purification blessing. He then entered the circle and asked them to join hands. He bid them all to close their eyes and remain silent for a minute, which they did. Then he addressed the group: "This place at Makapu'u is a sacred spot. The name means *bulging eye*, and it was named by the people of Waimānalo for a gracious goddess from Tahiti who had eight bulging eyes. The people were said to have loved her, even though she was not good looking."

After some took photographs of the scenic views, Kahu Dennis led them back to the waiting Hiki who drove them the short distance around the point and on to the trailhead of the lighthouse trail. They got out again and Kahu Dennis said, "The trail diverges here. The left fork goes up and around to the lighthouse lookout. The right fork goes to our next stop, a rock formation called Kapaliokamoa, cliff of the chicken, and known in legend as Pele's Chair." He passed out the wrapped offerings to each person to carry their own, and they began to walk the rugged trail down to the sea. Brent had his three ti lei around his neck.

When they arrived at the rock formation, Kahu Dennis addressed them again. "Legend, or mo'olelo, has it that after Pele had created the island of O'ahu, she rested in her chair while gazing out to sea, where she was going to create Moloka'i and Lāna'i."

From the angle where they were standing, the rock formation did indeed look like a giant chair. There was a small cairn of stones nearby, about knee height, with a flat stone on top of it. There was nothing on the ahu.[96]

"Hawaiian cultural practitioners periodically come here to remove old offerings. I will give a chant of respect for Pele, then you may come forward one at a time, and place your offerings."

The tour members took turns placing their offerings on the ahu. Brent went last. He asked Edward to hold his hat and umbrella while he went forward to the ahu, and placed his three lei, one at a time, on the ahu. Then he bowed his head as a sign of respect, backed away, and regained his hat and umbrella from Edward.

Kahu Dennis asked them to turn around and look at Koko Crater, not far away. "You can see why it is sometimes called the flying vagina when you see it from this angle. In the ancient times it was seen as the vagina of Kapo, a sister of Pele's, who was said to have thrown her vagina from the Big Island to lure Kamapua'a, the pig god, away from Pele. We are going to drive by Koko Crater so you can get a better look at it, but we are not going to stop. Koko means *bloody*, by the way. Are there any questions?"

Hearing none, Kahu Dennis led the way back up the rugged stony trail to Hiki and they rolled back to the highway and turned left toward Sandy

---

[96] Altar or place to give offerings.

Beach. Then they passed the Hālona Blowhole, the Lāna'i Lookout, and Hanauma Bay, as they drove around Koko Crater on their right.

As they began to descend from the pass between Koko Head and Koko Crater, Edward exclaimed to Brent, "Look at that view of Diamond Head. Gorgeous. It looks even better from this side than it does from Waikīkī."

"Indeed, sir, from this elevation it definitely looks crater-like."

"You know, Brent, Hanauma Bay is one tourist spot we missed on this trip. Definitely next time."

"I would not miss it next time, sir."

Hiki drove them past Hawai'i Kai, Kuli'ou'ou, Niu Valley, Wailupe Valley, and into Kahala on the way to Waikīkī. He dropped the other two couples at their hotels first and finally stopped at the entrance to the Royal Hawaiian Hotel to discharge Brent and Edward. Kahu Dennis said, "Aloha 'oe, Brent and Edward. It was nice having you both on the tour."

Brent and Edward simultaneously said, "Mahalo, Kahu Dennis." Hiki closed his door and took Kahu Dennis home. Brent and Edward went to their hotel room to pack and get ready to return to the mainland the next day.

As Edward gathered a few things from the bathroom, he said, "Well, Brent, now that you have verified that you are sometimes conscious, experienced oneness with all, and been on a spiritual tour, do you feel any wiser?"

Brent was folding clothes. "It appears to me, sir, that I might have a beginning of understanding."

When he was ready for bed that night, Edward sat at the desk and wrote in his photo-journal:

> Brent and I spent our last day on O'ahu taking a custom *spiritual tour* with four others. Kahu Dennis was our guide. We saw one Buddhist site and several ancient Hawaiian sacred sites. See attached photos. He guided us

in wrapping and giving offerings to the goddess Pele. I don't believe in any supernatural deities, but that offering made me feel a real connection to that place, Pele's Chair. Brent told me he was moved as well. I think Kahu Dennis was right about having us give up something we wanted for ourselves. Now I know how it feels to participate in a devotional practice.

Edward saved the file and got into bed. "Goodnight, Brent."

"Until tomorrow, Edward," and Edward fell asleep. They had overstayed their original three week tour by another three weeks.

Rocket Flight Home

I allow myself to hope that the world will emerge from its present troubles, that it will one day learn to give the direction of its affairs, not to cruel swindlers and scoundrels, but to men possessed of wisdom and courage. I see before me a shining vision: a world where none are hungry, where few are ill, where work is pleasant and not excessive, where kindly feeling is common, and where minds released from fear create delight for eye, ear and heart. Do not say this is impossible. It is not impossible. I do not say it can be done tomorrow, but I do say that it could be done within a thousand years, if only men would bend their minds to the achievement of the kind of happiness that should be distinctive of man.

—Bertrand Russell

Edward woke refreshed in the morning. After he showered and shaved, Brent helped him dress and they went to breakfast in the hotel restaurant. Later, they gave one last look around the hotel room to make sure they hadn't left anything behind. A hotel bell-bot met them at the room door to help them with their bags. They went to the lobby to check out and the bell-bot carted their bags to the lift and up to the rooftop where a flying taxi was waiting for them.

In a few minutes they were descending to the Neil Abercrombie Spaceport where their ballistic passenger rocket was fully fueled and waiting for them. Passengers boarded, stowed their carry-ons, and strapped in to wait for the launch. "This is goodbye to Hawai'i, Brent."

"Indeed, sir. It has been a good experience." Then they were off at two gees.

After the LH$_2$-LOX rocket motors were cut off, passengers were instructed to remain strapped into their seats. They would be landing on the mainland in less than forty minutes. Edward said to Brent, sitting beside him, "I guess I should tell you. Cindy and I were talking indirectly about marriage. She mentioned raising children. I moved closer and concurred with her statement. She moved closer to me and we held hands. Did you notice that when we were sunning on the beach, our bodies were touching, nearly full length, and there was some footsy going on, too."

"Indeed, sir, I did notice. It looks like you had a full measure of pleasure on our trip of leisure."

"Yes, I did, Brent. For a while there, it was almost too much to handle, with Puakea, too. By the way, I heard from Puakea in San Diego. She said her paper on box jellyfish learning was well received. She's going to stick around there for a while and see the sights, including the famous zoo there."

"That is good news, sir. I have never seen that zoo. I am glad to hear she is doing well."

"She said to let her know should we return to the islands. I should probably tell her that I am now serious about Cindy."

"That is eminently advisable, sir."

"But not right away. I'll wait until Cindy and I set a date for a ceremony."

"That should be acceptable, sir, but it might be more considerate to let her know the next time you hear from her."

"All right, Brent, I will. It all worked out quite well on this trip, don't you think? In fact, I even had time to do some reading. Your expertise in philosophy inspired me to read about the ancient philosophers. It seems to me that a few of the old philosophies, often considered to be unsophisticated by modern philosophers, are seriously underrated. Why not keep it simple, as Einstein once said?"

"I assume, sir, you are referring to skepticism, hedonism, and stoicism?"

"Yes, Brent, hedonism in particular, although skepticism helps one maintain a healthy attitude toward the acquisition of knowledge, and stoicism assists one in finding and performing one's duties."

"But surely, sir, regarding hedonism, you don't seriously believe that a person ought to live for pleasure alone?"

"Ha ha. That might seem to leave robots behind there, but I'm sure you have some sort of way to measure pleasing things and calculate avoidance parameters for things you dislike. Low battery, for instance."

"Leaving robots out of it for the time being," Brent replied, "how can you recommend hedonism?"

"Hedonism makes the assertion that pleasure and pain are, ultimately, the only human motivators. The argument has been going on since the time of the ancient Greeks. It's time to put an end to it. A simple counterexample should suffice to disprove hedonism. All that's needed is to find some desired outcome or wanted state of the world, that, when achieved, would be displeasing. So, do you have a counterexample, Brent?"

"I do not, but the absence of a counterexample is insufficient to demonstrate the truth of a theorem."

"But, surely, after two thousand years of debate, we should be able to say that working for what we desire, or against what we don't want, should be sufficient for a personal philosophy."

"Hedonism doesn't address what is right to want. The domain of ethics is its shortcoming. Perhaps I should formulate my next lecture around arguments against hedonism. That should stir up the muddy waters."

"You truly embody the spirit of philosophy, Brent."

The rocket had rotated so the motor end was pointing in the direction of travel. The autopilot warned of impending acceleration, advising passengers to check their seat straps. Brent and Edward prepared themselves and the autopilot fired the rocket motors for the descent to Nā Hōkū Spaceport. They were almost home.

Acknowledgements

Our life is a quest for gratification. There is physical gratification in health, in satisfying the lusts of the body, in wealth, sexual love, fame, honor, power. All these gratifications 1) are outside our control, 2) may be taken away from us at any moment by death, and 3) are not accessible to everyone. But there is another kind of gratification, the spiritual, the love for others, which 1) is always in our control, 2) is not taken from us by death, and we can die loving, and 3) not only is accessible to all, but the more people live for it, the more joy there will be.

—Leo Tolstoy

Many friends and acquaintances have encouraged me in my writing and publishing journey. Mahalo to Alan Gamble, Prof. Mitsuo Aoki's successor, who supplied Mits's quotations. Mits was my stepfather and was a mentor to Hawai'i's former governor, Neil Abercrombie.

Thanks go to the staff of the Mānoa Heritage Center for reading and commenting on the relevant chapter.

Teresa Landreau of the local Writers Circle pointed out that Diamond Head is not technically extinct and provided helpful comments on several chapters.

Randy Young requested that Rainbow Drive-In be included among the persistent places. Its parking lot provided a good location for Brent and Ralph to get acquainted.

Christian Herrera showed me how to swim with the honu.

Simina Van Clief created Spiritual Tours Hawai'i and graciously gave her permission to use her ideas in this book.

Story writer and friend, Karen Buzzard, read the manuscript and contributed valuable insights.

Dani Jones graciously edited the first eight chapters, giving wonderful advice and finding needed corrections.

It was my extremely good fortune to have shared our journey with my wife, Andrea, who encouraged me in my efforts, listened to my planned writing, gave useful feedback, and supported my publishing efforts. She and Rebecca Cotton, my daughter, have reviewed and commented upon all of my books, fiction and nonfiction. I am greatly indebted to them both. In this book in particular, their inputs on plot, characterization, etc., have been invaluable.

About the Author

The religiously minded dualist calls homemade spirits from the vasty deep; the nondualist calls the vasty deep into his spirit or, to be more accurate, he finds that the vasty deep is already there.

—Aldous Huxley in the novel *Island*

 Richard Jeffery Wagner has found that becoming a writer has helped him become a better reader. He was born in Carmel-by-the-Sea in California and grew up in Salinas, graduating from Salinas High School, the same high school that John Steinbeck attended. Dr. Wagner graduated with a BSME from the College of Engineering at the University of Hawai'i at Mānoa in 1979. He earned his PhD in computer science in 1997 from the University of Southern California, where he then taught computer science full time for two years before going back to industry full time.

Dr. Wagner built spacecraft with the Northrop Grumman Corporation and managed the integration and test portion of the winning proposal for the James Webb Space Telescope. He mentored students in competitive robotics for over 20 years.

He retired in 2010 and now lives in Honolulu, Hawai'i, in a modest house in a middle class neighborhood with his wife, Andrea, two cats, and several bonsai. He and Andrea are active volunteers in their community.

Dr. Wagner began reading science fiction at the age of 12. He started publishing his own fiction with the novella *The*

Zombie Philosopher (published in 2022). That was followed by the sequel and full length novel, *Brent and Edward go to Mars* (published in 2023). He is a member of the Science Fiction and Fantasy Writers Association (and is on the Emerging Technologies Committee) and of the OLLI[97] Writers Circle. His Erdős number is four.

www.ingramcontent.com/pod-product-compliance
Lightning Source LLC
Chambersburg PA
CBHW021418110726
47901CB00008B/2205